# BEDHEAD

A Romance

**KAYT MILLER**

*For the Beedle Babes.*
*You know who you are.*

*There are people you meet along the way that change your life. Make it better, richer. The women I met living on Beedle Drive remain some of the most important people in my life. Even though we're all busy with our families, jobs, and aspirations, I know that our bond will alway remain strong and constant.*

*I love you, ladies.*

*As for our Patsy , we lost her, sadly. Our Irish lass. The funniest person she knew. Cancer is a bitch —it took her from us way too soon. She was a force of nature and the life of the party.*
*We all love you, and miss you, Patty Jane.*

# CONTENTS

## CHAPTER ONE

*This isn't happening. It's just a dream.*

At least that's what's going through my head until the I hear, "Bloody hell, he's got a bird?"

"Oy, mate, I think we woke 'er." That comment comes from the second person in my little dream fantasy. He stepped up behind the first one, the *hot* one.

"What gave it away, genius?" says dream man numéro uno.

"Well, I'll tell ye... she's got bedhead and her spectacles are askew. But that's a nice pair of baps."

*Spectacles? Baps?* I laugh aloud, and it sounds rather hoarse and dry. So I shut my mouth and think about "askew." That's such a funny word. If you say it three times fast, it sounds like you're sneezing. *Askew. Askew. Askew.* I laugh again as I adjust my glasses so they're no longer *askew* on my face. I'd take them off but I need them to see since I took my contacts out before climbing into bed.

"You all right, love?"

I blink at the screen of my laptop and attempt to take in the sight before me. Without speaking a word, I stare at the two men who have called me using the FaceChat application. Two men who are shirtless and beyond gorgeous from what I can tell only seeing the top third of them. Maybe they're naked. Besides that, they're English, Brits, of the UK variety.

*God, I love accents.*

"It's just a mirage," I say again. "They can't be looking back at me at…" I turn to look at the clock on my bedside table. "Three thirty in the a.m. Right?"

"Excuse me, love?"

I look back at the screen and blink. "Huh?"

"We'd like to talk to our long-lost mate."

Mate? I've heard that expression. I'm sure I know what that means. *Shit, wake the hell up, Quinn!* "Your long-lost mate?"

"That's right. Our mate. Be a dove and wake up the lazy git."

"Um… your wife or girlfriend or whatever isn't here." I stare at the screen as both men burst into uncontrollable laughter. "What?" *God, wake up already.*

"Did you hear that, Cooker? She thinks you've got a wifey."

*Cooker? That's a strange name.* When he smiles at me, I stop worrying about his name because I nearly faint from the sight. It's a good thing I'm lying down. "Our friend, love. Max."

"Max?" Who the hell is Max?

"Maxwell Quinn," adds the other guy. I call him the "other guy" because the guy in front—"Cooker," apparently—is the hottest man I've ever seen. The "other guy" is cute too but nothing compared to the tattooed, blond god who is front and center on my computer screen. Okay, let me rephrase that. I've seen hot guys before, but none of them have called me in the middle of the night before. Unfortunately.

"Maxwell Quinn?" I rub my face with both hands and then look back at the laptop. I'm waking up, which is both good and bad. It pains me but I have to say, "I think you have the wrong number."

Mr. Hottest Man in the Universe replies, "We googled the eejit. One Maxwell Quinn. It gave us this American number."

"I think—no, I *know* you have the wrong number, because my name is Quinn Maxwell."

"Bloody hell," mutters my future husband. Snort. Just kidding. "Are you seriously telling me your name is Quinn Maxwell?"

"Seriously."

"Bloody hell," he repeats.

*Yeah, bloody hell indeed.*

# CHAPTER TWO

"That was weird," I mumble tiredly to myself as I bite into a stale piece of white bread that I toasted to make it not seem stale. It also helps that I slathered it with Dollar Bin-brand grape jelly. Good as new.

"What was weird?"

I blink several times before I'm able to focus on one of my new roommates, Patsy. I've been living in a house with five other women for almost a week. I moved in last weekend, right before classes started. It's a good thing too as I was getting desperate. I couldn't find any housing I could afford. Heck, I'm scraping by as it is even though this house is a bargain.

*I need to find a job.*

When Patsy, who I met last year when we lived on the same dorm floor, found out I was looking for a place to live off campus, she let me know there was a room open in this house. Besides Patsy, I live with her younger sister, Susanna; Kat, who is dating Patsy and Susanna's older brother, Ryne; and finally Robbi and Lindsay. I haven't quite figured out how they all know each other. Patsy's the only one I know, and that's not all that well. I hope I'll bond with the other girls in the house, but I'm not great at breaking the ice, as they say. My shyness and insecurities have always been a curse.

I stare at Patsy as she meticulously cuts fresh fruit into uniform shapes, all while humming a happy tune. How does she do it? I know she was out late last night. I heard her clomping around her bedroom at all hours because my room is directly below hers, so I hear just about everything that goes on in her room.

I gaze enviously at the grapes she's placing into her dish of a decidedly healthier breakfast than mine. Hers? Yogurt, granola, and fresh fruit. Mine? See above. Heck, if I could swing it money-wise, I'd have at least one of the things Patsy was having for breakfast. *Yep, I need a job.* When you're poor, carbs are about all you can afford. Take ramen noodles—no, please, take them. Ha! No, so ramen noodles cost like twenty cents per package. That means for only two dollars, I have ten meals. Heck, noodles in general are cheap. Bread? Same thing. One loaf of day-old bread is a buck at the local Dollar Bin.

I peek over at her again. It's obvious fruit does a body good, because she's got a killer bod, made all the more noticeable by the tight leggings and crop top she's wearing. "Did you work out already?" I ask her.

Patsy makes a humming sound that sounds like a yes. Then she says, "I ran. Made it three miles this time."

How's that possible? She's got to be hungover.

*I* should work out. We can do it for a discounted price at the Iowa State University Recreation Center. It's where some of our athletes work out, but there's a section in the building for us mere mortals. There are all kinds of treadmills and weight machines there. On a good day, you can walk on a treadmill and watch the football team run sprints. Too bad I haven't had the time, money, or inclination to trek over to the rec center. I look down at my body and internally shrug. I also have a body reflective of my food choices—dough. I release a soft snort as I bite down on my extra-crunchy bread.

"What's so funny?" she asks, looking back at me again.

"Nothing." I shrug. "You're the funny one."

"Right?" She smiles brightly. Pointing at the toast in my hand, she adds, "Cute nails."

"Thanks." I smile midbite. My fingernails are sort of my signature thing and have been since middle school. Because of that longevity, I have an enviable collection of nail polish in my possession. I love to change the paint at least once per week, it's therapeutic, so in honor of the first week of school, I've painted them Iowa State University colors, red and yellow, alternating each finger. Not as detailed as I usually do, but I was in a rush since I had to move and settle in just days before classes started. I'll do something more advanced for next week. Ooh, maybe multicolored Converse tennis shoes. I've done that before, and it's super cute.

After brushing my hands together to remove the toast crumbs, I clean up my spot at the circa-1950s kitchen table, gather my bookbag, and check my watch.

Patsy turns and begins walking toward the table. Setting down her bowl filled with yogurt goodness, she asks, "Hey, I thought you were going to tell me the weird thing?"

Oh. I ponder making something up, but "the weird thing" is far-fetched enough. "I got a FaceChat last night."

She blinks at me a few times. "We all get FaceChats."

"At three thirty in the morning?"

Patsy winks. "Sometimes."

"From two hot English guys?"

She blinks some more, then, with a hushed voice, steps closer, "No. Who were they?"

I shrug. "I'm not sure. It was a wrong number." I snort. "Obviously."

"Why 'obviously'? You could get calls from hot guys in the middle of the night. *Booty call,*"

she singsongs, then finishes it with "*You're* pretty."

Okay, Patsy is officially my favorite roomie. "That's real sweet, but they were looking for someone named Maxwell Quinn."

"No!" Her voice is all breathy and rushed again. "Seriously?" She chuckles. "What are the odds?"

"Since I'm an art education major, I'm going to just come right out and tell you that math is not my thing, so statistical analysis of the odds someone would call me, Quinn Maxwell, and ask for Maxwell Quinn is beyond my capabilities. I can draw you a pretty pie chart, but it'll have to be cherry."

Patsy laughs again. "You *are* funny. Maybe I'll let you join my club."

"Club?"

"Yeah, the 'funniest person I know' club."

"Oh, right." I shrug. "Okay."

Getting right back to the subject at hand, she asks, "What'd they say?" I start to speak, but she interrupts with "Then what did you say?"

I pause for a second to be sure she's going to let me respond. "They called asking for Maxwell Quinn...."

"You already said that." Gesturing wildly for me to get on with it, she adds, "What else?"

"I was half asleep."

She squeaks. "Do you think they were calling from the UK?"

"No idea. But"—this is going to blow. Her. Mind—"they were shirtless."

Slapping my arm, hard, she shouts, "Shut up! Were they built? How large were their arms?"

"Ouch." Stepping back out of harm's way, I nod. Patsy has a thing for muscly arms, but if she'd heard their sexy English accent, she'd have gone bananas. "I think they had nice arms. I'm not sure. I was only on the line with them for a couple of minutes.

Enough for them to figure out I wasn't the person they were seeking." Far from it.

Moving closer, she places her hand on my forearm. "Oh. Em. Gee."

Her excitement is getting me excited, sort of. Well, as excited as one can get at seven thirty in the morning. On the day of my first biology class.

*Ugh, science.*

"Did you get their number?" she asks, chewing on her unpainted middle fingernail. I should offer to do her nails sometime. It's the least I could do to thank her for letting me live here.

I'm sure I could call them back if I looked at the recent call log, but "Why?"

"Just curious." She shrugs. "Maybe we could drink some wine sometime and call them back."

"Don't you have a boyfriend?"

"So?" Her bottom lip juts out just a bit. "I can look."

"Sure, sure. You can look. But there's no way I'm calling them back. As soon as they realized their mistake, they hung up." Abruptly. They took one look at my messy head of hair and heard my croaking sleepy voice and wanted nothing to do with me. I shrug again. I can't blame them. I'm scary with bedhead.

"Still." Taking a bite of her breakfast, she smirks. "It'd be fun."

"Uh-huh." Checking my watch, I realize I'm going to be late for my first class. "Gotta go. See you later." I grab my bag and start for the front door.

"Think about it," Patsy shouts after me.

"Yeah, I'll think about it." *Not.*

Once I'm out the door, I pull the keys from the zipper pocket on my backpack and unlock the trunk of my scooter to get to my helmet. I smile down at my awesome wheels made possible by my oldest brother, Steve, who's extremely talented when it comes to mechanical things. He rebuilt it from the frame up on the cheap. I've dubbed my moped Frankenscooter since it's made up of a bunch of parts from other scooters. It's also multi-colored for the same reason. The gas tank is lime green, the frame is red, the seat is a dirty shade of white, and the trunk, the place that holds my helmet, is yellow. It's a mishmash of lots of things, and that's okay. Me and Frankenscooter understand one another. We're both misfits. And thanks to my big brother's talents, I'm not forced to ride Cy-Ride, our city bus system, every day. Don't get me wrong, Cy-Ride is a great option on rainy and snowy days, but it takes twice as long to get places on the bus.

Placing my helmet on my head, I press it down onto my topknot hard enough to latch the chin strap in place. With the key in the ignition, I press the Start button and silently pray that it will turn over. When it purrs to life, I smile and head off to my first and favorite class of the day, Ceramics 2. Having that class first takes some of the nerves away from biology later today. I take the neighborhood streets to campus to avoid Lincoln Way, Ames's main thoroughfare. This time of the morning, it'll be packed with people trying to get to work and class. Taking the back way will save me time in the long run, which is good since I spent extra time talking to Patsy this morning. I don't want to be late or else someone will snag my favorite potter's wheel. I learned that the hard way last spring when I took Introduction to Ceramics. And we can't have that.

I get lucky and find a spot right in the ISU Design Center parking lot. That never happens, trust me. Stowing my helmet, I jog down the back ramp that leads to the shipping dock, a shortcut to the basement where the ceramics classes are held. Well, lots of art classes are held on the lowest level, including painting, jewelry making, textiles, and woodworking. It's a hub of artistic-ness. Wait. That's not a word.

It's official, my brain is mush. Probably due to that phone call last night.

As I grab a few things from my locker that sits only a few doors down from my classroom, I pause to give those guys one last thought. How can you blame me? The two men on the screen were gorgeous, but the one who did most of the talking was the hottest. In all of my twenty-one years, I've never seen anyone like him. Okay, maybe on the cover of a fitness magazine or a romance book. I only saw him from the chest up, but that's all I needed to give me a lifetime's worth of material for any future fantasies. He was blond and tan. His eyes seemed like they were light, almost golden. He also had a big toothy smile the entire time that made me speechless. In a word, the man was perfect.

*That's enough!* There's no room in my life for *that* fantasy man. I've already got one of those. And *he* lives in Ames. Nope, I need to get my head out of the clouds and into class.

I pat myself on my back for keeping it real.

Snort. God, I'm such a dork.

# CHAPTER THREE

The second I step into the house, I'm swarmed. Not by locusts, even though it feels a little like that. No, this is a swarm of roommates. Roommates who got wind of a certain late-night call.

*Thanks, Patsy.*

"Quinn," someone yells from the living room. "Get your ass in here and tell us about the hot Brits."

Placing my bookbag on the floor, I walk slowly down the short hallway into the main living space. It's like walking into a living room from a 60s sitcom. There's an ancient stereo cabinet circa 1965, two old sofas, and three chairs from the same era. The only oddball is the flat screen TV. When I turn my head, I see Patsy point to the seat next to her on the long olive-green couch. "Sit here," she says.

I blow a gust of air out of my mouth and walk, shoulders slumped, over to the seat. I'm starving. All I want to do is make some ramen and get mentally prepared to study for my art history class. That class is all memorization of art, artists, dates, and genres. This could be a good way to bond with the other women in the house.

Once I'm seated, I look at the ladies. I quickly count six. There's one extra person in attendance. "Hey," I say to everyone.

"Quinn," says Patsy in an extra-perky voice. "Start at the very beginning." She turns to the rest of the girls. "Everyone keep your trap shut until she's done. Then she'll take questions. Got it?"

I want to laugh at the way she's taken control of this... whatever this is. Interrogation? Inquisition? Yeah, that sounds about right.

"Well, I was in my room." Duh. "I'd been watching something on Netflix, so—"

"What were you watching?" That question came from Susanna, Patsy's little sister.

"I said no questions until she's done," snaps Patsy.

Susanna must be used to her sister's ways, because she snaps right back, "Jesus. Who died and made you boss?"

"Me," Patsy retorts.

*Okay, then.*

"I was watching *Dead to Me*."

Before I can get another word out, Kat, another roommate interrupts. "Oh my God. Isn't that show great?"

I chuckle because this is going to take fucking forever if they keep interrupting me, but I find it funny nonetheless. "It is."

"What's it about?" asks Susanna.

"For crying out loud," shouts Patsy. "Shut the hell up and let her tell the frigging story."

I can't help it. I laugh, loudly. It must be contagious, because when I look at the other ladies, everyone is laughing—even Pats.

Without being told, I keep going. "I must have fallen asleep because—"

"The show must not have been *that* good." I'm not sure who said it because it sounds like it was mumbled.

"I swear on all that is holy, I will punch the next person who interrupts in the tit. Hard. You hear me?" Patsy huffs.

That's all it takes for the laughs to start again. I'm laughing so hard that tears are running down my face, and I may have peed a little bit. When I get myself under control, I start again, but faster this time. "*Ifellasleepwhilewatchingtheshow.*" Breathe. "*Theringingwokemeup.*" Breathe. When no one says a word, I slow it down. "I assumed it was my best friend, Tayler." Even though she just lives across town, she calls me at all hours of the night. "I reached out and tapped the Answer icon, and they appeared."

I watch as Susanna and Robbi, my fourth roommate, scoot closer. They're getting into this.

"It took a second for the screen to open up, but when it did, I had to blink a million times."

"Why?" Robbi asks.

"Well, I thought I was dreaming."

Susanna is next. "Why?"

"For cripes' sake. Shut the hell up." I can tell Patsy's on her last nerve.

"Fuck you, Pats," growls Susanna.

Attempting to stop the sister fight that's about to erupt, I keep going. "When he came into view, I know I must have gasped, because on my laptop was the most gorgeous guy I'd ever seen."

Susanna raises her hand, waving it about like she's in third grade and she's got the right answer. "Wait. I thought you said there were two guys?"

"There were, but at first it was just the one guy." The hottest one. "It took the other one a minute or two to get into the frame."

"What'd they look like?" asks Robbi.

"They were both shirtless," Patsy whispers.

"Hey!" Susanna protests. "You—"

"Nope. Not a shirt in sight. I could really only see from their faces to about here." I place my hand right under my breasts so they can get a visual. "They were both good-looking. The one in the back, the one who came onto the screen second, had short dark hair and eyes. He seemed smaller than the main guy but still muscled."

I look around the group. None of them are speaking, so I continue. "The guy in front was big, blond, and beautiful."

"You make him sound like a girl," snarls the only person I don't know in the room. I ignore her.

"He was definitely *not* a girl. He had tattoos on both arms. I couldn't tell what they were, but they came up over his shoulders." I stare at the faces around me. They're all rapt with attention. "So anyway, the guy said, 'Oy, he's got a bird.'"

"Oy?" Susanna giggles. "Did he really say that?"

I nod.

"I love it when British guys call girls 'birds.' So cute," sighs Lindsay—our resident romantic, apparently.

"I do too. So, I just stared at the screen until the one in front said, 'Get our mate for us, will you, love?' or something along those lines."

I choose to leave out the part about my bedhead, and I still don't know what baps are. That's unimportant.

"Oh, I love it when British guys call girls 'love.' So romantic." Lindsay again.

"Yeah, that's cute. So, I just stared at the screen because I had no idea what was happening. I was half asleep. So then the one in front, the hot one, asked me again, 'Love. Can you wake our mate?' Since I had no idea what he was talking about, I asked, 'Your mate? Your girlfriend or wife's not here.'"

"Yes. 'Mate' means 'friend' in British," Lindsay says with a nod.

"You didn't figure that out before then?" I look to my left at the girl I've never seen before. "Everyone knows what that means." I stare at the girl and do my best to hold my tongue. It doesn't pay to argue with someone like her. Though I should have, because she's not done. "Like *you'd* just get some random call from two hot guys."

Patsy steps in. "Don't, Kara."

"Yeah, don't be that way." That came from Susanna. I still don't know who Kara is.

"*You* invited me over here, Sus. You told me you wanted me to vet the new roomie. Well, I'm here vetting and she"—Kara points to me—"thinks she's hot shit."

I feel my face burn. I know it's got to be red as a tomato. It always does that when I'm embarrassed. Thank you, Irish ancestry. "I do not."

"Just ignore those two," Patsy says, patting my knee. "Finish the story."

It's not a story. It really happened. I just want to go to my room, so I choose to swallow all of my emotions and finish it up lickety-split. Nodding to Pats, I finish. "They asked for Maxwell Quinn, so I told them my name was Quinn Maxwell and that they had the wrong number. They said good night, and that was it." I pause, hoping that can be the end of it. The mean girl, Kara, is glaring at me.

"Well, that's rather anticlimactic," says Robbi. "Are they in the States? Are they coming to visit?"

I blink at her but keep my mouth shut. Okay, I guess I can't do that, so I shrug and say, "It was a wrong number."

"Yeah." Kara snorts, pointing at me. "And I can tell you with 100 percent certainty that they won't be calling *her* back."

"You really are a bitch, Kara," Robbi snaps.

"Whatevs." Kara rolls her eyes. "I'm out of here."

The only positive part about Kara? She doesn't live here. Thank God.

# CHAPTER FOUR

*What's that noise?*

I blink and see my room is filled with mostly darkness except for the screen on my laptop. It's glowing brightly. It's also where the noise is coming from. My FaceChat app is dinging repeatedly.

"Who the hell is calling me at"—I lean in to read the time on my computer—"three o'clock in the *freaking morning?*" At least this time I wasn't quite asleep yet. Studying for my art history class took me twice as long thanks to the fact that I'm not great at memorization. That and my roommates kept popping into my room last night to ask me more questions, and then Susanna came to apologize for Kara. It was a nice gesture, but I really hope I never see that woman again. She's got "mean girl" written all over her. I don't need that. I had that in high school, and I'd hoped it'd be different in college.

Somewhat irritated, I reach out and press the icon on the touch screen. When it opens, I see him. The guy from last night. The hot one.

Because I've got manners, I say, "Um, yeah?"

"Evening, love."

I stare for a second, waiting for the second man to appear. When he doesn't, I focus my attention on the blond Adonis on the screen. "Hi."

"You're awake?"

"I've been studying."

"Studying? You're a student?"

I nod. "Junior at Iowa State University."

"Iowa State? You're at uni?"

*Uni?* I think about that a sec. Oh... university. "Yes, in the state of Iowa. The midwestern United States."

"I've been to the States, love. New York and Boston."

"Cool." I nod again. I've never been to either of those places. The farthest east I've traveled is Chicago.

"Listen." I watch as he raises his arm so he can run his fingers through his hair. God, I wish I was taping this, because I think I could watch him do that a million more times. His arms are insane. Patsy would die. And his hair? It looks wet, and it's longish on the top. Long enough for him to run his fingers through it and mess it up but in a very sexy way. "My apologies for last evening."

"It was the middle of the night."

"Indeed. I believe we're six hours ahead of you."

I attempt to do the math, but as I've said, it's not my thing. "So, what time is it there?"

"Nine."

"In the morning?"

"Yes. Just had a workout. I'm a bit knackered."

"Knackered?"

"Tired. Like *you* must be. I just wanted to apologize for waking you up last evening."

"So you decided to do it again?" I deadpan.

He looks at me and smiles rather shyly. It makes him better-looking, if that's possible. "Barmy, eh?"

I stare at him for a second, wondering if that's good or bad.

When he says nothing more, I do what I've always done in awkward situations—I smile like a damn fool and say, "Sure."

"You've a lovely smile, Quinn Maxwell."

Oh shit. I know I'm blushing like a crazy person. "Thanks. What's your... uh..." Wow, I don't even know his name.

"Cooke. Cooke Thompson."

"Ah, that's why the other guy called you Cooker."

"My mate. Ian. He's a daft git."

I blink again, wishing I had an American-to-British translator app handy. So, what did I do? You guessed it, I smiled like a fool and said, "Sure."

That must have been the wrong thing to say, or maybe the right thing, because Cooke Thompson throws his head back and laughs heartily. He's got a contagious laugh. So much so that my own laugh starts off as a giggle but quickly devolves into a cackle and a snort. Not the prettiest laugh, ladies and gents. He must enjoy it, though, because before I know it, he's backed up a bit with his hand on his flat-as-sin stomach as he slowly bends forward. His phone isn't moving, so I assume he's got it on a table or something, because I get to watch the whole thing without interruption. It's a sight to behold, let me tell you. Not only do I get to see two-thirds of Cooke, but I get to see where he is—in some kind of workout room. There are weight machines to his left and other things like treadmills and ellipticals to his right.

By the time he's calmed down, I've checked out most of Cooke and his surroundings. From the looks of his amazing body, I'd say he's an athlete of some sort. The large logo of a rose on a shield painted on the wall behind him is a clue too, but I've never seen it before, so I'm only guessing.

"What is that sign behind you?" I ask.

He's stopped laughing enough to tell me, "Team logo."

"Team? What kind of team?"

"Rugby, love."

"Oh, right. Rugby," I repeat.

The look on his face is one of surprise. "You know rugby?"

"Well"—I play with my glasses nervously—"I've heard of it."

For some reason, he thinks that's funny too, and his laughter starts all over again. "Bloody hell, woman. You're a cracker."

Do I even need to tell you what I did? No? Okay.

"Sure."

And it all begins again. He's laughing so hard he's drawn a crowd now. A crowd of men in various stages of undress. So far, no one is completely naked, but they're pretty close. When one of them sees the phone with me peering back at them, several of them begin to move closer. I spy Ian in the bunch, but it's still a tad creepy the way they're staring at me, to be honest. They're looking at me like they've never seen a video phone call before and are trying to figure out if it's real.

"Oy, is that the lass from the other night?" Ian must be the one to ask. No one else would know me from Eve.

"Bugger off, lads," snaps Cooke from somewhere in the crowd.

One of the others responds. "We just wanted to see what the fuss was about, Cooker."

Cooke suddenly sounds angry. "I said feck off."

"Jesus, okay." And like they're being scolded, they all move away from the phone quickly.

Cooke must pick up his device, because now all I see is his pretty face. "Sorry 'bout that, love."

"No. It's okay." I mean, I just saw twenty or so beautiful British men. Why would I be upset about that? "No worries."

We look at one another for a second or two. "Well, I need to get to sleep. I've got class in the morning. A quiz, I'm pretty sure."

"What course?"

"Art history. It's over Gothic architecture." I roll my eyes. This quiz will be the death of me. Heck, all of Dr. Connolly's tests are going to kill me.

"Too bad about the cathedral, eh?"

Notre-Dame Cathedral in Paris was damaged by fire recently. Thankfully, the Rose Window appears to have been spared. "I know. I want to see it one day."

"At least the Rose Window survived."

Wow, he read my mind. "I know."

"Well, you best get to sleep. Nighty night, Quinn Maxwell," he says suddenly.

"Night, Cooke."

When the screen goes blank, I have several weird thoughts rolling around in my head. One, the guy doesn't really know how to end a phone call. Two, I get the feeling I'm going to hear from him again. And lastly, I know I'm not telling a single soul about this second phone call. Not a soul.

*Five minutes later:*

**Me:** Yo, Tayler. Meet me at the Hub tomorrow for lunch. I've got a story for you!

What? You don't expect me to keep my best friend out of the loop, do you? Oh, and the Hub is a building smack-dab in the middle of the ISU campus where you can get a decent cup of coffee and lunch, if you so desire. There are also vending machines along with lots of tables, inside and out on a patio, for people to gather. It's one of my favorite places on campus.

**Tayler:** Yep. C U there. Noon?

I knew my girl would still be up. She's like a bat. Nocturnal.

**Me:** Noon.

## CHAPTER FIVE

"So, who is this bitch Kara?" Leave it to Tayler to pinpoint a problem.

Taking a bite of my PB&J on stale white bread, I answer, "A friend of Susanna's. Apparently she invited her over to vet me."

"To *vet* you? Why? Patsy knows you. That's bullshit."

"I don't know. I haven't been there long enough to get to know them." I shrug. "It makes sense they'd want to know whether or not I'm psycho or whatever."

"No, Kara's job was to gauge whether or not you were cool enough to hang with them."

"Well...."

Setting her coffee cup down, Tayler sighs. I know the sound. It's one of her 'let me explain life to you' kind of sighs. "You always do that."

"Do what?"

"See the best in people when I guarantee they don't deserve it."

"I do not."

"Yes you do."

"Name one." I know what's coming. I shouldn't have challenged her. We've been friends since elementary school. She's seen it all.

"Where do I start? I'll leave middle school and high school out of it and start here"—she points to the ground—"at ISU. Shit, let me just use Bryant."

I wince. I knew she was going to bring him up.

"Even his name...." Tayler rolls her eyes.

"Hey! There's nothing wrong with his name. He can't help that. He was born with it."

"It's not his name that bothers me."

Here we go. This is where she launches into a fifteen-minute diatribe on why my crush on Bryant Falco is stupid. I know it's stupid, but it can't be helped. It was love at first sight. When he walked into my three-dimensional design class last spring, he looked around the room like he owned the place. When his eyes met mine, he smirked and made his way to my table. After sitting right next to me, he turned, gave me a devastatingly handsome smile, and said, "Hey."

*Bam*. Love.

Then he *kept* sitting by me, even though there were plenty of empty seats about and lots of attractive girls in the class. But he sat by *me*. Now, even though we don't have any classes together this semester, I still try to pop in to see him when he's working at the sandwich shop on Welch Avenue. I do my best to bump into him whenever possible, and I drag Tayler along with me. "We can't help who we love, Tayler."

"You don't love him."

Why does she do that? "You don't know what it's like when it's just the two of us."

I think I picked the wrong time to say that, because the sip of coffee she just took ended up all over our table and me. "Fuck. You did not just say that bullshit."

Grabbing napkins, I do my best to wipe the dark liquid from

the front of my white tee. Of course I wore white today. "It's true."

"And by alone, you mean the one and only time you two worked on a project together?"

I'm starting to feel picked on here. "We've hung out." No, we really haven't. I've seen him at Cy's a couple of times, and he's had a beer with me. Technically, I approached him and drank my beer as we chitchatted. He's nice. He's always very jovial and sweet to me. I don't know why Tayler is so down on Bryant Falco. "He's the perfect man for me."

"Okay, first off, there's no such thing as a perfect guy."

"Dylan is pretty perfect." That's her boyfriend. They've been together since junior year of high school and live together in an apartment on the east side of Ames.

"No, Dylan is definitely not perfect. Nobody is."

"But he's perfect for you."

Tayler shrugs.

"What? He is."

"Dylan's fine. But we're not talking about me. We're talking about you."

"Look. I'm not naïve. I know the chances of Bryant Falco liking me back are slim to none, but for once in my life, I'm doing my best to think positively. Even if we end up as friends only, I'm okay with that, because I'd rather have him in my life than not."

"You say all the right things, dearest friend, but I know you. You're going to be heartbroken the first time you see him with another girl."

"Wow." I gather my garbage to throw it away as I leave the Hub. "You have no faith that Bryant will ever see anything in me. Hell, you probably don't think anyone will like me as more than a friend."

"No. I didn't say—"

I hold my hand up to stop her from talking. "That's okay. I get it." I feel the burn behind my eyes and nose that always precedes tears. But I'm not gonna do it. I refuse to tear up in front of Tayler. "I'll die alone. Me and my thirty-six cats."

"Stop it." She tugs on the sleeve of my tee to keep me from leaving. "You're just trying to make me feel bad."

I halt because it hits me like a ton of bricks. Turning back slowly, I look at my beautiful best friend. Her long auburn hair practically sparkles, it's so shiny. Her perky little nose dotted with freckles that are obvious since she barely wears makeup. She doesn't need it. Then there's her petite body. She's never been bigger than a size four. When she was, she thought she was fat. Ha. That's a joke.

"I can't make you understand how I feel about Bryant, but you're supposed to be my best friend. You're supposed to support me even if failure is inevitable. That's when best friends come in handy—that's when they come to the rescue. But you don't even think I have a chance with him. Why is that? I'm not hideous." I look down at my big T-shirt and leggings with the tear in the knee, then back up at Tayler. "I'm fat. I know that. Some guys like a little meat on a girl's bones." I haven't met one of those unicorns yet, but maybe someday.

"Bryant isn't one of those guys."

"How do you know?"

"Because, my sweet, delusional friend, if Bryant wanted you, he'd have already made a move."

Oh. Wow. It stings like a thousand wasps getting me all at once. "I see."

"No, you don't. Guys like Bryant don't do girls like you."

Fuck. That hurts. One tear leaks out, but I don't give a shit. "Stop." I hold up my hand again. "That's enough." Sniffling, I turn away from her.

"Quinn, wait. I didn't—"

I ignore her and walk out the door. I've got to process this. I need space from the one person I thought I could count on.

## CHAPTER SIX

I needed and wanted space, but maybe not for this long. It's been almost a week since our fight, and Tayler hasn't tried to call me once. Nope. No voice mails, not a single text. I haven't contacted her either, because I know Tayler Sorenson, and if I call now, she'll want to rehash everything that we argued about. All of it. And I don't want to hear how I'm not the kind of girl guys like *that* way. I mean, I already knew that. I've heard it pretty much all my life thanks to my brothers. Heck, even my dad calls me "my chunky monkey." Ugh. Such a terrible nickname. I don't have the heart to say anything, because for him, it's not offensive. My mom's favorite endearment is "pleasantly plump" because she and I have the same body type. She obviously doesn't have the negative self-image that I do. She's lucky. But those parental expressions are nice compared to some of the things I've heard in the past. My older brothers were particularly cruel growing up, calling me "thunder thighs" and other mean things.

Listen, I'm not feeling sorry for myself, I swear. I'm just trying to make my point. I know I'm no man's ideal woman. But I've read enough books and watched enough reality television to believe there's someone for everyone. Mine may not be Bryant, I get that. I'm not naïve. But if I don't put myself out there, how will I ever know for sure? She knows me better than anyone. I've had crushes before, and she knows I get over them, eventually. So why is Tayler making a point about *this* guy now?

Since our fight at the Hub, I decided I was going to do something I've never done when it comes to Tayler: I'm going to wait her out. It's going to have to be *her* who contacts *me*. And when she does, it'd better start off with an apology. In the meantime, I've been doing my thing: going to class, studying, working up the courage to apply for jobs, and I've decided to hang out with my new roommates. Tonight, we're going out for Thirsty Thursday. It's what we college students call the night we all go out and drink too much. It's also the night bars such as Cy's Roost have drink specials like two-dollar pitchers of crappy beer. I know, hangovers make Friday classes almost unbearable, but I need to get to know my roommates, and having a drink—or three—with them is one way to do it.

Speaking of which, I look at my clock. I've only got thirty minutes before they're off to the bar. I jump off my bed and search my little closet for something decent to wear. Generally I wear oversized tees and either jeans or leggings. Scanning my closet, I don't see anything that inspires me, so I search for my black V-neck tee and black jeggings. For those of you who haven't heard of those, they're jeans that stretch like leggings. The best of both worlds.

Crawling around on my floor, I find my black Converse sneakers underneath my bed along with some pretty scary-looking dust bunnies. Scary because I think I just saw one skitter away from my hand. *Shiver.* After sliding on my shoes, I pick up my small crossbody purse that's just large enough to hold my cell phone, a debit card, and some cash. I stop in my tracks when I catch a glimpse of my face in my mirror. "Shit." I didn't do a thing with my hair or makeup. Instead of that, I took forty minutes to paint my nails. I did the Converse sneaker nails. So cute.

Peeking at the clock, I see I've got a few minutes to spare, so I pull out the tie in my hair, brush it, and put it back up into a knot on top of my head. Looking at my little bit of makeup, I swipe some mascara on my lashes and a soft pink lip gloss on my mouth. Looking in the mirror one last time, I shrug. "As good as it's ever going to get."

Upstairs, I meet my roommates hovering near the front door. Correction, my roommates and Kara. Great.

"That's what you're wearing?" says guess who.

"Knock it off, Kara," snaps Patsy. Looking at me, she smiles. "You look good. I like the all-black ensemble." Except she pronounces "ensemble" like she's French. It makes me laugh.

One by one, the girls start to make their way out the door. As we move, I hear Kara muttering something to Susanna. "She could have at least done her hair."

"Shhh," says Susanna. "Leave her alone."

"Why?"

"Just... she's nice."

"Fuck nice. She's—"

"Enough!" shouts Robbi. "Stop being a bitch to her, Kara, or you can go home."

"Yeah," Kat agrees. "If you can't be nice for once, go home."

"Fuck you," mumbles Kara.

But, sadly, she doesn't leave.

"Who's turn is it to buy the next pitcher?" asks a drunk Robbi.

"Mine." Sliding out of our big booth, I hold up two fingers. "Two?"

"Two!" shouts Susanna. "And get some fries."

I shake my head. Cy's serves bar food most days, but I know

for sure they aren't serving food tonight. They never do when they know the bar is going to be wall-to-wall people.

"They don't serve food when it's like this." I point to the sea of people.

Susanna gives me a sad face as I begin the long trek up to the bar. There's only one here at Cy's Roost, and since this place is packed due to the beer specials, it takes me a while to weave through the hordes, but not nearly as long as it's taking me to get served now that I'm at the bar. Being short is not in my favor right now. I'm waving my arm like a maniac to get the attention of one of the bartenders when I hear my name.

"Quinn!"

Turning my head to the right, I hear it again but from my left. Rotating my head toward the voice, I smile when I see him. Bryant. Quick as I can, I squeeze past several people until I'm next to him. "Hey."

Bryant chuckles, and it's so adorable. "This place is insane, huh?"

"It is. I'm supposed to be getting beer for my roomies, and it's taking forever."

Before I can say another word, Bryant has flagged down a bartender. Leaning close to me, he whispers, "What do you need?"

My God, his breath just hit my right ear. It made my skin pebble with goose bumps. I even got a whiff of his breath—minty. His cologne is subtle but manly. My goodness, this guy.

"Hello. Earth to Quinn." He chuckles again.

"Oh." I flush bright red. "Sorry. Two pitchers of Light, please."

I watch as he leans over several people to order my beer. In no time, he's got both pitchers in his hand along with an empty glass. Then he says, "I'll follow you."

"Oh, okay." I start the long walk back, but this time, he's right behind me. And I mean *right* behind me. He's bumped into me several times, and I'm not going to lie, it felt amazing each and every time.

When I get to the table, the girls are all huddled together, laughing.

"Finally, Jesus," Kara grumbles. "Where'd you have to get it, China?"

She really is a bitch. Without another word, Bryant sets the pitchers down on the table. Turning to me, he asks, "Mind if I join you?"

Oh hell. "Of course not." I quickly slide into the booth, and he follows close behind.

"Hey," says Kara with a fake-ass smile. "Who's your friend, Quinn?"

"Oh, right." I giggle like a dork. "This is Bryant." I point to him. "Bryant, these are my roommates." I pause for a second and point at Kara. "Well, not her."

Bryant leans forward with his hand out to her. "Bryant Falco. What's your name, not a roommate?" Then he chuckles. It sounds stupid.

"Kara," she says sweetly. "Kara Becker."

I stare in stunned silence as she places her hand in his. It stays there for a long time. When he gives her hand a squeeze, it feels like he just squeezed the hell out of my heart. What the ever-loving—

"Quinn!" shouts Kat from across the table. So, like two feet away.

"Yeah?"

"Did you hear from those hot Brits again?"

"Yeah, like that'd ever happen." Kara snorts.

I look at Kara and see she still has her hand in Bryant's. Giving their hands the evil eye, I turn to Kat. "I did, actually."

I know, I know. I swore I wouldn't tell anyone about the second phone call, but, well, I can't let Kara get away with her snide remarks.

"What?" squeaks Patsy from the far end of the table. "When?"

"The next night."

"The night of our powwow?" asks Kat.

"Yeah. Another late call. Three in the morning."

Kat asks, "Was it both of them?"

"No, just one. The one who made the call the first night."

I watch Kara open her mouth, but I jump in first. "He called to apologize for waking me up and for the wrong number."

Robbi asks, "So, what'd you say?"

"That it was okay. I don't know. We talked for a while. I found out a few things about him."

Susanna joins the conversation. "Like what?"

"He's a rugby player."

"How do you know that?" Kara snaps.

I quickly glare at her, then answer, "He was in a gym. There was a team logo behind him, so I asked him what it was." I decide to add more. "There were other guys working out around him."

"Rugby?" asks Bryant. "Where is this guy from?"

"He's British," responds Patsy.

Bryant has taken an interest now. "Is he professional?"

I shrug. "I don't know. He looks like he could be a professional athlete. His body, I mean."

"Jesus. Do you guys really believe this shit?" Kara spits, crossing her arms in front of herself like a petulant child. What the hell is her problem with me?

"Fine. Here." I pull the phone out of my little purse. Searching the FaceChat for recent calls, I find his number. Without another thought, because beer has given me courage, I hit the Call button. My roommates have squeezed in closer. If Kat could crawl onto my lap, I think she would. Turning on the speaker, we hear it ring once, then twice. When it rings a third time, I assume he's not going to answer. Just as I'm about to hang up, I hear him. "Quinn. Love."

Thank. Fuck.

He's lying on white sheets. His hair is messy, and he's shirtless. I can see more of his tattoos from this point of view. "Hi, Cooke. Did I wake you?"

"You did, love. Turnabout's fair play, eh? Where are you? It's noisy. Are you in a pub?"

I snort. "A bar. I'm with my friends. They didn't believe me when I told them about your wrong number. They thought I made up the whole Maxwell Quinn debacle."

"Debacle." He chuckles, and it sounds sexy and sleepy. "I'd call it kismet rather than a debacle, love, because I met you."

"Oh." *That was nice.*

"God damn it, Quinn. Let us see him." Kat's bouncing in her seat.

"Right." Talking to Cooke, I tell him, "I'm turning the phone so you can meet my friends."

"All right. Only fair after me mates the other day."

Without another word, I hold my phone up so everyone can see him. I start with Bryant. "That's Bryant. Then Patsy." I skip Kara. Ha! "Then there's Kat, Lindsay, Robbi, and Susanna." I pull the phone back to face me.

"Who was the blonde? You didn't mention her name."

Of course he noticed that. "Oh, that's just Kara."

I feel the phone being wrenched from my hands. I'm gobsmacked that Kara just took my phone. "Hi, Cooke was it?" Kara preens. "You'll have to forgive Quinn. She's very rude. We're used to it, though."

Cooke sounds surprised. "Oh?"

"Yeah, we barely tolerate her. She—"

I reach over and grab my phone from her hands. Without another thought, I end the call. I've had it with this girl. I tried to keep my mouth shut, but no more. "Kara," I say loudly. "I have no idea what I ever did to you, but I'm only going to say this once. Back. The. Fuck. Off."

"Or what?" She sniffs. "You going to sit on me?"

When Bryant chuckles, that's it. It's like a stab in the back with a bowie knife. So, I turn to him. "Let me out, please."

"Quinn," he starts.

I give him my best glare. "Bryant. Let. Me. Out."

He quickly slides out of the booth, and I follow him. Stepping away from the table, I move as fast as I can toward the back door. Thankfully, the place has thinned out a little, so it's not a struggle to get through the crowd. When I'm nearly at the back door, I hear Patsy or one of them yelling my name, but I ignore them. I need to go home. I want to be by myself.

Stepping out onto Hayward Avenue, I turn north. When it meets up with Lincoln Way, I take a left just as my phone rings. I look down and see the FaceChat icon flashing. Without thinking, I press the button to answer. "Hello?"

"Quinn?"

My goodness, I could listen to him say my name forever in that pretty English accent. "Yeah?"

"What happened? You're no longer at the pub, love?"

"I left."

"Are you crying, love?"

"N-No." Okay. A little.

"Why? Did I do something?"

"No." My voice cracks. "Of course not. It was K-Kara."

"She's a right cow, eh?"

That makes me laugh. "If that means she's a bitch, then yes." I blow out a breath, trying to calm myself. "I barely know her, but she never stops saying terrible things about me."

"She's jealous, love."

I know I should laugh at that, but I can't. "I gotta go." I hang up the phone again and shove it in my back pocket. "Jealous? Of me?" What a fucking joke.

I make it another block when my phone rings again. "Hello?"

"We keep getting disconnected."

"Uh-huh."

"Are you walking? Alone? After dark, love?"

"It's not far. Ames is very safe." I stare down at my phone and blink a few times because I can't believe what I'm seeing. Cooke is getting dressed. Don't worry, he's not naked—not completely. He's in a loose pair of shorts that show off his perfect abdominals. Now he's sliding on a shirt. When he pulls it down, I can see it's got the same logo, the flower, as I saw in the gym, and there's an O and a 2 with it. "Is your team famous?"

He's still moving around in what appears to be a hotel room. "We're the best, love."

"Are you on a college team?"

Cooke chuckles. "I'm going to send you a link later today. Check it out and that will answer your question."

"Oh. Okay." I pause. "So, not a college team?"

"No, love." Cooke chuckles as he picks his phone back up. "You almost home?"

Oh, he wants to hang up. "Yep," I lie. "Just walking up to my door now."

"Okay, then. Sleep tight, Quinn Maxwell. I need to dash."

"Bye, Cooke." I'm about to press End as I cross the street. Looking up, I'm barely aware of the car turning the corner toward me. I don't think he sees me. I attempt to pick up my pace, but I'm forced to take corrective action, launching myself forward until I feel hard concrete against my palms and knees. As I fall to the ground, my phone skitters across pavement.

The passenger in the car leans out of the open window and yells, "Pay attention where you're going, dumb bitch!"

I roll over onto my butt and assess the damage. My jeggings are ripped on *both* knees now, and blood is oozing out of the scrapes beneath. My hands feel like they're burning. When I peer down at them, I wince. They're really messed up, and rocks and dirt are embedded in my palms. "Shit." I suck in a sharp breath as I try to wipe them on my legs.

"Quinn? Love?"

*What the hell?* I look to my left, searching for my phone. I spot it in the grass. Gingerly, I roll in that direction and pick it up. "Cooke?"

"What happened?"

"Oh. Erm...."

"Quinn."

"I fell." I'm not about to tell him I was an idiot and almost got hit by a car. "I guess I had too much to drink." Which is not a lie.

"I thought you said you were home. There's a shop behind you."

I slowly turn my head and see the bright lights of a convenience store. *Damn.* "Well, I... you sounded like you were busy. I—"

"Darling." It sounds like "Dahling." So cute.

"I'm fine. Just a klutz. Go. Get on with your day. I'm almost home, I promise."

"I'll walk with you." He chuckles. "If you're tipsy, I want to make sure you're safe, love."

"Fine." I push up to standing and stare down at myself. I'll live. "So, you don't play college rugby."

Cooke starts to laugh, and it reminds me of our last call. It's contagious, and I laugh too.

"No, I guess you could call me a professional footballer."

"Like the Minnesota Vikings?"

"I suppose it's similar. I'm paid to play the sport. Not as much as your famous American footballers, but enough."

"Ah, I see."

"Just click on the link I'm going to send you and watch it. It'll explain everything."

"Man of mystery, huh?"

Cooke laughs again. "Indeed. I'm extremely mysterious."

It's my turn to laugh. He seems very open to me. Nothing secretive about this man. But what do I know? We've only spoken three times. Well, more if you count the times I've hung up on him.

I look up and see my house. "Now I'm really home."

"Oh? Prove it."

Turning the phone around, I point it at the white house with the red door. "That's my house."

"You live with the girls from the pub?"

"There are six of us."

"That's a lot of females in one house." He pretends to shiver.

Pushing open the door, the first thing I notice is the silence. Nice. "It's not bad." Looking at our small kitchen, I silently wish I had something good to snack on, but I can't bring myself to eat toast right now. "I'm home," I say tiredly. "Time for bed. I've got an early class tomorrow."

"All right. Nighty night, Quinn."

"Night, Cooke. Have a good, er, workout?"

"Aye, lass. Thanks."

And he was gone.

# CHAPTER SEVEN

Taking a coffee break at the Hub the next day, I use the time to study my notes for Introduction to Biology. We aren't supposed to have a quiz today, but it's Friday, the day of the week that lots of people skip, so a lot of professors give pop quizzes to punish those who can't get their butts out of bed. But I'm a good student and woke up on time—mostly—and was out of the house and on my scooter in time for Ceramics 2. Yay!

Just as I'm about to write down some vocabulary, I hear his voice. "Hey, Quinn."

I look up and blink. The sun is shining through the floor-to-ceiling windows in the Hub. "Oh, hi, Bryant." I know I should ignore him, be angry with him for laughing when Kara... never mind. She's a hag.

"How're you feeling today?" He smirks.

"Fine. Why?"

"You were pretty wasted last night."

"Um." No, I was tipsy, as Cooke called it, but not wasted. "Right."

I watch as Bryant sidles up close. "Mind if I sit?"

I nod to the chair across from me, but he chooses the one

next to me. Not unusual, but still. I'm a bit leery. I'm not sure what to do, so I jot down a vocabulary word into my notes.

"What're you doing?" he asks.

I want to say, "What does it look like?" but I decide to keep the snark in check. "Studying?" Why the heck did I say it like it was a question? I shrug. "Friday is pop quiz day."

"Right." He places his hands on the table and begins to tap nervously. "So."

I sigh, set down my pencil, and look at him. "So."

"I was curious about that guy you were talking to?"

"Yeah?" Why on earth for? I arch my brow.

Bryant chuckles and flips the front of his hair out of his eyes.

I used to think that little hair flip was cute. Now? Oh, who am I kidding? It's still cute.

"My roommate is on the Iowa State rugby team."

"We have one of those?" *Who knew?*

He laughs again. Patting my hand a tad too condescendingly, he says, "Of course. It's a club team, so it's not like our other big sports. They travel, though. Play teams from the other Big12 schools."

"Huh. Who-da-thunk?"

"Is your friend famous?"

I shrug because I have no idea.

He's not giving up on the questions. "You mentioned the logo?"

"It's a flower."

"Wait." Tapping on his phone, he stops and turns the phone my way. "This logo?"

Wow, he found that fast. "Yep. That's the one."

"So, he plays professional rugby." He pauses, then punches out, "For. England."

I shrug again. "I guess."

Bryant chuckles. "Wow." Looking back down at me, he smiles.

"Leave it to ditzy Quinn to befriend a professional athlete and not even know it."

Hold the gosh dang phone. Ditzy Quinn? I'm not ditzy. "I'm not ditzy."

Patting the top of my hand again, he smiles, but it's not sincere. "You know what I mean."

No, I really don't. But I'm not going to argue with him about this. It gives me some things to think about, though.

"What's his name again?" Bryant picks his phone up and holds it like he's ready to go.

"Cooke."

"Cooke?"

Why is he asking? If I let on that I probably know more than I should about the hot guy from England, Bryant might get the wrong idea. "Cooke the rugby player from England."

Bryant chuckles, shakes his head, and types. I wait in silence as he stares down at his phone. Looking up at me, he asks, "Cooke Thompson?"

I lift both shoulders and attempt to show him that I have no idea. *Why do I care what Bryant thinks?* I doubt he'd be jealous of a guy half-way across the world.

Reaching out, Bryant slaps my back. Hard. So hard that I wince. "Leave it to somebody like you to fall into something like that. Jesus. You're friends with fucking Cooke Thompson."

I lift one shoulder. "I wouldn't call us friends." I wouldn't. We've talked on the phone a few times. So what? "I didn't realize you followed rugby." Honestly, I know very little about Bryant. *Except that I thought I loved him.*

"I'm a *big* rugby fan. My team is Wales." There's a weird silence between us. Uncomfortable. That is until he says, "Yeah, well, the reason I stopped by...."

*Oh, here we go.*

"Do you happen to have your friend Kara's number?"

*Oh. No. He. Didn't.*

Before I can even think to speak, I slam my book shut, then slap my notebook down on top of that. Then I take both and shove them into my backpack. First off, "My *friend* Kara?" What the ever-loving hell? Secondly, why would he ask *me*? I'm—he's supposed to like *me*.

"Quinn?"

Grabbing the handle of my backpack, I stand. Turning to him, I say the only thing I can and still save face. "Kara is *not* my friend." I mean, didn't he hear the shit she was saying about me last night? I doubt it stopped when I left. "I just met her, and I've been doing my best to stay as far away from her as possible."

"Why?" He's standing up now too.

"She's mean."

"Mean? She seemed nice."

"To you," I spit. I'm not doing this.

I start to step away when I feel him grasp my upper arm. I quickly pull back because I hate my arms. His voice is soft. "Quinn. Stop."

I stop, but I don't look at him.

"I'm sorry," he continues. "She was a bitch to you last night. I shouldn't have asked you for her digits."

*Digits?* God, that sounds so stupid, especially since I already know he's not sorry for wanting her number. He's just sorry he asked *me*.

"No problem." I step away from him, picking up my pace. I'm out the door and on my way to biology—one hour early. Great.

As I'm walking out the door, he shouts, "Hey, tell Cooke he's got fans here. If he's ever in Ames—"

The door slams behind me, so I don't get to hear the rest of it, thank goodness.

## CHAPTER EIGHT

Tayler was right, but I refuse to admit that to her. If I do, she'll just rub it in my face. Not only that, but she's never the one to apologize first whenever we've had a fight, and I'm tired of it. She claims it's because I'm too emotional (I am), that I take things too personally (I do), and she doesn't have time for it. God, just thinking about it pisses me off. I've lasted over a week without my best friend. While it makes me sad, I know I need to hold out for her to extend the olive branch this time. Can I do it? Time will tell. In the meantime, I'll get to know my roommates a little better—hopefully sans Kara—and see where that goes.

~

As I wait for my biology class to begin, I use the time to go over my notes again. Biology is not my thing. You can lump science right in with math, *thankyouverymuch*. Exception? I took Geology 101 my freshman year, dubbed 'Rocks for Jocks,' and I loved it. I learned a lot of good stuff about Earth, like tectonic plates. Plus, the professor was cool and funny.

The door opens to the lab and our teaching assistant steps in.

She's in charge of these labs while the actual professor does the lecture portion of the classes. At least the labs let us *do* things. Sitting in a lecture for ninety minutes is not my favorite thing, but it's just part of it, I guess. Today, we're continuing to talk about ecosystems, and happily, our task is to work in groups to make a poster about our experiments, which is right up my alley. Whoever I get lumped with will appreciate my artistic skills.

Just as class is about to end, I feel my phone vibrate in the front pocket of my hoodie. We're not supposed to have phones in class, so I want to be discreet. Looking down, I reach into my pocket and pull it about halfway out, enough for me to see the text

**Unknown:** Hey, this is Cooke. Just wanted to check on you after last night.

I'm honestly shocked. I mean, I've video chatted with this man several times, and it's strange because he's very easy to talk to. Sure, it could be the fact that he lives a million miles away and obviously unattainable for someone like me, so there's none of my usual nerves like when I talk to hot guys like Bryant. Cooke seems to be a nice guy who happens to be drop-dead gorgeous and definitely out of my league.

I look up to make sure the TA can't see me on my phone. Holding it under my table in an attempt to hide it, I quickly add him to my contacts and type:

**Me:** Hi, Cooke. I'm good. In biology lab. Can't get caught with my phone.

He responds immediately.

**Cooke:** Biology, eh? I think you need to tell me all about your biology lessons.

I blink a few times. *Is Cooke flirting with me?* I shake my head. "Nah." So I type the least sexy thing I can think of.

**Me:** We're learning about ecosystems.
**Cooke:** Well, that's a shame.
**Me:** It's not my thing.
**Cooke:** What's your "thing"?
**Me:** Art. I'm an art ed major.
**Cooke:** Art ed?
**Me:** Art education. I want to be an art teacher someday.
**Cooke**: Wonderful profession, educator. You must be a talented artist.
**Me:** I'm okay.

"Quinn Maxwell."

Shit.

I look up and see my TA glaring at me. "Choose. Your phone or this class."

Wow, she doesn't mess around. But I knew that. She's said the same thing to several others in class. "Sorry." I quickly slip the phone into my pocket and get back to work. I feel it vibrate several more times, but I don't dare look at it. No matter. I've only got a few minutes left in class; I can check after.

As I'm walking out the door, I half expect the TA to pull me aside and give me a good talking-to, but she doesn't. Luckily.

Once outside, I hoist my heavy backpack behind me and start the long trek back to my scooter. Just as I step onto central campus, my phone chimes. Pulling it out of my back pocket, I quickly hit the FaceChat icon. "Cooke?"

"Hey, love. You didn't write back." Why does he sound a little miffed about that?

"Oh, sorry. I got caught with my phone in class, and that's a no-no. I'm just leaving now."

I glance at the time on the Campanile, the ancient clock

tower in the middle of ISU's beautiful campus: 2:00 p.m. Doing some quick math, I ask, "So, is it eight o'clock at night there?"

"It is, love, and I'm knackered."

He's used that word before. "Why are you tired? What did you do today?"

"Up with the chickens for our first workout. Then meetings, a workout, lunch, more meetings, a scrimmage, more meetings, dinner, then off to the physio."

"Physio?"

"Oh, let's see if I can give you the Americanized name." He chuckles. "The therapist for my leg."

"You hurt your leg?" Oh no.

"Years ago, but it still gives me fits now and then."

I've stopped at one of the concrete benches in the grassy park-like spot on central campus. I look around me and sigh. It's so pretty here, and people love hanging out in this spot. Students are sitting on their sweatshirts talking, and there's a guy taking a nap to my right. He must be tired, because the other people aren't quiet.

"What are you sighing about?" Cooke asks with a look of curiosity on his face.

"Campus. It's pretty. Here." I turn the phone around and scan the large courtyard. It sits smack-dab in the middle of four of the oldest buildings on campus: Beardshear, the Memorial Union, Catt Hall, and Curtiss Hall.

"It's lovely."

So are his accent and the words he says with said accent. "It is. The weather is perfect. Not too hot, not cold yet."

"It sounds ideal."

In many ways it is. "So, are you going to bed now?"

"I'm not my granny." He chuckles. "But I'm no spring chicken either."

Okay, now we're getting into some personal questions. "How old are you?"

"Twenty-six, love. And you?"

"Twenty-one." I almost say "and a half," but that sounds childish.

"A babe."

I blush, thinking he means I'm attractive, but then I remember who I'm talking to and who I am and snort as I think better of it. He means I'm still young. "Sometimes I feel ancient." Without giving him a chance to comment, I ask, "Have you always played rugby?"

"Since I was a lad, yes. My father was quite good, so he taught me the sport."

I'm almost nervous to bring it up, but he did send them to me. "Oh, I watched those videos."

On the screen, Cooke goes from standing somewhere in a room to lying on his bed. A white pillow fluffs up around his head as he places one hand behind his head while the other holds his phone above him. It gives me a bird's-eye view of his chest. The pose makes the arm behind his head look corded with muscles. I'm staring like a dang fool, but I'm forced out of my daze when he asks, "What did you think?"

What did I think? About what? I shake my head. "Oh, about your little rugby movies?"

Cooke chuckles. "Yeah, our little movies."

There were two short videos about his team and their road to the Rugby World Cup. He was in it a lot: getting measured for a suit, being hooked up to a heart monitor, doing a lot of running around with his teammates. "I liked it." The truth is, I know nothing about rugby. "My, erm, friend Bryant's roommate plays rugby for Iowa State, my university."

"Have you been to a match?"

"No. I... he just told me." God, why is talking about Bryant making me all squirrely?

"Are you blushing, lass?"

Yes. "No."

"Who is this Bryant fellow? Boyfriend?"

Now I feel the heat on my cheeks. "I wish," I whisper. "No. We're just friends."

"Friend-zoned, eh?"

I nod. "Exactly."

"He's a fool. You're lovely, Quinn Maxwell."

"Ha," I say too loudly. "He's out of my league."

I stare down at my phone and watch Cooke's face change from one that's smiling and jovial to one that's serious and rather angry. "I've only just met you, love, and I happen to think you're in a league all your own."

"Well, therein lies the problem. You just met me, and anyway, I don't think FaceChat really counts as 'meeting' someone."

"The feck it doesn't," he snaps. "You've become the bright spot in my day, Quinn, and we've only just met on FaceChat. If we met in person, I'm sure I'd fall madly in love with you."

I'm blushing, but not in a good way. Why do I get the feeling he's fucking with me? I don't need this. "Well, it's a good thing you're not here, because you'd be disappointed." I feel my eyes water, but I'm not about to let him see me upset, so I quickly say, "Hey, Cooke. I need to, uh, get to class. I'm late."

"Quinn."

"Bye," I chirp, doing my best to sound happy, though it's hard to when it's been a shit day. "Nice talking to you."

It's true. I take everything way too personally. I'm not sure I know how to stop doing that, though. I grew up as the youngest of five kids, three of whom weren't especially nice to me. It probably stems from that, I guess. Don't get me wrong, I love my family. I do. Now that we're older, I think they get that they weren't very nice to me. Hell, I'm sure they know now. My mom likes to tell everyone that I pretty much cried the first sixteen years of my life. I've no doubt that's partially true. It's probably why I hate crying now. It's also why I internalize everything people say, even if it's not intentionally mean-spirited. Like what

Cooke just said. He meant well, but I know without a doubt that if he were here in person, he would *not* be attracted to me. How could he be? I'm a size sixteen on a good day. Guys like Cooke Thompson don't fall in love with the Quinn Maxwells of the world. They just don't.

# CHAPTER NINE

Entering my house, I set my backpack down next to the kitchen table. The first thing I notice is the house is unnaturally quiet. With five roommates, there's always someone home, and they're usually watching a movie or listening to music loudly. When I step into the living room, I see four out of the five huddled together, whispering. So I'm not a creeper, I say, "Hey."

They jump apart quickly, three of them giggling and Robbi merely smiling. "Shit, girl. You surprised us," Susanna says with her hand over her heart.

"Sorry." I'm not actually sorry. "Hey, Pats," I say, nodding in her direction.

"How was your day?" asks Kat sweetly.

"Goo—" I'm about to say "good," but I decide not to lie. "Shitty, actually."

"Oh?" all three say in unison.

"Why? What happened?" Patsy sounds sincerely concerned.

I know I shouldn't say anything because this is going to get to the rest of the roommates and probably to others, but what the hell. "Bryant wants Kara's number."

"Yay," Susanna squeaks as she claps and bounces up and down in her seat. "She'll be so—oh."

"You like him?" I think it was Kat's question.

"I do." I shrug. "Or I did. But I know he's out of my league."

"Oh," Susanna coos. "That's not true. You have such a pretty face."

Now, here's the thing. I know she means that as a compliment, but it's not. Sure, she said I had a pretty face, but what I heard was "It's too bad the rest of you is hideous."

"Thanks." Looking over at Susanna, I tell her, "I've got Bryant's number if you want to give it to her."

"Oh, um, sure." She smiles weakly.

"Also, I really like you guys. I've enjoyed hanging out with you at Cy's and here, but if you go out and Kara's going to be there, please let me know so I can bow out gracefully."

"Not over a guy." Robbi sounds indignant. "Hoes before bros, Quinn."

Shaking my head, I say, "She's not nice. To me, anyway. I don't need that in my life." I had to deal with that enough with my family and the bullies in middle and high school. I'm not doing that again.

Patsy nods. "Sure. We'll tell you if she's going out with us."

"But...," Susanna starts but then hesitates.

I arch my brow, waiting for it. I know what's coming. Susanna is going to tell me, "*Kara's not so bad.*"

"Kara means well."

Close enough.

Susanna feels compelled to continue, I guess. "She had a rough childhood."

I stand in silence, waiting for Kara's sob story. No matter what it is, there's nothing so terrible that should make her into such a vile human being.

"Her sister died when she was a baby."

"Sorry to hear that." I really am. "It's sad."

Robbi scoffs, "It's still no excuse for being the world's biggest bitch."

"Robbi..." Susanna whispers.

"Welp," I say with my happiest voice, "I'm going to make some ramen, and then I've got studying to do."

"You know...."

Holy shit. Is today going to be the world's biggest fucking cliché day or what? When it rains, it pours, as they say. I look over at Patsy. "Yes. I know ramen is bad for me. If I didn't eat it, I'd probably lose weight."

Patsy nods.

Shrugging, I say, "But, it's cheap and I'm broke, so that's just the way it is."

"I could help you."

I'm doing my utmost to *not* roll my eyes hard. I smile instead. "Yeah?"

"You could start running with me."

She's right. I could. I could also win the Nobel Prize in math. *Definitely not.* "I'd have to walk. I'm going to start working out at the rec center as soon as I save up enough money for the membership." Save up? How am I going to do that? I don't have a job.

"Good." She smiles. "I just care—"

Interrupting her, I return her smile. "I know. Thanks, Patsy."

"No problem."

I turn on my heel and grab my backpack from the dining area. Instead of making ramen right now, I opt to go down to my room instead. I'll make it later, after everyone gets settled in their rooms. I've had enough interaction with people for one day.

Knock. Knock. Knock.

I lift my head off my textbook. "Yeah," I say sleepily.

"Quinn? It's Patsy. Can I come in?"

"Sure." I quickly scan my room to make sure I don't have anything out that would embarrass me—you know, like dirty undies and such.

When she steps in, she looks first at me, then around my room. "Do you like it down here?"

"Yeah. My room is big." And it is. It's twice the size of my room at home. It's also super moist, and I'm pretty sure there's a colony of spiders living under my bed. So, I've got that goin' for me.

"Good." She points at my desk chair.

I nod.

Turning it to face me, she sits. "Look. About earlier."

"No, it's okay."

She holds up her hand, and I stop talking. "You and I met last year, so you didn't know me before."

"Before?"

"Before I lost just over one hundred pounds."

"Wow. Really?"

"Really. It took me two years and a fuck-ton of work." She giggles. "Keeping it off is twice as hard thanks to beer."

We both laugh at that.

"So, when I said I'd help you, I meant it."

I open my mouth to speak, but she holds her hand up again. "But with the caveat that you need to know that I meant what I said. You're beautiful." I'm about to roll my eyes when she adds, "*All* of you."

She knows. I'm sure she heard about her pretty face a time or two.

"If you want to go for walks, I'd love to go with you. They're free, and it beats the hell out of running." She laughs. "I fucking hate running."

"Me too. Running hurts."

"Heck, thirty-minute walks every day will give you more

energy. You know, endorphins or whatever. If that's all you do, then you're still doing something proactive and healthy."

I walk a lot already. Going across campus several times a day is good enough, right?

"I know what you're thinking. Yes, we walk a lot on campus, but you're probably not getting your heart rate up since they're short distances."

I swear, the woman is a mind reader. "Tomorrow?" Might as well bite the bullet. I have a feeling Patsy won't let this go anyway.

"Meet me downstairs at six. We'll do thirty minutes. On the days we have class, it'll give us time to get ready for class afterward."

"Ugh, six? In the morning?" I whine, but then I laugh. "Sure. See you then."

After she leaves, I scowl at my textbook. I'm tired of studying, so I grab my nail polish supplies and set to work to give my nails a new look. Since it's now September, I'll do autumnal colors. A different one for each nail.

With my supplies out, I sigh. Doing my nails is my stress reliever. I lose myself in the process—just what I need right now.

# CHAPTER TEN

Six o'clock came faster than I'd hoped. I tossed and turned all night, though I'm not sure why. I'm usually like that right before a big test, but that's not it this time. It could have been because I knew I had to get up early. I don't know how many times I looked over at my clock on the nightstand and calculated how much time I had left to sleep. Yeah, that doesn't help.

When my alarm finally buzzes, I roll out of bed with a groan and turn on the lamp by my bed so I can search for something to wear. I blink rapidly because I swear I saw something move across my floor, and it wasn't small. I release a shiver, then race over to the light switch. Once the entire room is illuminated, I scan the floor. "Nothing." I sigh with relief, figuring I was probably just hallucinating. I groan again and pick up a pair of my leggings that are only a little dirty. *I'm exercising. I don't need perfectly clean clothes for that.*

In my top drawer, I find my one and only sports bra. I struggle to get it over my chest, and it's not because my boobs are big. They're not. It isn't easy, but I finally get it on. Panting and sweating from the effort, I rationalize that *that* was a pretty good workout, so why do I need to go for a walk?

Who am I kidding? Patsy would never agree to that. Next, I slip on an old ISU tee from my bottom drawer and glance at the clock. I'm late, so I grab my tennis shoes and a sweatshirt and head upstairs.

At the top of the stairs, I hesitate at the sight.

"Hey, Quinn," says a hoarse Kat.

"Morning, uh, everyone." I say everyone because all five of my roommates are standing in the kitchen slash dining room. "Are you all going for a walk?"

"Yep," mutters Susanna. "We could all use some exercise around here."

I smile. They're doing this for me, and it's the weirdest feeling. I swear my heart just jumped a little in my chest.

"It'll be fun," says a way-too-perky Patsy.

"Uh-huh," Robbi grumbles. "Sure."

I laugh and it feels good.

"Here," Robbi says, handing me a bottle of water. "Let's get this shit-show on the road."

I laugh again but say nothing else.

We walk for thirty minutes, and it's not easy. Patsy set a brutal pace. We're all breathing heavy and sweating by the time we turn the corner onto Beedle Drive.

"You're a bitch, Pats," Susanna says, panting.

"I know." She doesn't appear to care if she's a bitch or not.

Nearing the house, I'm taking a drink of water when I see movement to my left at the house across the street.

"Jack!" Kat yells.

When he looks up, he flashes a big smile and begins to walk toward us. "Beedle babes. You're out early."

*Beedle babes?* I scan the group. Yeah, I can see that.

"And who do we have here?"

I turn my head and meet Jack's eyes. They're nice. Blue with little crinkles in the corner. Crinkles that tell me he smiles a lot.

"Jack, this is our new roommate, Quinn." Patsy turns to me.

"Quinn, this is Jack Monroe, just one of the cute boys who live in that house." She points to the dark green ranch house directly across the street from ours.

"Boys?" He puffs out his chest. "We're manly men." Then he laughs. Turning back to me, he smiles again, but it's a little shy. He holds out his hand for a shake. "It's nice to meet you, Quinn."

"You too," I say, shaking his hand like I'm running for mayor. Ugh, I have no game.

"Well, we should celebrate the newest babe. Barbeque at our place?" he suggests.

"Hell yeah," says one of the girls.

"You ladies bring the beer; we'll provide the meat."

Susanna snorts, and it makes us all laugh.

Before Jack turns to leave, he leans down and kisses my hand. "You, beautiful Quinn, don't need to bring a thing."

"Oh, well...."

"Thanks, Jack," says Robbi as she takes my free hand and pulls me away. A good thing since I was frozen in time.

"I'll talk to the guys, see what date works. I'll let you know." He smiles brightly. "Have a wonderful day, ladies."

"You too," several of us say at once.

The minute we walk into the house, they start.

"Oh. Em. Gee. He likes you, Quinn," squeals Susanna.

"No, he—"

"He does," Kat jumps in. "He's never flirted with any of us."

I shake my head. "I'm sure—"

"We'll see at the barbeque, won't we? Hm?" says a smirking Patsy.

"No."

Oh geez. What will I wear?

---

## CHAPTER ELEVEN

---

**Cooke:** What is a scrum?

The past few days, Cooke has taken to texting me weird questions like that one. I know it's related to rugby, because after looking up the first two, I saw a theme—*Day one: What is a fly-half? Day two: What is a sin bin?*

**Me:** Scrum is another name for that gross soapy ring around the bathtub.

See what I did there? I made something up. I've been doing that for all of them because it's funny. I'm not sure he agrees, because after my latest funny, he wrote:

**Cooke:** Quinn, love. Don't be cheeky. If we're going to be mates, you need to learn all about the first love of my life.

I know what cheeky means, but when he says "mates".... I know it means 'friend' in British.

Fine. I can stop being cheeky.

**Me**: A scrum is: *an ordered formation of players, used to restart play, in which the forwards of a team form up with arms interlocked and heads down, then push forward against a similar group from the opposing side. The ball is thrown into the scrum, and the players try to gain possession of it by kicking it backward toward their own side.*

Thank you, Google.

**Me**: You know I just pasted that from Google, right? I still don't know what it means.

Before I know it, he's sent me a link to a video tutorial about scrums. It's only three minutes long, so I watch it.

**Me**: Oh, I get it.

Sort of.

**Me**: Thanks for dumbing it down for me. ;)
**Cooke:** Cheeky lass.

I shouldn't like that last text. Not at all. But I do.

~

Day four:

**Cooke:** Who is the best fly-half in the entire world?
**Me:** Um... you?
**Cooke:** Quinn Maxwell, you're bloody perfect, you are.
**Me:** So, all I need to do is stroke your ego and I'm "bloody perfect"?
**Cooke:** That about sums it up, yeah. Stroking is always encouraged.

**Me:** Ugh. No you didn't.
**Cooke:** My apologies. That was ungentlemanly.
**Me:** Apology accepted.
**Cooke:** ;)

~

DAY FIVE CAME AND WENT. SO DID DAYS SIX, SEVEN, AND eight. It bugged me just a little, because I was getting used to waking up to a text every morning. No matter, I've got other things to fill the void. After all, Cooke isn't real. Well, okay, he's a real person, but he lives in another country, he's a professional athlete, and he's gorgeous. It was just a matter of time before he grew tired of the stupid girl from Iowa. In the meantime, I've been keeping myself busy with school and my roommates. We've gone for a walk every morning so far. Most everyone makes it, but there have been mornings that one or two couldn't drag themselves out of bed due to hangovers or, erm, company of the manly variety.

No one is very talkative at six in the morning, but by the end of the walk, there's a lot of chatter. And laughter. The girls make me crack up. They're all so different, but every one of them has a great sense of humor. We bumped into Jack again one day this week. There's still no date set for the barbeque. No biggie. I haven't been thinking about that at all. I swear.

Day nine brought about a text from Cooke. I was happily surprised.

**Cooke:** Tokyo. Ever been?
**Me:** To Tokyo? As in Japan?
**Cooke:** Aye.
**Me:** No. I've barely seen the States.

When he doesn't respond, I send another text.

**Me**: Are you in Tokyo?

If so, it'd make sense why he hasn't been texting.

**Cooke**: Aye, it's our World Cup. You should watch. We play your USA team tomorrow.

*The US has a rugby team?* I'm not going to ask that question. I'm pretty sure he already thinks I've got something wrong with my brain.

**Me**: I'll see if it's televised here.
**Cooke**: Or online.
**Me**: I'll find it.
**Cooke**: Good. Nighty night, Quinn.

I look at the clock and blink. I wonder what time it is in Japan.

# CHAPTER TWELVE

"I know nothing about rugby."

"Me neither, Kat." Well, I take that back. I know some things thanks to the videos Cooke has sent me, along with his sporadic rugby terminology quizzes.

Patsy sighs. "I guess we'll figure it out together, huh?"

I nod as Robbi adds, "It's cool we know someone playing, though. We've got skin in the game, as they say."

I think that refers to gambling, but it could work here too. "We'll just have to watch and see what it's like."

The six of us are all sitting around a large square table at a local sports bar in downtown Ames called The London Underground. When I called ahead, they promised they'd have the game —or as Cooke called it, the match—on starting at eight. That means it's ten in the morning in Japan. Hooray for Google.

So here we are, and we're not alone. The place has a good crowd. Turning to the girls, I say, "I'm going to go get us a pitcher of beer."

Walking up to the front, I can't help noticing how cool the bar is. It's all dark wood and brass beer taps, just like the British pubs I've seen on television and in movies.

I scan the bar and notice a large group of guys sporting Iowa State rugby T-shirts. I'm going to guess they're the team that Bryant was referring to. It's not just the shirts that give them away but their size. They're all big guys. Not fat but thick, and some are quite muscly.

When the game starts, the bar comes alive. The few rugby fans and the team make the experience more exciting. When the bartender slides the pitcher to me along with six glasses, I wince at the price quoted. I'm going to have to cut back somewhere to make up for this night out. Grabbing the pitcher of beer, I turn and see my spot at our table has been taken. I scowl when I see Kara. *Great.*

I do my best to keep my scowl in check as I set the glasses down on the table. Because Kara took my spot, there's no longer a chair for me. Sure, I could ask her to find another place to sit, but I'd prefer not to engage her right now. I look around for another chair and see none. Instead of lamenting, I take the pitcher and a glass back up to the bar. There's an empty seat next to one of the big guys.

"Hey!" shouts Susanna, "don't take off with the beer."

I swivel in my seat. "Well, my seat was taken, so I had to find a new one. If you want some beer, you'll need to come up and get it."

Several of the girls laugh, but I distinctly hear Kara say, "She's such a bitch."

I'm ignoring it *and* her. I'm here to watch my friend Cooke play rugby, and that's what I'm going to do.

"Go, Cooke, go!" I shout at the television. He's got the ball and is running down the field, weaving between and around opposing players. "Run, run, run!" I yell louder.

"You're really a fan, eh?" asks the mammoth guy next to me. I bet if we stood next to each other, he'd be a foot taller than my five feet five inches. He's wearing the red and yellow rugby shirt, same as the other guys.

Ignoring him until the play is done, I then turn to him. "Cooke Thompson." I point at the screen. "Number ten for England is a friend of mine."

"Yeah, right." He snorts, then chuckles.

I shrug because it doesn't matter if this guy believes me or not.

"He is," says Patsy from behind me. Pointing back at their table, she adds, "We were all there when she called him on FaceChat."

"No shit?" The big guy nods. "Cool."

"Yeah." I nod back. It is cool.

"That guy is the best ten I've ever seen."

"Really?"

For those of you who, like me, are rugby challenged, let me explain. Each player's number, from one to fifteen, tells us what position they play. So number ten is always the fly-half. Number two is called the hooker, and so on.

So to hear that Cooke Thompson is "the best ten" means he must be very good at his position, which doesn't surprise me. I am surprised Cooke hasn't bragged about his skills. Sure, he's joked about his talents, but he'd have to be good to be a professional. Now, after seeing him on television and hearing what this guy next to me has to say, maybe he *should* be tooting his own horn a bit more often.

"Yep, the best," says the big guy next to me.

I smile at him, then hold out my hand. "I'm Quinn."

He places his giant hand in mine. "Mulroney."

"Your first name is Mulroney?"

"No, it's Dan. I thought Quinn was your last name."

"Nope. Quinn Maxwell."

"Hmm, cool."

I turn to the television and see play has started again. Cooke really is amazing. He's got a *C* on his jersey, which I already know stands for captain because Dan told me so. I can see why. He's the guy who seems to be organizing the plays. Not only that, he kicks the ball well, and he's made some passes to his teammates that seem impossible.

"He's so good." I'll have to tell him so the next time he sends a text.

Hell, why wait? I pull my phone out and shoot off a quick text.

**Me:** At a local pub watching you kick ass on the pitch. You're amazing, Cooke, and my new friend Dan thinks so too.

# CHAPTER THIRTEEN

C *ooke*

AS SOON AS WE'VE DONE OUR CELEBRATING AND OUR MANAGER has said his "good job, lads" speech, I move to my locker and grab my phone. Unlocking the screen, I see the usual congratulatory messages from me mum and me baby sister, Saffron. I also see one from Quinn and smile. That is until I read it.

**Quinn**: At a local pub watching you kick ass on the pitch. You're amazing, Cooke, and my new friend Dan thinks so too.

I feel my teeth grit and my nostrils flare because "Who the bloody hell is *Dan?*"

## CHAPTER FOURTEEN

I haven't gotten a response from Cooke all week. I knew he had another match in Japan because I looked up his schedule online, so I've no doubt that he's been busy preparing for that. The fourteen-hour time difference between Iowa and Japan makes chatting more complicated, and I don't really want to call him since I have no idea what he's doing.

What the heck am I saying? *Of course* he hasn't written back or called. I'm an idiot—just some stupid girl from the US who he called accidentally. He doesn't have time for me now that his season has started. His life is much more exciting and interesting than mine. I was probably just a little distraction before his rugby stuff started for real. But I can't help it. I looked forward to hearing from him. He made me laugh, and I think I did the same for him.

*Sigh.*

I need to accept that my little friendship with a rugby super-star, English dreamboat, and a very nice guy are over. Sadly.

It doesn't matter. I'm busy too, especially since I've added my daily walk at the ass-crack of dawn into my routine. So far, the other girls are still on board with our walks and have gotten up with

Pats and me. It's been nice to have everyone walk in the morning. I've gotten to know them much better because of it. It helps that they don't put on any pretenses. They're not awake yet, so to say my roommates are blunt at six in the morning is an understatement.

Another good thing is we ran into our neighbor Jack again. He's cute in a hipster kind of way. You know, with his perfectly trimmed beard, light brown hair cut short on the sides but longer on top that he puts product in, and his plaid shirts and colored jeans. Yeah, I'm making him sound like he dresses like an A-hole. He doesn't. It's too bad I weigh more than he does.

As Susanna sips her breakfast smoothie, she asks, "What're you doing today?"

I've showered and changed after our walk and am enjoying a delightful piece of toast with peanut butter. *Yay, protein!* "I've got to find a job." I've put off the job hunt for long enough since I'm now seriously low on funds. My financial aid only goes so far. I've got just enough for rent, utilities, school, and books. That's it. After that, I'm on my own. I shouldn't have spent twenty bucks at The London Underground last week. I could sure use that today.

"Have you tried the mall?"

"I haven't." The mall is clear across town. My scooter would get me there, but in the winter, I'd have to take the bus. That'd be at least an hour each way. But it's an option, at least. "I'll check it out."

"Cy's is hiring," Robbi says, stepping into the kitchen. "My friend Chris works there, and he said they had to fire one of the bartenders." She turns to face me. "They were stealing."

"Really?" That question is in response to both things, the stealing and a potential job. "I don't know how to bartend."

Robbi shrugs. She's been kind of surly this morning. "I'm just telling you what I heard. It doesn't hurt to apply."

No, it doesn't. I look up at the old brass clock on the wall. My grandparents had one just like it in their house. "It's almost ten. I should go now." I'm kind of excited about the idea of working at Cy's Roost. It's my favorite bar in Ames, and it's where everyone goes to hang out.

"No more going to football games or any other Iowa State event," says Robbi with an arched brow. "You'll have to work all of those."

"I don't do that anyway. Too expensive."

"Then go for it," Susanna chirps.

"Robbi?" I look up at her. "Can I mention your name?"

She snorts. "Sure. I'm quite important there," she says sarcastically. "Mention my name and I'm sure they'll hire you on the spot."

Wow, she's grouchy. "Okay," I say, smiling. "Thank you so much."

"Mm-hmm."

I look over at Susanna just as she rolls her eyes, then giggles. Ignoring that because I don't want to make Robbi mad, I quickly run back downstairs to find clothes that are decent enough for job hunting.

"This will have to be good enough," I say as I slump my shoulders. All I've got to fit the job-hunting bill is a pair of black leggings and a long black shirt since wearing a dress is not a great idea on a scooter.

I search the floor for my black flats, spying one near my closet. Slipping that one on, I lift items off the floor, hoping the missing shoe is there. I finally spot it underneath my bed. I shiver thinking about the creepy-crawly things under there that I'd rather not disturb, but it must be done.

On my knees, I reach beneath the bed and grasp the shoe. Yanking it out as fast as I can, I jump up and peek inside the shoe, making sure there's nothing hiding in there. When the coast is clear, I slip it on my foot. With a quick glance at the mirror, I grimace. My hair, in a low ponytail, isn't very professional, but the alternative is my signature messy bun. That's even less professional.

"It'll have to do."

～

"Hi," I say to the irritated-looking male behind the bar. "I'd like to apply for your bartender position."

The tall, surly man throws a whitish towel over his muscular shoulder, then places his hands on his narrow waist, making his black tee pull tight against his chest. It's enough to tell me the guy is built. I can't help staring at the tattoo on his left arm until he says, "What bartender position?"

I quickly stop staring and reply, "My... uh, Robbi told me there was a bartender opening."

"Who the fuck is Robbi?"

Oh shit. I'm doing this wrong. "My roommate?"

"Well, wow, okay, that's all I need to know. You're hired."

I quickly smile but then realize that was sarcasm. That's okay. I'm feeling like I've got nothing to lose since the mall was a bust, so I keep the smile on my face and say, "Great. When do I start?"

The guy's hands fall to his sides, and his chin drops down to his chest. It's moving up and down. Is he laughing? Yes, he's laughing. I hope it's a good sign.

"Sweetheart." He looks up at me and smirks. "It doesn't work like that."

I'm going to keep trying. "What doesn't? You hired me, I accepted. It's all good." Keep in mind that the smile is still plastered on my face. I'm not giving in. I need a job, and since the mall produced zero job prospects....

"Fine," he huffs. "Hop up and sit at the bar. Let me ask you some questions."

*Oh holy hell. Is this actually working?* I do as he asks. As gracefully as possible, I lift one thick thigh onto the bar stool, then pull my body up until I'm seated, mostly. I use the edge of the wooden bar to help with my ascent. In the end, my ass is hanging off more on one side of the small stool than the other, but no worries, sheer will should keep me seated. I place my hands on the old wooden bar, one on top of the other. "I'm ready."

I watch as he drops the towel somewhere next to him. Placing his palms on his side of the bar, he leans forward. It makes his arm muscles bulge a little more, and I can't help staring. "What's your name?"

I nod. I'm ready for this. "Quinn Maxwell."

Hesitantly, I ask, "What's *your* name?"

"Luke." Without missing a beat, he asks, "How old are you?"

Luke fits him. "Twenty-one."

"Good. Where have you bartended?"

Shit. I knew this was coming. "Um, nowhere?" I make it sound like a question, then add, "But I love to drink."

It must have been the right thing to say, because he laughs again. His entire body rumbles when he does it. "Wow, that's a great answer. I can't believe I've never heard it before."

"You haven't?" I smile with pride.

"Have you done anything in the hospitality industry? Waitressing? Food service? Anything?"

"I worked at the ice cream shop in my hometown one summer." I gained nine pounds and vowed never to work near ice cream again.

"That's something, I guess."

"I was a receptionist at a dental office in high school, and I've worked at the state fair selling tickets at the Midway for the last two years." Then I remember, "Oh, and I detasseled corn once, for one day."

He chuckles again. It's rich and deep. "For one day?"

"Um, well, I'm not really very outdoorsy."

"You don't say?" He says it sarcastically again, but this time it isn't funny.

My smile vanishes and I nod. *Stop it, Quinn. He was just teasing. Don't take it personally.* Feeling the need to clarify or maybe defend myself, I explain, "There was only one day left of work." That's part of the reason. The other is I got lost in the field. The foreman had to hunt for me, and I missed lunch, which sucked because detasseling is hard work and I was super hungry. But I'm not going to tell him that part.

"So, you have customer service experience but that's it."

It wasn't a question.

"I'm smart. I learn quickly."

Luke rolls his eyes. Crossing his arms over his broad chest, he stares down at me. I'm not sure if I should be speaking—you know, doing more to sell myself so I can get this job—or if I should just get up and walk out. I'm seconds away from sliding the rest of the way off the stool when he says, "Fine. I'll give you a shot. Two weeks. If you can't handle it, you're done." He turns away from me and starts to load bottles of beer into a tall fridge. I'm about to leave when he turns back with a pad of paper and a pen. "Here. Write down your shit, including your class schedule."

"Okay."

I begin to write my name, address, and phone number when he asks, "Can you come in tomorrow to train?"

It's Sunday. I've got nothing planned other than walking. "Sure. What time?"

"Noon."

"I'll be here."

I quickly write out my class schedule and am about to ask him if he needs anything else when he reaches for the paper. "This is fine for now. You can fill out the other shit tomorrow." He tosses the pad of paper down onto the counter next to the register and then continues to load the refrigerator. I sit for a minute or two, wondering if I should leave, when he answers for me. "We're done. You can go."

Wow, I'm pretty sure Luke is an asshole. But he's an asshole who just gave me a job, so there's that. Sliding off the seat, I smile. "Thanks. See you tomorrow, Luke."

He mumbles something, but I ignore him. It's best to get out while the getting is good. He may not like me now, but I'll change his mind because, damn it, I'm awesome.

Ha! Where did that self-assuredness come from?

I smile all the way down the sidewalk and around the corner to my scooter. Unlocking the trunk, I grab my helmet and slide it on my head. As I throw my leg over the seat, I nod to myself, because you know what? I just got a job. I *am* awesome.

When I get home, the girls and I celebrate my new job with popcorn and a movie in the living room. I also get an earful from Robbi about Luke Green, the owner and resident asshole of Cy's Roost. I listen as Robbi tells tales of Luke's many quirks and idio-syncrasies. They're too numerous to list, but apparently Luke likes things a certain way behind the bar, and if you can't do as he says, you're out. It doesn't bother me that he has his own way of doing things, but I am glad I now have a heads-up about him. I have to do a good job and make it past that two-week mark.

# CHAPTER FIFTEEN

Just as I'm about to finish a paper for my art history class, my computer begins to buzz. I check the time and see it's nearly nine. Tapping the icon, I wait a second or two for Cooke's face to appear and feel a smile spread across mine. When he smiles back, I take a second to see where he is. He must be using his phone, because all I can see is his head and part of his upper body, but nothing in the background. He's dressed in what looks like a zip-up sweatshirt with his team logo on the upper left side.

"Hey, Cooke."

His voice is quiet, a whisper. "Allo, love." He sounds tired.

"It's been a while." I do my best to speak softly too. It seems like the thing to do.

"Sorry. Been a mite busy. We're leaving Japan. We'll be home by tomorrow."

"Oh, you're leaving Japan right now?"

"Aye."

He does sound tired. I watch as his image moves around, almost bouncing. "Are you in a vehicle?"

"On the team bus. Heading to the airport."

"Oh, I see." I'm not sure what to say. I could ask him about his other match, but I already know they won because I checked the web for the score.

"Where are you? It's rather dingy-looking."

He's right. My room is dingy. Probably due to the fact that I've only got one tiny window that's covered by a dark curtain. "In my bedroom."

He gives me a funny look.

"I call it my subterranean slumber chamber. Spiders included."

I watch as he throws his head back and a laugh escapes his lips. It doesn't end right away either. "E-Excuse me?" he chokes. "Subterranean what?"

"Slumber chamber. The basement. I live in the basement. Everyone else lives above ground."

"Oh, poor dove."

"It's not bad if you don't mind moist conditions and spiders. Lots and lots of spiders."

I watch him visibly shiver. "Arachnids are bloody disgusting."

"That they are, my man. Worse than snakes."

"Bloody hell, woman. Snakes? You live with snakes?"

"No." I giggle. "Just spiders. Well, I'm pretty sure there's another type of nocturnal lurker too, but I'm afraid to know what it is."

"Poor lass."

Just then, someone else moves onto his screen. I stare at a bearded man with a white-blond mohawk.

"What's so funny, Cooker?" the hairy man asks.

Cooke's smile is gone. "Feck off, Ollie." Ollie does as he's instructed and disappears from my view. I'm about to say something else when Cooke asks, "Who's Dan?"

"Huh?" *Dan?* "Dan?"

"The bloke you mentioned in your text. The one who watched rugby with you?"

"Oh." I giggle again. "Just some guy at the bar. We all went to watch your game at a pub, and the Iowa State rugby team was there. I sat next to him at the bar." Since my seat was taken at the table by she-who-shall-not-be-named. "But I don't know him."

"Good."

*Good? What does that mean?* I stare at the screen, then snort. *No. Way. Is Cooke jealous?* "I've got news too. Though not as good as yours with your wins and you getting to go home and whatnot."

Cooke chuckles. "Let's hear it."

"I got a job!" I practically squeak when I say it.

"A job? Do you need money?"

Okay, that was a weird question. "I'm a college student. Of course I need money." I giggle.

"I can send you—"

I stop giggling. "No." My face serious now.

"I've got loads."

"No. Why would you suggest that, Cooke?"

"You should be focusing on your courses, not a job."

"I am. I've got time in my day to work. No worries." I smile again in the hopes that I can move this little conversation along. "I'm going to bartend at a pub and restaurant." See, I said "pub." "It's one of my favorite places, called Cy's Roost."

"Cy's Ruse?"

I laugh at his pronunciation. "Cy's *Roost*. You know, like a chicken roosts? Cy's our college mascot, so the bar's named after him."

"I see."

Ignoring the frown on Cooke's pretty face, I tell him more about the place, how it's been around a long time, that my mom and dad used to hang out there when they attended Iowa State, how I carved my initials in the same table as my mom and dad did years ago, and that it's where we all like to hang out.

"So it's a family tradition." Cooke nods like he gets where I'm coming from.

"It is."

"Well then, I'm very happy for you, love."

"Thanks." I pause thinking of a new subject. "So, have you enjoyed Japan?"

Cooke's mouth lifts on one side. "Japan is a lovely place. I think you'd like it. But I'm ready to be home, to sleep in my own bed. I miss my flat."

Flat. I know this one. It's an apartment. "Where do you live?"

He arches a brow. "Are you a stalker now?"

I quickly lose the smile. He thinks of me like a weird fangirl. I knew it. "No. I'd never...." I look down at my hands. "Um, I need to go, Cooke. My mom is call—I need to go. Bye."

I hit the End button just as I hear him start to speak and quickly shut my laptop. I'm tempted to turn it completely off, in case he tries to call back, but I need it to finish my paper. My computer does, in fact, buzz again, but I ignore it.

The last thing I want is for Cooke to think I'm some weird stalker chick, though I don't think he meant that the way he said it. He doesn't seem like he'd intentionally hurt my feelings. He's just tired.

I hope.

~

"ARE YOU LISTENING TO ME?"

I blink as I look up at Luke. "Yes."

"I said make sure each label is turned toward the front."

I'm loading more beer into the glass beer fridge, as Luke calls it. He's a tad particular about the way the bottles need to line up. Anal retentive is probably the term I'd use to describe Luke's habits. No worries. Robbi gave me a heads-up, so I was ready for it. I quickly turn the labels forward.

"If you're busy and you need to grab a beer fast, you'll want to be able to see the label," he explains.

"Makes perfect sense." And it does. Luke is going back over

some of the basic things that he showed me last Sunday. He really is anal retentive.

"Now, as you're working, you need to be cleaning as you go. Wipe down the bar with this." He holds up a yellow cloth. "This is only for the bar top."

I nod. I *know*.

Holding up a blue cloth, Luke says, "This is for the stainless top here." He points down to the part of the counter customers can't really see. "Keep the dirty dishes to a minimum. Run glasses back to the kitchen as soon as this bin is full." He lifts a square plastic tray meant to put glassware through the dishwasher. "When you take it back, pick up an empty tray and bring it back here."

"Okay." I'm so tempted to roll my eyes because he's repeating the same stuff we covered last week, but he's not in a joking mood. I snort and his head snaps back to me. "Sorry."

He keeps going. Repetition is good, right? "A good chunk of your job is to make sure it runs smoothly. Having glasses piled up back here makes it harder to be efficient."

I can see that too.

Just then, a woman approaches the bar. She's tall, blonde, and focused solely on Luke. I smile but say nothing. "What can I get ya?" he asks.

"Gin and tonic, please." The woman smiles as she leans against the bar giving both Luke and me a glimpse of her cleavage. I know what she's doing. She's trying to get Luke's attention, and I think it's working.

"Quinn, grab a rocks glass."

Yay, I finally get to mix a drink. Last Sunday was all about paperwork, using the computer, and the stuff he just went over again. Since I now know what a rocks glass is—the short one—I pick one up and wait for my next order from the bossy boss.

He doesn't disappoint. "Fill it with ice."

I move to the ice machine. Using the glass, I scoop up enough ice to fill it.

"No!" Luke shouts. "Jesus."

I jump and nearly drop the glass.

"What?" I squeak.

"Do. Not. *Ever*. Use the fucking glass as a scoop."

I nod but feel my eyes start to burn. I'm not used to someone shouting at me. But I will not cry.

Stepping closer, he looks down at me. No longer sounding angry, Luke says, "If the glass breaks while you're scooping out the ice, we'll have to empty the entire icemaker, clean it out, and start over. We can't have glass in the ice."

I nod again, doing my damn best to hold it together. "Sorry." My voice cracks.

In a softer voice, Luke adds, "Sorry. I didn't mean to upset you, Quinn. You're doing a great job. I'm used to working with idiots. I know you'll never do that again."

I slowly shake my head back and forth. "I-I won't. I swear."

"Good." He turns and smiles at the blonde woman. "Now, let's make this lovely lady a drink."

As I make the drink, the two of them flirt. It's sort of annoying, to be honest. By the time I've placed a lime wedge on the glass, he's got her number, and I think there was a promise of getting together later. But it's none of my business.

I worked until five, the point in time when Cy's gets busy on Sundays. Luke doesn't think I'm ready for prime time yet, and I agree, but I'm proud of myself. I did well. I drew beer without much head—that's the foam at the top of the glass, you dirty-minded minx. I made several gin and tonics, as well as a whiskey sour. Luke gave me a chin lift as I left, which is a good sign, I think. Another good sign, I'm going to be working with Chris several days after school. That tells me Luke trusts me to be here when he's not. Besides, Cy's isn't very busy in the later afternoons, so I should be able to gain more confidence and speed. I'd just be in the way right now.

# CHAPTER SIXTEEN

On my way to my scooter, I check my phone for the first time tonight because personal phones aren't allowed when we're working. Luke's words. And seeing how he feels about ice, I don't want to be on the receiving end of his wrath again. Ever.

Glancing down at my phone, I see I've got several text messages. Tapping the icon, I notice they're all from Cooke.

**Cooke:** I'm home, love.
**Cooke:** My sincerest apologies. I know you're no stalker.
**Cooke:** My address: 35 Haliburton Road, Twickenham, TW1 1NZ. UK Pop by if you're in the area. :p

He even added the happy face/tongue out emoji.

**Me:** Since we're giving addresses, mine is 205 Beedle Drive, Ames, Iowa 50010, USA. In case you're in the area. ;p

I'm not sure why, but I get a chill thinking of Cooke Thompson stopping by. Wouldn't that be something?

~

I'M STARING DOWN AT AN EXPRESS DELIVERY ENVELOPE IN MY hands. An envelope with a return address of Twickenham, England. It's handwritten, and I can only assume it's in Cooke's hand. It's a little messy but still readable. I run my fingers along the letters of my name, imagining him taking the time to write this out. Shaking that off, I flip the envelope over and carefully tear it open. Inside is a single sheet of white, lined paper. I open it and see something slide out and fall to my feet. Bending, I pick it up and read the front: Visa Gift Card. I close my eyes and look at it again. "No, Cooke."

With the letter in my right hand, I read his words.

---

*Quinn,*

*As you said, uni students always need money, and I have more than I need. Please use it as you wish. Throw a bash for your mates, or buy yourself something you've always wanted. Have some fun.*
*Yours, Cooke*

---

God, I'm not sure where to start with this. I stare at his words, then back at the gift card. Flipping it over, I gasp. "A thousand dollars?" That's just... ridiculous. I'm instantly angry. Okay, maybe angry isn't the right word. Flummoxed. That's a better word. I told him I didn't need his money, but he sent it anyway. Yeah, flummoxed and frustrated. Oh, and flabbergasted. Now there's a good word.

Without thinking, I pull the phone out of my pocket and shoot off a text.

**Me**: Cooke, no. What were you thinking? This is too much. I don't need this.

I stare at my phone, waiting for a response. When nothing comes immediately, I glance at the clock and do the math. It's late evening there. He should be up. When there's still no response, I gather my book bag and letter and make my way downstairs. I'll study for my next test while I wait for him to reply.

By seven that evening, there was still no word from Cooke, so I decide to seek the advice of my roommates. I'm sure I'll get a variety of opinions about what to do about this thing, but that's good. I need to hear all sides.

When I step into the living room, Susanna, Lindsay, and—ugh—Kara are watching something on the television. "Hey." I look at Susanna. "Are the other girls here?"

"In Patsy's room," mumbles Lindsay. "They're getting ready to go out."

Since her room is right around the corner from the living room, she must have heard us, because soon the room is filled with the girls. I wish Kara weren't here. She's always here, and I don't understand why.

"What's up?" asks Robbi. I've come to realize she's the no-nonsense roommate. She doesn't pull any punches, nor does she put up with much bullshit. I can respect that.

"Well...." I pull out the folded letter from my back pocket. Carefully, I remove the card and unfold the letter. "I got this from Cooke today." I hand the letter to Robbi, who quickly reads it. Her eyes grow round, but she passes it on to the next person. I watch it move around the room, deciding to wait until everyone has read it before I speak.

When it's Kara's turn, she reads it, then snaps, "How much?"

I ignore her for as long as possible, since Patsy and Kat still haven't read it. When they do, I clear my throat. Holding up the card, I say, "He sent me a thousand dollars."

"Wow." Patsy gasps. "That's a lot of money."

"It is."

"What're you going to buy with it?" asks Kat.

"I don't think I should keep it."

"Why the hell not?" Kara snaps. "He sent it to you. He told you to have some fun."

"It's not my money. I didn't ask for it."

"Sure you didn't," mumbles Kara.

"I didn't. I told him about my new job."

Robbi asks, "Is Luke still an asshole?"

I shrug. "Pretty much."

"God, I'm so sick of you holding court about this guy," grumbles Kara as she stands up, taking a step or two closer. "You think the world revolves around you."

*Yeah, well, I'm sick of you being here all the time.* "No, I—"

Kara keeps right on going. "You're pathetic. You're stroking his fragile ego, and now he's paying you." She stops. "Wait." She snorts. "Priceless."

"What?" Do I want to know?

"Are you sexting him?" She starts to cackle.

"No, of course not." *What is sexting? Oh, wait.* "No!"

"Well, if he's *just* your friend, then why not spend it? It's a gift."

"Kara, it's not my money. I can't just spend his hard-earned—"

My words are cut off the second Kara reaches out and takes the card from me. "Then *I* will. He said you could give it to your 'mates,'" she sneers.

"Well, you're not my mate, Kara." I look around the room, wondering if these women are truly my friends. My eyes focus on Susanna. "Are you just going to stand here and let her do this?"

"Me?" Susanna squeaks. "B-But her sister...."

Oh, wow, seriously? "So, she gets away with treating me and probably lots of other people like shit because her sister died?"

"Quinn!" Patsy finally speaks.

"What? That's the reason, right?"

The room is silent for way too long until Lindsay finally says, "*Kara* was supposed to move in."

I look over at Lindsay. "Who was?"

"Kara. She was told she could have the room downstairs."

I look at Kara, who has her arms crossed in front of her and a smirk on her face, then back at Patsy. "Is that my fault?"

Patsy looks sheepish as she says, "No, it's mine. I, erm, didn't realize it was promised to her."

"I see." Because I do. She's the roommate they wanted. Not me. I turn to Kara. "I'll start looking for a new place to live." I look for the letter that is now on the coffee table. Picking it up, I step toward Kara, who backs up like I'm going to hurt her. "Give me the card." She places it in my outstretched hand.

I start marching out of the room, then turn back to her. "Enjoy the spiders." I pause. "And whatever is lurking around at night. I named it Aragog." *Let's see if Kara gets that Harry Potter reference.* Then I'm out of there, getting back in my room so I can sulk in private because I'm sure as shit not going to cry. Not over Kara. I can't get over what an emotional roller coaster this semester has been, and it's only October.

I flop onto my bed. "I miss my best friend." If I could talk to her about everything, she'd... she'd probably tell me to stop being a pussy and tell those people upstairs to suck it. But I'm not Tayler, no matter how much I wish I could be.

I roll over to my side to face the faux wood–paneled wall. Or walls. All four of my walls are covered in brown paneling. I'd call it vintage or even retro if I weren't positive it's been here since the seventies. I had plans to make this room more personalized. Covering up the paneling was stage one. I planned to use posters. I have a bunch of them in my room at home that I was going to bring back after the holiday break. But there's no reason to do that now.

Sighing, I squeeze my eyes shut, trying to think of something other than my roommate issues. I do my best thinking—or meditating, as Tayler likes to call it—when I'm lying on my bed, eyes closed, so I do just that. But just as I'm about to get into the zone, my phone pings.

**Cooke:** It's just money. It makes me happy to help you, but if you don't want to spend it right now, save it and buy a plane ticket to the UK for a visit sometime soon.

I read his text, then reread it. *He wants me to visit?*

**Me:** You want me to visit?
**Cooke:** Sure. Bring along some of your mates.

Oh, okay. For a second there, I thought he wanted to see *me*.

**Cooke:** How's the pub?
**Me:** Fine.
**Cooke:** Only fine?
**Me:** No, good. I've a lot to learn, but it's a useful skill. I can always fall back to it if I need to.
**Cooke:** ?
**Me:** You know, if I need a second job down the road, I can always bartend.
**Cooke:** I see.

I can't think of anything else to say. I'm not feeling very talkative tonight.

**Me:** I'm probably moving out of my house.
**Cooke:** Why?
**Me:** Long story.

My computer buzzes suddenly. I hit the FaceChat button. "Hello?"

"Love. Tell me the long story."

With a sigh, I do.

"Where will you go, Quinn?"

I love how he says my name. Lying down on my stomach, facing the computer, I honestly answer with "I don't know. There's not a lot available, especially in my price range." I decide to add, "I didn't say that so you'd send more money, either. Please don't send more money."

Cooke chuckles. "You could use the money I already sent to—"

"No."

He chuckles louder this time. "You're a lot different than any of the girls...."

He doesn't finish his sentence, so I ask, "How so?"

"Most women have only wanted me for my money."

"I highly doubt that, Cooke. Have you looked in the mirror?"

"Aye. But I hope *you* see there's more to me than a pretty face."

"Sure." At that, he laughs loud and long, which makes me start to laugh right along with him. "I think you're going insane, Cooke."

"Aye. Insane for you."

*Huh?* I'm about to ask him what he means by that when there's a knock at my door. "Hang on, Cooke."

Pushing myself up to sitting, I yell, "Come in." I blink as I watch all five of my roommates enter, single file, into my room. This ought to be good.

Crossing my arms over my chest, I ask, "What can I do for you?"

Patsy speaks first, because of course she does. "We wanted to tell you that we don't want you to move out."

I look at each roommate one at a time, ending with Susanna. "Oh?"

"Look. We know Kara is...."

Oh, I'll finish her sentence. "Mean?"

"She's, well, challenging."

"Oh come on, Pats," mutters Robbi. "She's a bitch and you know it. And not just to Quinn." She looks over at me. "But she's especially terrible to you, Quinn."

"Fine." Patsy sighs. "The thing is, her dad is our mom's boss. We don't want to rock the boat with her because our mom really needs her job."

I want to scoff, but I don't. "You think Kara has that kind of power?"

I look at Susanna, who is slowly nodding. "She's a daddy's girl."

"So, you want me to move out so she can give your mom job security?"

"No, we don't want you to move out," says Kat. "None of us can stand her, okay?"

"So, when she took the gift card and wanted to use it herself, you were okay with that?"

"Pardon?" says the man on my computer screen. When he says it, it's like there's no *o*, so it's just "Pardn?"

"Oh, sorry, Cooke." I turn the screen around so he can see the girls.

"You're talking to Cooke?" asks Lindsay.

"Cheers, ladies," he says in a husky voice.

"Hi, Cooke," they all say at once.

"Did you say this other person took the gift card I sent to *you?*"

"She tried to," Robbi snaps. "But Quinn took it back."

"Quinn." He looks at me. "That's naff. She sounds like she needs a good bollocking. Would you like me to take care of that, love?"

I have no idea what any of those words mean, but it sounds like he may want to beat her up. "That's very kind of you to offer, Cooke, but I can handle Kara."

"I've no doubt. You're quite something, Quinn."

Looking back up at my roommates, I say, "So, now you *don't* want me to move out?"

Kat speaks first. "We never did."

I glance at each woman. "You never did." It's not a question.

"No, we were fucking relieved when Patsy said she promised the room to you," Robbi adds.

Awkward. That's how I feel right now. They're telling me they want me to stay, *and* I can feel Cooke's eyes burning a hole in my side. "Well, finding a new place was going to be impossible. Doesn't Kara have an apartment?"

"A nice one," mutters Susanna.

"So, why does she want to live here?" *With the spiders?*

"Because she lives alone. She doesn't like it."

Probably because she couldn't find someone to bunk with her. "So, now what?"

Patsy has all the answers. "Nothing. We'll tell her you can't find a new place."

I look down at Cooke, who seems concerned. "Fine." I sigh in relief. My shoulders don't feel as tense either. I can barely afford this place, and it's cheap. Well, maybe with my new job.... I just need to make it one more week, then maybe....

I watch the ladies file out, saying good night as they go. A couple of them say goodbye to Cooke too.

"That was interesting," Cooke says with furrowed brows. "Do you believe your mates?"

"I do." I don't have any reason not to. "I've gotten to know them some over the past few weeks, and I really like them. I believe they're sincere. It sounds like Susanna and Patsy are in a tough spot."

"What will you do about this Kara? She's a right cow, she is."

That makes me laugh. I love those British euphemisms. "She is that." I sigh. "I had to deal with a girl just like her in high school. I found it easier to ignore her rather than engage. I could never win."

"I think it's bollocks that your other mates won't stand up for you."

"It's not their job. I'm a grown-up, Cooke." Well, most of the time. "There will always be Karas in the world." I need to learn how to deal with them effectively. "It'll be fine."

"Bollocks," he grumbles. "You weren't taking the piss about the gift card? She took it from you?"

"She did, but I took it right back. You know...." I look up at the ceiling and see one of my eight-legged friends skittering across the tile. He's small, so I decide not to freak out.

"You know what?" Cooke asks.

"Maybe if I tried to be her friend...." Maybe she's just misunderstood. It's possible that the death of her sister has really made her that way.

"Love...."

"I mean, maybe she's lonely." I know what that feels like. It feels like shit.

"If she is, it sounds like she did it on her own."

"Maybe." I need to think about this.

Cooke and I end our video chat, and I get ready for bed. As soon as I lay my head on my pillow, I do my best to put myself in Kara's shoes. I ponder the issue for so long, I fall asleep with the light on and a plan to take the high road. I'm going to be the better person. Maybe then she'll see I'm not the enemy. We could be... not friends. No. But we could tolerate one another. And that's good enough for me.

It's decided. The next time I see her, I'm going to make an effort to turn things around.

# CHAPTER SEVENTEEN

I don't have to wait long, because the next morning, Kara is standing in the kitchen with the rest of the girls to go for our walk. Before I speak, I think back to the night before. You know, when I decided to take the high road. Stepping up to Kara, I smile as much as possible this early in the morning. "Kara?"

She turns her head and scowls. "Yeah?"

"I'm sorry."

"For what?" she snaps.

Wow, she's not making this easy. "I think we got off on the wrong foot." Her fault, totally.

"How so?" She's now turned to face me, her hands on her tiny waist.

"Um." Shit. How so? "We just did."

"Wow, you're a real wordsmith."

"Look." Now it's my turn to snap. "I'm trying to get along here."

"Why? So you don't have to move out? Sorry, but you're in *my* bedroom."

This is so not working. "I was just trying to...." To what? What's that expression? Oh, right. "To extend an olive branch."

"A what?"

"To make peace."

"Don't worry about me. I'm at peace with how things are," she deadpans.

"Well then…." I look at the rest of the girls. Shrugging, I say, "I tried." Then, looking back at Kara, I add, "I'm not moving out."

"What?" she squeaks, then points to my roommates. "But they told you it was supposed to be *my* room." She presses her thumb into her chest. "Besides, they don't want you here."

I look at the girls and know they aren't going to say a word, but at least now I know why. "I can't find a place. There's nothing available."

"Here." She grabs a folded piece of paper from somewhere behind her. "I found some rentals."

I scan the sheet and scoff. Every place on this list is double what I'm paying now, if not more. "I can't afford these places."

"You can with your fancy gift card."

"No."

"No?" she sneers.

"No."

Turning to Patsy, Kara barks, "Aren't you going to do something about this?"

Patsy shrugs. "What can I do? I can't kick her out; she signed a lease."

No I didn't. She made that up. Jesus, this is getting ridiculous. "Can't we just get along, Kara?" I mean, seriously.

"No!" Kara screams. She *literally* screams. I'm a little afraid the neighbors will think there's a murder in progress thanks to the volume and intensity of the sound. Piercing. That's the best way to describe it. Or horror movie worthy. That's another good one.

In shock at the scene before me, I step toward the door to get out of the house. I need to get away from all of this, but Kara isn't having it. As I pass her, she grabs hold of my ponytail and yanks.

Hard. So hard that I'm pulled back and off balance. I swing my arms around, doing my best to stay upright, but it doesn't work. I fall back, hitting my head on one of the old kitchen chairs.

"Kara!" shouts Patsy. I hear the others yelling too. I just can't make out what they're saying. Looking up, I see everyone yelling and screaming all around me. The women are all in one giant scrum. Ha! Did you see what I did there? I used one of Cooke's terms.

I do my best to roll onto my side and scoot back from the melee so I don't get trampled. And that's when I hear it. Sirens.

"Great," snaps Robbi. "This is bullshit."

I'm not sure who she's upset with. Hopefully not me. When I see her glare turn to Patsy, I think I know.

Before I can figure it all out, Kat is on her knees next to me. "Quinn? Are you okay?"

I push myself up until I'm sitting. The back of my head hurts, but I'm not bleeding. At least I don't think so. I run my palm over the back of my head, then look at it. Nope, not bleeding. But I'm definitely going to have a headache, along with a nasty bump.

"LADIES."

I look over to where all of my roommates and Kara are sitting on the couch. The cop in front of them has both of his hands up, attempting to talk over all of the voices, while I'm on the other side of the room talking to the other policeman, Officer Golden. He's nice. He's checked my head several times and asked me to tell the story of the events of the morning—multiple times.

"Ladies!" the other officer shouts.

It's enough to get everyone's attention.

He takes a deep breath before he continues. "I'm going to write up a report. If Miss Maxwell would like a ride to the hospital—"

"No," I say instantly, shaking my head too hard. It hurts, yes, but there's no way I can afford a visit to the emergency room. "I'll go to the University Health Center later today." It'll get me through the weekend. Good thing, because I've got to work all day at Cy's tomorrow. It'll be my first day working on a football game day.

"Miss Maxwell?" asks Officer Golden. It's a perfect name for him. He's blond and tan and, well, he reminds me of Cooke, if Cooke were the boy next door rather than a badass rugby star. "Miss Maxwell?"

"Oh." I giggle. "Sorry."

"Will you be pressing charges against Miss Becker?"

"What!" the she-devil screeches from across the room.

She stands up and begins to move toward me at a fast clip until the other cop steps in front of her. "I wouldn't do that if I were you, miss."

"B-But—"

Part of me would love to press charges, but I have a feeling I'll need a lawyer and lots of time to deal with that when all she'll get is a slap on the wrist. Okay, I know none of that for sure. I'm basing that solely on my binge-watching of police procedural shows. "No. I'd just like her to stay away from me."

"You'll need to seek a civil protection order, then. We can help you get that started," says Officer Golden softly.

"I'm not going to hurt you," Kara spits. "It was an accident."

I look up at the blond policeman, then over to Patsy, but she's on her phone. I scan the rest of my roommates, but I can't read their expressions other than they're a combination of pissed and worried. Well, except for Lindsay. She's got tears in her eyes. This whole thing is upsetting everyone.

I shake my head. "No. That's okay."

He looks surprised. "Are you sure?"

"Yeah." I shrug. As evenly as possible, I add, "I think she was just overzealous. She reacted without thinking in the heat of the moment." Heat she created herself, but whatever.

Officer Golden hands me his card. Before I take it, he flips the card over and jots something down. "My personal cell number is on the back if you change your mind, or if you just need to talk."

Grasping the card, I pull it from his fingers. "All right. Thank you." When I look up, he's smiling at me. It's not a big smile, but it's warm and kind. "Thanks," I say again and give him a smile of my own.

Just before he turns to leave, he leans down and quietly says, "Be careful, Quinn. And go to the clinic today, yeah?"

I nod and whisper, "Yeah."

Patting my shoulder, he moves toward our front door, the other officer following.

When they're both gone, that's when the yelling begins. It starts with Patsy. "I think you need to leave, Kara."

Her reply? A smug "I know. I'm late for class."

I look at my phone for the time. Shit. I missed ceramics, and if I don't get a move on, I'll miss art history.

As I begin to stand, Patsy adds, "And don't come back."

Uh-oh.

"What!" Kara shouts. "Why?" That time it was more of a loud whine.

"You can't be seriously asking me that." Patsy has her hands on her hips and her feet in a wide stance. She's ready for a face-off.

Kara points at me. "She started it."

"No, I—"

"She didn't," Patsy cuts in. "She was trying to make peace. You have five witnesses to that fact, but you wouldn't have it."

"Why should I? She's in my room."

"First of all, that's not her fault. That's mine. I wanted her here. She's my friend." Patsy must be feeling brave.

"I-I'm your friend too."

Susanna steps up next to Patsy. "Kara, a friend wouldn't threaten to get our mom fired."

"I didn't."

"You did," snaps Patsy.

"Well, if your mom—"

"Nope." Patsy holds up her hand and shakes her head. "Do *not* go there."

"Well, my daddy—"

"He knows. I just called and told him the police were at our house and the reason they were here."

"You didn't," Kara sneers

"I did. I also told him about your threat to get my mom fired."

Kara's mouth is opening and closing like a fish out of water. It's not a very good look for her. She finally says, "You're lying."

Patsy shrugs. "Call him. You'll see."

With her nose up in the air, she huffs. "I will." We all stare as she marches out of the living room and down the short hallway to the front door.

When it slams, Patsy releases a gust of air like she's been holding it for years. "I should've done that a long time ago."

"Did you really call Mr. Becker?" asks Susanna.

"I did. After I called Mom. She gave me his cell number."

Kat then asks, "Was he angry?"

"You could say that. He said Mom is his oldest and most loyal employee. He'd never fire her just because his daughter says so." Pats sits back down. "I suspect that's all true; however, if Kara went to him claiming we hurt her physically or something, he'd fire Mom."

"For sure." Susanna nods.

"That's why I thought he should know. I offered to let him talk to the police, but he said he'd talk to Kara first."

"She could lie to him."

"I'm sure she will. But I'm going to scan this"—Patsy leans

over, picking up the police report from the coffee table—"and email it to him."

"Good idea," mumbles Robbi. "I need to get going. I'm late." She points to the police report. "I may need a copy of that for proof since I missed a test in my first class."

"Me too," says Lindsay.

Patsy nods. "I'll make everyone a copy."

With that, I'm out the door with my backpack in hand. I'm still in my walking clothes, which consists of tight leggings and a T-shirt that's shorter than I'd ordinarily wear, but I'm late, so it's just the way it is. At least I brushed my teeth before everything happened, and my hair is still up but in a low ponytail now. Sliding on my helmet, I wince at the pain. The bump has grown to the size of a baseball. I should have iced it. Officer Golden told me to, but I don't have time now. If I hurry, I can just make it to art history.

## CHAPTER EIGHTEEN

I haven't seen Kara for a week, and it's been bliss. To be honest, I haven't given her much thought after last week. Partly because I've been so busy with work and my classes, and partly because, well, I got invited to a party. A *rugby team* party. I ran into Dan one day at the Hub. He walked right up to me and said, "Hey, Karen, how you doin'?"

Yeah, I know what you're thinking. He got my name wrong. That doesn't bug me. Neither does the real reason he's inviting me—because of Cooke. The truth is, I'm not about to miss a chance to go to a *real* college party. So, when he asked me how I was doing, I laughed and said, "It's Quinn, but Karen is close."

Dan chuckled. "Sorry." He stared at me for a second, blinking. "You look nice."

I blinked right back at him and then looked down at my outfit. Jeans and a T-shirt. My standard look Monday through Sunday. "Oh, thanks."

"What're you doing tomorrow night?"

I knew I didn't have to work. "Erm, nothing?"

"You want to come to a party? It'll be mostly rugby players and our friends."

"Oh, wow." I know I blushed like a crazy person. "Sure." Then I thought, *What the hell? I can't just go to a rugby party –alone. Can I? No!* "C-Can I invite my roommates?"

"Sure, the more the merrier. Give me your number, and I'll send you the address." He leaned closer as I recited my phone number. I heard my phone ding and knew it was Dan sending a text. "There you go. See you tomorrow."

"Right. Great. See you."

Oh. Em. Gee.

I quickly pulled out my phone and sent a group text to my roommates telling them about the invite. I received immediate excited responses from Lindsay and Susanna and one grumbly affirmative from Robbi. Nothing from the other two. Since then, Patsy and Kat have said they'd have to see. They both have boyfriends, so I suppose their men wouldn't like them going to a rugby team party. At least I hope that's all it is.

In addition to that, the barbeque that the neighbor guys promised is now going to be on Sunday. My weekend is booked solid with the party on Friday, work on Saturday, and the barbeque on Sunday. I feel like I'm starting to like my life a little bit. It could also be the fact that I think our morning walks are helping me. I haven't lost any weight to speak of, but I feel better. I have more energy, and with that, more optimism.

I haven't heard a peep from Cooke since that last time. I don't know if I overwhelmed him with drama over Kara and the money card or what. Part of me would like to message him, but what would be the reason? He's busy or else he'd get in touch with me.

Right?

"Yo! Listen up!" shouts Dan. "This is the girl I was telling you about, Corinne. Her best friend is Cooke Thompson, the greatest fucking fly-half in the fucking world!" He's so loud I have to cover my ears. The other guys must agree, because they all start howling like wolves.

I start to laugh, and after the howling subsides, I correct him. "It's Quinn, and we're just acquaintances." *Acquaintances?* Ugh, I'm a total dork. Not a surprise.

I was so nervous for this party. I wanted to get here early, but the girls told me that's a no-no. So, it helps that I drank a couple of beers at home before we left for the party. Not only that, but Lindsay and Susanna decided I need to step up my look, so they did my hair and makeup. They wanted me to wear something more suited for a dance club, but unfortunately, the nicest "club" clothes I have are black jeggings and a black tunic. So that's what I'm wearing. It doesn't matter; my face and hair look spot-on thanks to their talents.

As soon as we walked in the door, the girls scattered. Robbi saw a friend from one of her classes, and Lindsay and Susanna wanted to mingle. I guess they talked to a couple of the guys that night we were at the London Underground. It's just the four of us, since Kat and Patsy went out with their boyfriends instead. While I wish they were here, I get it.

"Queen!" shouts a half-naked man. In all fairness, most of the guys are half naked, and there's one guy who's completely naked. According to Dan, it's just "how they roll." Anyway, the half-naked man rushes toward me, wrapping me up in his arms. They rest right below my ass, so when he stands up, I feel myself being lifted from the ground.

"Oh, no...." I pat the top of his head because I'm not sure how else to get his attention; plus it's the only part of him I can really reach. "Put me down," I squeak. "Please?"

We've begun to move around the room like that. Then, suddenly, he stops and releases me.

"Here she is, cap."

I slowly turn to face the biggest man I've ever seen. He's got to be almost seven feet. Okay, maybe not quite that tall, but he's close. My eyes roll from his stomach, where my head is, up to his face. He's... well, he looks like he may have been in a fight or two, recently. He's got one black eye and a white piece of tape running across the bridge of his nose. I'm about to ask him if he's okay when he grunts, "You Corinne?"

"Quinn."

"I'm Bull. Here." He holds out his hand. In it is a piece of yellow cloth. "Give that to him."

Him? "Cooke? You want me to give this to him?" I unfold the fabric to see it's a T-shirt. An Iowa State University rugby tee, to be exact. It's just like the ones they wore at the bar a few weeks ago. "Ask him to come here."

"Oh, he's in England." No way am I asking him to come here. He'd think I was insane.

*"I'm insane for you," he said.*

"Ask him."

I nod. "I will. I'll ask him."

"Call Dan when he gets here."

I'm biting my lip to keep myself from laughing. This entire thing is so comical. I don't know why, but I start to giggle.

"Why are you laughing?"

"Nerves." I wave my hand in front of my face to get myself under control. "You're sort of intimidating, Bull."

He smirks. "Yeah." Then grunts, "Ask him."

"I'll ask him."

"Good." Bull turns and walks away, and that's that.

I fold up the tee and shove it into my small purse. Half of it is poking out, but I'll make sure it gets home safely. The truth is, I'm excited to send it to him. Maybe I'll throw in a few other things—you know—, make him a care package. Not to mention how cool it'd be to see a picture of him in an ISU tee.

We stay at the party for another hour after that. By then, almost half of the rugby guys are stripped down to their underwear; the rest were naked. I don't know why, and it's strange. And it isn't like they're trying to be sexy or anything. Nobody is trying to rub their you-know-what on any of us; they're just hanging out naked.

Maybe it's a rugby thing. I should ask Cooke. Yeah, I know I said earlier that I didn't like to be the one to make first contact, but this is important. It's for science.

**Me**: Is it normal for rugby players to hang out naked all the time?

Not quite a second later, he responds.

**Cooke:** What the bloody hell are you talking about, Quinn?

I giggle at his response.

**Me:** I went to a rugby party, and by the end of the night, a bunch of them were naked. Is that a rugby thing or an Iowa State rugby thing?
**Cooke:** Bloody hell, woman. Stay the feck away from ruggers. Dirty wank stains, the lot of 'em.

*Wank stains?* I don't know what it means, but it makes me giggle anyway.

**Me:** So it's not just the ISU team?
**Cooke**: You're giving me a coronary. Did any of them touch you, love? I'll fecking kill them with me bare hands.
**Me:** They'd like that. They want you to visit.
**Cooke**: Jesus, Mary n Joseph.
**Me:** LOL. I'm sending you a shirt from them. They wanted you to wear it when you come to visit.
**Cooke:** Please, love. No more interactions with the rugby team. Promise me.
**Me:** But you're on a rugby team.
**Cooke**: I'm 7000 km away.
**Me:** Sadly, I know.
**Cooke**: Sadly?

Oh shit. I typed that. Now what do I say?

**Me**: Well, I need to get to bed. I have work all day tomorrow.
**Cooke**: I see you changed the subject. No matter. I'm sad too. Nighty night, fair Quinn. Stay away from those fecking arseholes.

I laugh and it feels good.

**Me:** For the record, they were all gentlemen. Naked gentlemen.
**Cooke:** Feck me. Stay away from 'em, love.
**Me:** :) Sure.

I throw myself onto my bed and laugh again. I've never had so much fun messing with someone as I just did with Cooke Thompson.

# CHAPTER TWENTY

"How was your first time working on a game day?"

I look over at Patsy, who's sitting in the lawn chair next to me. "Crazy. I was the barback. But I made it past the two-week trial period, so I'm officially a bartender at Cy's."

Patsy claps her hands and smiles. "Yay! Go, Quinn! Wait. What's a barback?"

"Everyone's bitch." I laugh. "I basically restocked beer and everything else the bartenders needed to keep everything running smoothly." The beer is stored in the basement, so I had to run up and down the stairs a million times. My legs are killing me today, among other things. "Next Saturday is going to be ten times worse."

"Oh, right. It's the Iowa versus Iowa State game."

"Yep. And it's in Iowa City this year, so everyone will be at Cy's to watch the game. So, I'm going to enjoy Jack's relaxing barbeque today, because this time next week? I'll be broken."

Pats giggles. "True. This backyard is so nice. We can just kick back and let the guys treat us like queens."

I nod, then sip my beer. The neighbor guys are great. When

we first arrived, I was introduced to Jack's roommates, Aaron, Ron, and John. They all seem so nice. I haven't worked up the courage to talk to any of them yet, but I'm working on my second beer, so maybe that will help. I look around the backyard and marvel at how well kept it is. There are even flowers planted all along the fenced-in yard, and outdoor lanterns hang from the one and only tree. It's old and massive, so there's no need for more than one.

"This yard...," I say to Patsy.

"I know. Aaron is in the landscape architecture program. This is all his doing."

"If he needs a project, maybe he could do this to ours." The backyard of our house is much smaller than this one, so it'd be easier, right? "I could help."

"You should ask him." Patsy turns her head to lean in. "Actually, you should talk to Jack."

"Jack?"

"Yeah, he keeps looking over here."

I hadn't been paying attention to Jack—or anyone for that matter. I look over toward the grill where Jack and Ron have been working. They're grilling burgers and hot dogs, and they seem to take it very seriously. At that precise moment, Jack turns to face the crowd and yells, "Food!"

There are about fifteen people here for this thing, and ten of them are charging toward Jack and Ron.

"I guess they're hungry." Patsy giggles.

"I'd say."

We wait until the crowd clears out to make our way over to the table. By the time we get there, everything is picked over. Now I see the reason for the stampede. But Jack must have been prepared, because he opens the grill and reveals a new batch ready to go. "Ladies." He smirks. "Burger or dog?"

"Burger," Pats and I say together. "Please," I add.

He places a burger on each of our plates, then says, "Hang on," and races back into the house. When he returns, he's holding a large tray. Bowing, he says, "Milady." I laugh as I see he's got fresh everything: buns, condiments, cheese, chips, and coleslaw.

"Wow, this looks amazing, Jack."

He blushes, at least what I can see above his perfectly trimmed beard. "I'm glad you approve, Quinn."

Patsy nudges my arm, but I ignore her. Instead I quickly fill my plate and return to my chair. There's no way Jack likes me. Not like that, anyway. And as the evening progresses, my theory is proven when I watch as his attention moves from me to Lindsay —who appears to be just as taken by him.

"See?" I slap Patsy's hand. "Lindsay and Jack."

Patsy's head turns slowly until she sees them together sitting on a bench at the back of the yard. "Well, I'll be."

"Yeah, see? Told you."

"Well, I guess it's okay to leave some of the guys for the rest of us." Patsy giggles.

"Huh?"

"Oh, come on." She rolls her eyes. "You've got men panting for you."

Heat rushes up to my cheeks. "No I don't." That's not true. Nobody likes me. Not like that.

"You didn't notice how that cop was totally smitten with you?"

"Officer Golden?"

"Yes. The blond god."

"No, he was just being nice."

"To you. I think he wanted to kill Kara after he heard what she did to you."

"No, he was just doing his job."

Ignoring me, she adds, "And what about Cooke?"

"Cooke?" I practically screech. "We're just friends."

"Sorry, but I have guy friends, and none of them FaceChat with me at all hours of the day and night."

"He's in England. And... and we're just friends. Have you seen him?"

"I've seen the way he looks at you."

"Oh, come on. He could have anyone. I'm just...." I look down at myself and notice two things. One, I've got a blob of ketchup on my tee that I hadn't seen before, and two, my stomach. "No. He's just bored."

"You don't see it, do you?"

"See what?" I'm getting a little defensive. And embarrassed by all this talk.

"How beautiful you are."

I'm blushing so much my eyes hurt. Trust me, it happens. "No. I'm too—"

Patsy moves her chair closer. "You're one of the prettiest girls I've ever seen, Quinn."

"No."

"Yes, Quinn. Look in the mirror sometime." She pauses. "And not just at your face. Of course your shiny dark hair set against bright, blue eyes is stunning, and you've got a perfect nose and adorable freckles. But your body is curvy and sexy. You just choose to wear those huge T-shirts all the time. The morning Kara went to crazy-town—"

I laugh at the expression. It's true, though. Kara definitely went to crazy-town.

"Anyway, that morning, you were wearing tight workout clothes. Officer Golden couldn't keep his eyes off you."

I shake my head. "You're wrong."

"Okay, fine. But I'm telling you, if you wore clothes that actually fit you, you'd have guys falling all over themselves."

I smile at Pats. "I appreciate what you're saying. I really do. Thank you." But she's wrong. And the depressing part? She didn't mention Bryant. The one man I've been pining for this past year. I've spent the better part of a year trying to figure out how to get him to like me back, but so far, I've come up with nothing, because that advice your mom gave you growing up, the "just be yourself" advice? Yeah, that doesn't work.

Why do I bother thinking about Bryant at all? He asked for Kara's freaking number. The jerk.

# CHAPTER TWENTY-ONE

"We need more Bud," Luke yells from the other side of the bar.

I quickly drop the bar rag and race down into the basement to locate a case of Budweiser. It's dark, so I slide my palm around on the brick wall in search of the light switch. When I find it, I flip it on, then quickly wipe my palm on my jeans. The basement is extra damp today. Not a surprise since it's been raining basically nonstop for two days. Rain's not typical for Iowa in October, but it's been unseasonably warm this year. *Thank you, global warming.*

Weaving my way through the stacks of inventory, I spot the Budweiser next to the rest of the domestic beers we carry. Reaching for it, I pull it down from the top of the stack and turn toward the stairs. The box isn't terribly heavy with its twenty-four bottles, but carrying box after box up a long flight of stairs is starting to take a toll on my back, legs, and arms. At the top of the stairs, I pause to catch my breath. Luckily, the entrance to the basement is sort of obscured from the rest of the bar, so I can do so in private. Lugging the box to the beer fridge after a moment's reprieve, I quickly fill up the Bud section in the refrigerator, lining up each bottle with labels out, just as Luke taught me.

"Yo, get me some fries."

I look behind me and see a group of guys sitting at the bar. They've been here a while, probably too long. Since the bar is loud, I raise my voice and say, "No fries today."

He yells back, "Okay, then rings. I'll have some onion rings."

I shake my head and step closer so I don't have to raise my voice. "No rings either. No food."

"Did you hear that, guys?" He looks at his friends, then back at me. "No food. She ate it all."

I blink for a second or two, trying to wrap my head around his words. *She ate it all?* "No, I—"

"Yo, Luke," the guy yells.

Luke steps over to the group, the usual scowl on his face. "What?"

"You'd better keep an eye on that bottom line because this one"—he points to me—"is going to eat all your profits."

I'm holding my breath. My face has got to be magenta, because it feels like it's burning up. Tears are sitting right below the surface, so I blink a million times to keep them from falling. *Why?* I mean... *I'm going to eat all the profits?*

*Who says shit like that to people?*

This guy doesn't know me. He knows nothing about my life. I mean, what if I'd just lost 100 pounds? What if I had a thyroid condition that prevented me from losing weight? This asshole doesn't know; he just sees my size and judges me based on that.

I've taken in some much-needed air now that I've worked through some of my thoughts, but I still don't want to say anything especially with Luke right there.

Ugh, Luke.

How embarrassing. He just *had* to hear that guy's words. Of course he already knows I'm fat, but still. When someone says something rude like that to your face, you don't want anyone else to hear it. Worse still, the guy's dick friends are all laughing and slapping the guy on the back like he just won a championship.

Yeah, if there was a world series of douchebags, this guy would win. No contest.

Just then, I'm pulled away from my thoughts by Luke. "Get out," he snaps.

"Wh-what?" the champion douchebag sputters.

Luke points one long finger at the guy. "You don't say shit like that to a woman, especially Quinn. Get the fuck out."

"Luke, man... listen."

"Don't fucking *Luke* me, asshole. Who says shit like that? Huh?"

The guy tries to reply, but Luke keeps going.

"This girl"—he jerks his thumb at me—"is the sweetest, hardest-working girl I've ever met. And besides that, she's fucking beautiful. You'd be lucky to have a girl like that, you pecker-head."

"Whoa, man, I didn't know—"

"Didn't know what, fucker?"

"That she's your girl."

"She's not my girl, but that doesn't matter. Grow up, dickhead. This ain't middle school. A real man never demeans a lady, especially *that* lady." He points to me again. "Now get the fuck out of here. The next time you come in, you apologize."

"I'll do it now," he sputters. "I'm sorry, Luke."

Luke rolls his head around in a circle. "Not to me, you fucking dumbass. Her."

"I'm sorry—"

"Next time. When you're sober. And you'd better mean it, or you and your fucking pussy-whipped followers are banned. For. Life."

"Luke...," the guy whines.

"Out!" he shouts so loudly that the people lined up at the bar immediately stop talking.

"Fine," the guy grumbles as he stands up from his seat at the bar. "Fuck you," he mutters.

"Banned!" Luke shouts even louder. "All of you."

He glares at me. "Thanks a lot, you fat bitch," he spits.

Oh, like I'm the one who got him banned. I'm getting looks I don't deserve. "I didn't—"

"No worries, Quinn," Luke says, patting my shoulder. "Get back to work."

So I do. I play barback, pour beers, and mix drinks—the ones I know, anyway. The ones I don't, I get Luke or Chris, the other bartender, to make. The night is hectic, but it seems to be flying by.

Until I see *him* with *her.* I glimpse Bryant from the corner of my eye. I turn to smile at him, and that's when I spot Kara. She sees me too. And when she does, she wraps herself around him like a python, pulls his head down to kiss him. With tongue. The sad part? He kisses her right back. He kisses her like he's done it before. Lots of times.

I watch for a second or two, but as soon as I gather my wits about me, I run down the basement stairs as fast as I can, almost taking a tumble. At the bottom, I take in deep breaths and release them slowly. "I will not cry." I won't shed tears over the guy I thought I was supposed to marry because he's kissing someone else. And not just someone else. *Her. He* was kissing *Kara.*

Once I've gathered myself, I find what I need and head back upstairs. Tromping up the steps, I whisper to myself, "Think happy thoughts." I squeeze my eyes shut and do my best to think of something happy, but nothing comes to me because all I can see is how my life is a fucking failure. How did I get to this place? The one where I put all my hopes and dreams in the hands of *one* guy. I know it isn't realistic, but when you lose your heart to someone, how *can* you be realistic?

"Why doesn't he see what I see?" I mutter to myself.

"Quinn!" shouts Luke. "Hurry the fuck up." At the top, Luke is waiting. "What's the matter?" he asks, taking the case of beer from me.

I must look flushed or something. "Nothing."

He looks nervous, and it surprises me. I've never seen him look tentative about anything. "You sure?"

"Yeah."

His tentativeness gone, he snaps, "You can't let shit get to you here, Quinn. People are assholes."

"I know." He thinks this is about the other guy. "Thanks." I pass him and wait by the fridge for the case so I can get right to work restocking the refrigerator. I do my best to stay busy, but every now and then, I see them. One time, she's sitting on his lap. She looks over at me every few minutes, and when we make eye contact, she smirks. At one point, Bryant approaches the bar. I hear him call out my name, but I pretend not to hear him, and Chris waits on him.

The next time he comes right up to me. "Quinn?"

I give him my best 'I'm surprised to see you' look. "Oh, hey, Bryant. When did you get here?"

"Halftime."

"Oh, well, what can I get for you?"

"A pitcher of Busch Light."

I quickly pour the pitcher. "Need glasses?"

"One. For you. Why don't you come over and hang with us for a minute?"

I pause for a moment, looking at Bryant, maybe for the first time. And it hits me. He has no idea. He has never seen me as more than a friend. Why else would he invite me over to his table to hang with him and his girlfriend? I raise my palm and place it on my chest, right over my breaking heart. It hurts. Pain is radiating from my center outward. No, I'm not having a heart attack, but I suspect it feels a little like this.

"You okay, Quinn?" Bryant asks, concern crossing his face.

No. "Yeah. Just tired." Sick and tired of being the last person anyone would ever want. "Thanks, but I can't while it's this busy."

"Oh, sure. Right. It just looks like you're not really doing much."

I swallow and it's painful. "It probably seems that way." I look to my left, where Chris and Luke are quickly making drinks and pouring beers, essentially doing all the work while I stand off to the side waiting for Luke to tell me what to do next. It's true. They really don't need me. Nobody does.

"I can't. Not until later."

"Okay. Well, I'll hang on to this." He holds up the glass. "Come over when you get the chance."

"Sure thing." I nod and put on a fake smile just as Luke yells for me to head to the basement again.

Time to get back to work.

# CHAPTER TWENTY-TWO

Have you ever had one of those days where you think things couldn't get any worse? Well, I'm having one of those. Luke finally kicks out the last remaining stragglers at one forty-five in the morning. We'd been able to get things restocked and cleaned up as we went along, so I'm out the door by two. Exhausted, I cover my head with a plastic bag I found in the kitchen at Cy's and walk as fast as my tired, sore feet can carry me toward the spot where I parked my scooter.

I turn left onto Lincoln Way, and that's when I see it—my scooter. Or what remains of it. I stop dead in my tracks. Dropping the plastic bag, I walk slowly to the wreckage. My scooter is totaled. I can't be sure, but from the looks of it, I'd say someone ran over it. Several times. The handlebars are several feet away from the main part. What used to be the trunk is shattered into pieces. I look around and frown. "Where's my helmet?" I turn left and right, but there's no sign of it. It's gone. I loved that helmet. It was retro and cool—a jet helmet reminiscent of those from the 60s. I splurged on it with the money I made working at the Iowa State Fair, and now it's just gone.

I stand completely still like an idiot because I'm not sure what to do. I can't carry it home. It's too heavy and in too many pieces. Not to mention, I'm too tired. I sniffle. Not because I'm crying but because I'm waterlogged. This rain is unrelenting. Okay, there are one or two tears. Don't judge. I'm mourning the loss of Frankenscooter. Just thinking his name makes me want to sob. I lift my head and peer down Lincoln Way in the direction of my house. It's a good three miles home. I'm sure I could make it, but I can't just leave him here. It's not right. Someone could scoop him up and throw him away. Besides, maybe some of him could be salvaged. Maybe my brother Steve could rebuild him. I stare down at the motor and wince. It's completely crushed. Flat as a pancake.

"Now what do I do?" Technically, it's a vehicle accident. I have insurance but only liability. That means they won't replace him. "I should call the police." Pulling my phone out of my bag, I remember I've got Officer Golden's card. I'll call him first.

I move to stand beneath an awning that hangs over the door of a little coffee shop. Once I'm out of the rain, I dig through my bag and find the card in my wallet. Taking a deep breath for courage, I dial the number on the back.

After only one ring, he answers, "Golden."

I wasn't ready for him to answer so fast, and I can't manage to form words.

"Hello?" he prompts.

"Um, Officer Golden?"

"Yes."

Sniffling, I say, "It-It's Quinn Maxwell." How must I sound?

"Quinn? What's wrong?"

"M-My scooter."

"Your scooter?"

"Someone broke it." Broke it? God, that's a dumb thing to say. "It looks like they ran over it. A lot."

"Where are you?"

"Lincoln Way and Welch."

"I'm on patrol. I'll be there in ten." He hangs up before I can even thank him.

Leaning back against the glass, I'm tempted to call Tayler, but I can't. Not at this time of night, and not yet. She still hasn't made a move to contact me. In all the years we've been friends, this is the longest we've gone without speaking.

Without another thought, I open my FaceChat app and hit Cooke's number. For some reason, I feel close enough to him to tell him my current woes. He'll make me feel better. He'll say all the right things. Maybe Patsy's right and Cooke has a crush on me. That would certainly cheer me up. What if he jumped on the first plane out of England and made it here by tomorrow to save the day?

*Oh my God, Quinn. What the hell are you thinking? He's not a super-hero, and he certainly doesn't have a crush on you.*

He's my friend, at least. Thinking of him as more than that is fairy-tale land, a fantasy.

His phone rings several times, and I worry I called too early. It's after eight in the morning there, but it's Sunday in England. Maybe he's sleeping in or at breakfast or church.

Just then, the screen comes to life. "Cooke?" I say frantically. I'm blubbering more like it. My nose is all runny, and I sound hoarse.

"Allo?" says someone who is definitely *not* Cooke. Hell, they aren't even male.

I stare at the screen, shocked by the sight before me. She's gorgeous and perfect. Just Cooke's type. *There goes my fairy-tale land.* Why does that bother me so much? It shouldn't. We're *just* friends, after all.

"You there?" she asks in a perfect English accent.

"Cooke." It's all I can choke out between sobs. This day has sucked beyond belief. Hell, my entire life keeps getting worse and worse.

"Oh, dear. You're upset. You want Cooke?" asks the woman.

When she says something like "Cooke, bruv..." that's all I need to hear. I hang up. She called him "bruv." I'm sure that's just a term of endearment for them.

When I hear sirens, I know it's for me. I look down at the phone and turn it off in case he tries to call back. I need to cut my losses. Facing Cooke now is not the answer, especially if he has company. He isn't going to want me to interrupt him now.

As the police SUV pulls up, I step out from beneath the safety of the awning.

"You're soaked," Officer Golden says as he climbs out. "Here." He jogs around the SUV, opening the passenger door. Get in."

Without a word, I slide into the car. The next thing I know, I've got a blanket wrapped around me, and he turns the heat up in the car. I watch through the window as Officer Golden walks around what's left of my only mode of transportation. At least he's got on rain gear so his uniform won't get soaked.

I'll have to take the bus now. Everything gets more complicated without my scooter like getting to class and to work.

As I do my best to get myself under control, I watch as Officer Golden gets pummeled by the rain as he takes photos of the wreckage. After that, he begins to pick up the pieces to place them in the back of the SUV. I open the door to help him, but he waves me off. The main part of the scooter has to be heavy, but he's able to roll it—drag it, really—to the back of the police car. He must be strong to be able to lift the carcass into the back of the SUV. When everything's picked up, he hops back into the car. I hand him the blanket, and at first, he waves that off too, but he finally takes it to wipe off his face and hands.

When he finally speaks, his words shock me. "Your tires were slit."

"What?"

"Someone slit your tires."

"Why?"

"And it appears they may have run over it. More than once."

I swallow. "Who would do that, Officer?" My poor scooter.

"Call me Gage."

"Gage Golden?"

He shrugs. "All my siblings have G names. So... have you seen Kara lately?" he asks quietly.

"Tonight."

"Tonight?"

"She was at Cy's tonight."

Turning his head, he scowls, "You been drinking?"

"No. I work there. Bartender."

"Oh, good. You saw her there?"

"I did. Strangely, she was with... well, with a friend of mine."

"Why strangely?"

"Well, I introduced them a while ago. I knew he liked her, but I didn't think they were dating or anything. Not until I saw them tonight."

Then Gage asks, "Did you tell your friend about the attack?"

Attack? I don't know if I'd use that word. "No, I haven't. Not yet."

"Perhaps you should warn your friend."

How do I do that? He's going to think... oh, what does it matter what he thinks? "I will." The car is quiet. "Do you think she did that to my scooter?"

I watch as Gage grabs a clipboard from beneath his seat. "I'm going to write up a report. Since I don't feel comfortable speculating, I'll investigate it. May I keep your scooter so I can look it over more closely?"

"Sure. Of course."

I answer each question Gage has for me, and then I sign the report.

"I'll give you a copy for your insurance," he tells me.

"I only have liability."

"Keep it for your records, then." He clears his throat. "Maybe get full insurance next time?"

"My brother built that for me from parts." I shrug. "Nothing to insure."

"I get it," he says, putting the car into gear.

Pulling out onto Lincoln Way, I stare out the front window as we move west, in the direction of my house. When he pulls into our driveway, I look over at him. Releasing a shuddered breath, I say, "Thank you for helping me."

"Anytime, Quinn." Opening the car door, I feel his hand on my wrist. I look up at him as he repeats, "I mean it. Anytime."

"Thanks, Gage."

Sliding out of the SUV, I wave.

Rolling down his window, he says, "I'll let you know what I find out."

I feel like I need to say something before I shut the door. "My helmet was missing."

He looks back over the seat where the scooter parts lie. "It is?"

I shrug. "It was pink and super cute." Using my hands, I attempt to help him visualize it. "It's sort of a half helmet, but they call it a jet helmet too. Just thought you should know."

He chuckles. "Pink? Jet helmet. I'll keep an eye out for it. Night, Quinn."

"Night, Gage. Thanks again."

"Anytime."

# CHAPTER TWENTY-THREE

From inside the house, I watch Gage's car pull out of our driveway. The house is silent. It's late, so I'm not surprised. It's got to be after 3:00 a.m. by now. With my phone in hand, I remember I turned it off earlier. Pressing the On button, I wait for it to come to life. When it does, a series of dings alerts me to new texts. I know who they're from.

**Cooke:** Quinn? You called? My sister said you were upset. Are you all right, love? Call me or text. Please.

Wait. His sister?

**Me:** I'm sorry I bothered you. Bad day. That's all.

I smile for the first time in hours as I make my way down to the basement. But the smile is short lived. The second my feet hit the basement carpet, I hear a splash sound. It takes a second for the water to seep into my Converse tennis shoes. Flicking on the flashlight on my phone, I'm shocked at the sight before me. The basement is filled with standing water up to my ankles. I slowly make my way across the room to my bedroom, pushing floating debris away with my foot as I go. I'm doing my best to remember how I left things in my bedroom this morning. I know I was rushing around....

At my bedroom door, it feels like my heart is about to jump out of my chest. I don't want to know the state of my room, but I have to. I turn the knob slowly. It takes extra effort to push it open because of all the water. The second I have it open all the way, I hit the light switch and nearly choke. All of my things— well, most of my things—are floating in four or five inches of water. Things like my $200 biology textbook and my laptop are sitting just below the surface. Clothes that I'd discarded throughout the week are lying in soggy clumps as well. Those can be washed, but things like my headphones, charger cables, and other schoolwork are lost. The sob that comes out of me is loud. I know it is because I felt it in my entire body. "How will I ever be able to replace my stuff?" My laptop was my high school graduation present. My parents won't be able to afford a replacement. And the textbooks? I know one of them was a rental, so I'm going to have to pay full price for that one.

Without thinking, I throw myself onto my bed and hear the water gush beneath it. It won't be long until it seeps up through the box spring to the mattress, but I still have a little bit of time to lose my fucking mind. Honest to God, I've never had a day like this one. A day that makes me want to give up on everything. Because right now, it's not worth it. None of it is worth it.

When my phone rings, I place it in front of my face. It's Cooke wanting to FaceChat. I'm tempted to ignore it, but fuck if I don't need a friend right now. I hit the button. I hear him saying things, his voice sounding sweet and reassuring. I've been doing my damn best to keep my emotions under control and seeing Cooke's sweet smile almost puts me over the edge but it also gives me strength. Especially when he says, "My love." Cooke's voice is strained. "Tell me what happened."

So I do. I tell him about my long day at the bar. I even tell him about the rude guy and the terrible things he said to me. I mean, he needs to hear the entire story, right? I mention Bryant and Kara, and when I get the part about Frankenscooter, the sobs start up again, but I quickly get them under control. I explain how helpful Officer Golden was, and then I go back and talk about the incident with Kara and the hair pulling, and then, finally, I set the scene for my flooded bedroom. I turn the phone so he can see the water and the damage. "See?" I whimper. "Ev-Everything's ruined."

"I see. Are you insured? Is the home insured?"

"I... I'm not sure. I can ask Patsy."

"That's your first step. Perhaps you need to wake your mates so they can see the damage. You can find out what's covered."

"Okay." That's a good idea.

"As for the rest, I'd like to kill the men at the bar for you, love. You're beautiful. And I'll buy you a new scooter. Hell, I'll replace your bloody—"

"No, Cooke. I didn't call you so you would buy me things."

"I know, dearest."

"I just wanted—"

"You needed a shoulder."

"Yeah," I whisper. God, I'm tired.

"I'm your shoulder. I'll always be."

"Thank you, Cooke."

"Now, go wake your mates. Get them to help you. I bloody wish I was there with you."

"M-Me too." I hiccup.

"I'll be in touch, love."

"Okay."

God, I sound pathetic.

∽

"Holy shit." Patsy gasps.

"What the fuck?" says a sleepy Robbi.

Kat blinks. "You just got home?"

"It's a long story, but someone ran over Frankenscooter. He's totaled. I had to wait for Gage to get there to write up a report. When I got home, it was past three, and I walked into this."

Kat has her hand over her mouth. "Shit. Your textbooks. And laptop."

"Who's Gage?" Kat asks, looking perplexed.

"Officer Golden."

"Gage?" Kat asks again.

Patsy stops her. "Focus, Kat. We'll ask her about her hot cop tomorrow."

I don't mind the questions about Gage. It makes me smile, truth be told. I seem to be much calmer now. Cooke was right, I needed my mates.

Patsy turns to me, placing her hands on my shoulders as she says, "No worries. I'll call the landlord about the insurance first thing in the morning."

"Oh, I hope this is all covered," Susanna says between sobs. "We're so sorry, Quinn. This has never happened before."

"It's okay." It's not, but I can't blame my roommates. "It's been raining nonstop."

Patsy reaches for my comforter. "Grab what you can, and we'll move it all upstairs to the second level. We can get you set up in that small niche at the top of the stairs."

"Oh, yeah. Great idea." That cheered Susanna right up. "You can be up there with me, Robbi, and Lindsay." She claps happily. "Yay!"

Robbi is feeling around on my bed. "We can grab your mattress. It's not wet."

"Perfect." Lindsay is giddy now.

So that's what we do. As a team, we gather up all the dry items first and carry them up to the top floor of the house. The small niche is sort of a perfect bedroom. Sure, there are no walls, but it's dry and warm.

After the dry things are gathered, we fill clothes baskets with my wet items. Robbi sets the baskets in the garage for now while Susanna and Kat work on the papers and textbooks. They seem to think that drying them out will work. I love their optimism. I wish I felt the same.

As for my headphones and laptop? I'm sure they're gone, but we'll let them dry out as well. When it's all said and done, all that remains in the basement is an old dresser that was on its last leg anyway and the bed frame. Those we can grab when the water recedes.

By the time we're done, the sun has risen, and we're all crashed out on the floor near my bed. "Thank goodness it's Sunday," someone mumbles.

I nod. "Yeah. I have to work later, but not until five."

"Well, you sleep," Patsy says, patting my leg. "I'll go call the landlord. If I find out anything, I'll let you know."

"Sounds good." I feel gross, and I really want a shower, but my body won't move. I feel like I need to say one last thing before I go to sleep.

**Me**: Thanks, Cooke. You said all the right things last night. I'll never forget it. Now... I'm going to sleep. Night.
**Cooke:** Aye. I'm glad I was useful. Sleep well, lovely Quinn.

*Lovely Quinn.* Those are the last words I think as I fall asleep.

# CHAPTER TWENTY-FOUR

You know that old saying about bad things happening to help us see all the good things in life or something like that? I think it's true. Four days ago was possibly the worst day of my life so far. Granted, no one I love has gotten ill or passed away, thank goodness. With that said, it was a pretty shitty day. Sunday wasn't super great either. We found out that the owners do have insurance, but only on the house itself. None of my belongings were covered under their policy. I'd have to have renter's insurance for that. Ask me if I have renter's insurance.

The answer is No.

I sort of expected that to be the case anyway, so I didn't get upset again. By the time I woke up at noon on Sunday, I had gotten sort of Zen about everything. I went to work, which was fun because the bar was dead, and Luke was off. Chris and I got to know each other, plus he taught me some new mixed drinks. Apparently, the cosmo is "very popular with the ladies," as Chris noted. I also made a Moscow mule and a sour apple martini. I've got to say, martinis aren't my thing. It sounded good, but boy was it strong. I did like the mule, though. That was delish.

Chris let me leave early after hearing about my Saturday. It's a good thing, since I was still tired, and I had a paper to rewrite because the last one was saved on my drowned laptop. Kat is letting me borrow her laptop tonight, thankfully. If I'd been smart, I'd have put all my work that was on my computer on a cloud somewhere, but I'm not smart, I guess. I also emailed all my instructors about the flood damage and the ruination of my school supplies. I hoped they had a heart so if I happened to turn anything in late, they'd let it slide.

I haven't heard anything from Gage yet. I was hoping he'd have a lead on the person who ran over my scooter. I'm tempted to call him, but he's probably busy. I'll just have to wait.

"WELL, I'M NOT GONNA LIE. I DIDN'T THINK YOU'D LAST THIS long."

I'm sitting in the Hub with one of my art history classmate's textbooks. She's letting me borrow her book for an hour so I can take notes while she's in another class. I need to buy her a coffee or something to thank her. Just as I'm finishing up my vocabulary list, a shadow crosses over my white notepaper. Looking up, I stare into the eyes of my long-lost best friend, Tayler. "Me neither. There were times when my fingers itched to make the move to call you, but I had a point to make."

"Point made." Tayler gestures to the seat next to me.

"Of course. Sit."

"God, I've missed you so much, girl."

"Me too." I reach out, holding my arms wide. She moves closer into the hug. I swear I hear her sniffling. "Dylan cheated on me. He moved out three weeks ago."

"What!" I screech. "No way."

"Way." She wipes away a tear on her cheek. "I really needed you last month." Several more tears slide down her face.

I move back in for another hug. "I'm so sorry, Tay."

Pulling back, she shakes her head and wipes away more wetness from her face. "I'm so sick of this roller coaster of emotions. I just want to move on with my life."

"So, you're living in that apartment alone?"

"Yeah, but not for long. I can't afford it on my own. Dad said he'd help me for a month or two, but that's all."

"Poor Tayler."

"Oh, stop." She waves me off. "Tell me about you so I can stop feeling sorry for myself. I'm sure you've got some gossip or drama for me to enjoy, right?"

"Oh, boy. Do I ever." I smile but then pause. "Are you sure you want to hear all of this? There's a lot."

"I'm positive. Spill, bitch."

So I do. I basically start where we left off that day over a month ago. I talked for over an hour, which included a bunch of questions from Tayler along the way. In the end, I had her laughing her ass off at my horrible, terrible, very bad fucking day. It's okay, I was laughing too. I mean, if you can't laugh at the stuff life throws at you, then you're in trouble.

"So, you work at Cy's? How have I not seen you?"

"I was in training for the first two weeks, so I only worked on Sundays and a few hours after classes at first. They're slowly getting me used to bartending. My boss, Luke—"

"Ooh, Luke Green. Yum," she hums. "That man is delish."

I think she's feeling better about Dylan. "He doesn't seem like your type."

"What? Hot and tattooed and muscled isn't my type?" She looks toward the door. "Guys like that"—she points—"are so my type."

I look over at the door and blink. Then I blink again. "No. Way." My voice is squeaky and breathless at the same time. I drop the pen I was playing with, slide off my stool, and run right into the open arms of one Cooke Thompson. When I get there, I wrap my arms around his neck and pull him down to me. "Oh my

God. I can't believe you're here." My voice catches in my throat, because seeing him in the flesh is amazing, but knowing the reason he's here choked me right up. "You're the best, Cooke Thompson. The absolute best thing that ever happened to me." God, I want to kiss him, but that would be weird.

I hear him chuckle in my ear, then feel his arms wrap around me and pull me into the best frigging hug I've ever had.

I pull back just enough to look up at him. Holy shit, the man is gorgeous. The screen did not do him justice. "How did you find me?"

"Your mate Patsy. She led me here."

"Oh my God. Your voice. Hearing it in person is amazing, Cooke."

"Yours too, love."

I feel wetness on my cheeks and quickly wipe it away. "I can't believe you're here."

"I booked a flight right away. I had to finish up a few things. I got here as soon as I could."

My breath catches. "You...."

"What?" He's smiling down at me, and it's the sweetest smile I've ever seen.

He pushes a piece of my hair out of my eyes, and I confess, "You're amazing."

"Nah, you are, love."

I quickly grab him again, this time wrapping my arms around his waist. God, he smells so damn good. I let my face plant itself on his hard chest. I blink a few times because of all the yellow in front of me. I pull back and look at his T-shirt. It's the Iowa State rugby tee. "Oh my God. You're wearing the shirt. Dan and Bull are going to flip. Out." I'm tempted to grab my phone right now and let them know he's here, but no, I want him all to myself for as long as I can.

"Are you going to introduce me, Q?"

I turn my head and see Tayler. "Oh, right." I step to his side and point at his stomach area. "Tayler, this is Cooke Thompson." I look up at him and point at my friend. "Cooke, this is Tayler Sorenson, my oldest and dearest friend."

"Delighted," he says, taking her hand and kissing the top of it.

It makes me break out into girly giggles. When I look at Tayler, she's blushing and doing her own version of a girly giggle. It's something to see, because Tayler isn't the type to blush, and I swear I've never ever heard her giggle. But something tells me Cooke Thompson makes *all* women giggle.

Pulling farther away from him, I take his hand in mine—it feels amazing—and pull him over to my table. As I gather my things, I start chattering at about one hundred miles per hour. "Are you hungry, Cooke? Thirsty? Tired? Do you need to rest? I need to get to class, but I could skip it. I can't skip work later, though. I'm new, so I don't think Luke would appreciate it, you know?" *Wait! How long can he stay?*

Tayler snickers, "Slow down, Q. You're sort of acting like a crazy person."

"Well, of course I am." I point in Cooke's direction. "This guy flew across the pond to see *me*." I pause to look at him for a second. "Right?"

"Absolutely."

"So, are you hungry or tired or thirsty?"

Cooke laughs softly. "I'm all of those things, but more than any of those, I'm just happy to meet you in person."

I smile wide. I know all my teeth are showing. "You are?"

"I am. But you must be off to your course. I don't want you to skip anything. I've booked a room at a hotel. I'll head back there, have a bite and a lie down, and then I'll come to... what's it called? Cy's Roof?"

I roll my eyes and laugh. "Cy's *Roost*."

"Right. Roost. I'll be off and see you there this evening. How does that sound?"

Without saying a word, I move closer to him, holding my arms out for another hug. He doesn't disappoint. Cooke does what he did before, wrapping me up and holding me tight.

"I'm so glad you're here," I murmur.

"Me as well, love. Me as well."

IF YOU ASSUME I PAID LITTLE TO NO ATTENTION IN MY afternoon class, you'd be correct. I could barely contain my excitement. I mean, Cooke Thompson is *here*. In Ames, Iowa. To. See. Me. So as soon as we were dismissed, I literally ran out of the room and was out the door to the nearest bus stop in minutes. From there, it took me at least thirty more to get home. That's okay; I still had plenty of time to shower, change, and actually put on some makeup before I needed to be to work. As the bus moved at a snail's pace to west Ames, I decided I needed to ask Cooke a question.

**Me:** Do you mind if I let Dan know you're here? I can tell him you'll be at Cy's later.

I send that message, then add:

**Me**: And can I invite my roommates? And Tayler?
**Cooke:** Of course, Q. (I'm using your friend's moniker.) I'd love to meet the rest of your mates.

I quickly shoot messages to Dan and the girls. I hope they're up for going out on a Wednesday. Patsy quickly responds.

**Patsy:** Way ahead of you. LOL. I told the girls he was in town. Sounds like totes fun.

*Totes fun?* She makes me laugh. People on the bus are staring at me now. They probably think I'm a crazy person for laughing out loud. Oh well. Not going to worry about that now. No, I need to worry about what I'm wearing to work tonight. You know, real-world problems.

**Dan**: Holy shit. Seriously? Fuck. Bull is going to shit himself. We have practice, but we'll cancel it. See you at Cy's.
**Me:** Yep. C U

## CHAPTER TWENTY-FIVE

The joint is jumpin', as they say. When I first got to work, there were only a handful of people here. Now there's an entire rugby team and their entourage, my roommates, and Tayler. It's a party. Luckily for me, I've only had to pour beer so far. Luke has decided to let me try it on my own. He's still here, lurking in the kitchen and his office. Well, correction—as soon as the rugby team got here, he's been staying close to the bar area. But I've been holding my own.

When the door opens, I stop what I'm doing and hold my breath. Then I release the breath and slump. Still no Cooke. I guess I should have asked him what time he'd be here. I'd text him, but Luke would frown upon that, even though I warned him that everyone was coming to meet my friend. Apparently, Luke doesn't pay much attention to sports. His words. He said his life is this bar. That's sort of sad, really.

As I start to pour a pitcher for Bull—get this... the pitcher is his glass—the door opens again. I turn my head in time to see the man himself step through the door. What was especially strange was the noise in the bar. There was none. The second he stepped foot into the place, it went dead silent. Well, until one of the rugby guys said, "Jesus, look at the size of him." Several people laugh, me included.

But once the shock wears off, he's practically attacked by the hordes. I watch as he talks, jokes, and laughs with everyone around him. At one point, Bull looks over at me, and I swear he's crying. Maybe I underestimated Cooke's fame. Hell, even Luke seems to be a little starstruck. Since Cooke's been here, Luke's been bombarding me with questions about him like, "How do you know him? Where did you meet him? Are you sure you can trust him?" I wasn't sure what he meant by the last question, but I quickly answered it, and he seemed to be satisfied.

Once everyone has had a chance to talk or just touch Cooke, he steps up to the bar. "Hey, Q."

"Hi, Cooke. What can I get you?"

"Guinness, please, lass."

"Bottle or tap?"

He arches a brow at me like I asked him something stupid. "Tap. Always tap."

"Right." I laugh and pour him his Guinness. God, I hope I did it right. Sliding the glass to him, I hold my breath, half expecting him to critique my pour, but he doesn't. Instead he places the glass to his lips and drinks fast. Almost half the beer is gone in one go. I watch his throat bob up and down as he drinks. It's sexy. Okay, I know that sounds weird, but everything about Cooke Thompson is sexy.

"You look beautiful, Quinn."

"Huh?" I'm taken aback by his words.

He chuckles. "I said you look beautiful."

"Oh." I look down at myself. Black tee, black jeans, black Converse. "Thanks?" I guess I did do something with my hair. I flat-ironed it and left it down for once. And I have makeup on, so there's that. "Are you okay with everything?" I point to the crowd behind him. I'm worried he's annoyed by all the attention.

"I'm perfect. No worries. Your mates are cool."

Just then, I let my eyes move to Cooke's left. Bull is seated next to him, staring at Cooke. "You need another beer, Bull?" I ask.

He nods, so I pour another pitcher.

"Cooke, I think you've got a true fan there." I nod to Bull.

Bull grunts. "You're the bomb, Corinne."

"It's Quinn," Cooke snaps.

Bull quickly corrects himself. "Right. Sorry, Quinn. I asked you to get him here, and you did." He holds his palm over his chest. "I'm at your service anytime you need me or any of us." He picks up the phone he's got in front of him. "Give me your digits."

I start to laugh but stop when I look at Cooke.

"And why is that?" he asks, anger written all over his pretty face.

Bull stares at Cooke, and I see real fear there. "So I can text her, so she has my number, sir. If she needs protection or whatever, she's got the entire team at her disposal."

*Sir?*

Cooke nods, but his expression is still steely. "I appreciate that, mate." He slaps Bull on the back. "Keep my girl safe."

I'm not sure what to say about all that, so instead of overthinking it, I move on to the next customer. Everyone is having a good time, especially when Cooke rejoins the raucous rugby guys. They're taking turns getting pictures with him, and at one point, the entire team lines up behind him for a group shot. I'm sure that'll end up on the web. And for those people who know and love rugby, it'll be a big thing.

I'm just finishing up making my first mule for a customer when I see Bryant walk in the door. I haven't seen him since my horrible, terrible, very bad fucking day, and I'm okay with that. I half expect Kara to follow him in but he's alone. He makes a beeline to Cooke, introducing himself as "one of Quinn's best friends." I'm not sure how I feel about that, but I'm not about to correct him right now. When he finally approaches the bar, he says, "Hey, Quinn." Pointing his thumb back to Cooke, he adds, "How'd you get him here? Promise him homemade cookies or something?" Then he smirks.

I'm speechless. Honest to God speechless. I'm not sure whether to laugh or cry. I recall him referring to me as ditzy not long ago, also insinuating that I'm not a useful bartender, and now what? I had to lure Cooke Thompson from England with baked goods? What the ever-loving fuck? "No, he came to support me."

Bryant snickers. "Is that what they're calling it these days?"

I lean closer. "For your information, Kara assaulted me, then someone ran over my scooter and destroyed it, and my bedroom flooded with half a foot of water, ruining my textbooks and computer. *He's* my friend. I was upset, and he came to see what he could do."

"So, he's going to buy you a new scooter?" Honest to goodness, I don't think he means it the way he said it, but it still pisses me off. I mean, why he didn't lead with "What! Kara assaulted you?" I have no idea.

"No," I growl. "He's here because he was worried about me."

"Why didn't you tell me about any of that?" Now he looks affronted. "I would've helped."

"You're dating Kara."

"Dating? I wouldn't say dating." He smirks again, and I want to punch him in the face.

Stepping back from the bar, I pick up the bar rag and ask, "What can I get for you?" He still hasn't asked me about the first thing I mentioned. He doesn't care.

"Busch Light, please."

"Glass or pitcher?"

"Glass. I'll bum some beer off the guys after that. Hopefully your friend Cooke is buying."

Wow, he's a cheap-ass mooch too. "He's not a frigging ATM," I mutter to myself. Pouring his beer, I place it in front of him. "Three-fifty."

He pulls out a five and hands it to me. I ring him up and place his $1.50 on the bar. Usually, people leave at least the fifty cents on the bar. Not Bryant, though. He leaves nothing. "I'll get ya next time," he says with a wink and the pistol hand gesture.

"Sure." There won't be a next time, since he's planning on mooching off everyone else in the bar. "What did I ever see in that guy?"

"No idea," says Tayler. She must have snuck up on me.

I roll my eyes. "How are you doing?" I'm worried about her. She and Dylan were inseparable going on four years. That's a long time.

"Good." She leans closer to the bar. "We're going to sit down and have a long-ass talk about all of this." She uses her thumb to point behind her. "But right now, tell me how to get Luke Green's attention."

"I have no idea. You know me. I'm the last person to dole out advice about a guy. Besides, you're absolutely stunning." Especially tonight. She's wearing a short, tight dress in an emerald green color. It looks amazing with her deep red hair.

"Introduce me, then."

I can do that. I head toward the kitchen and yell, "Luke."

"Yeah?" He steps out, wiping his hands on a towel. I wonder what he was doing. No matter, he looks damn hot in jeans that fit him perfectly and a tight Cy's Roost tee. His tattoos are peeking out of each sleeve, giving us a glimpse of some beautiful art.

"I want to introduce you to my best friend. A best friend I will never give free drinks to." Crossing my fingers, I add, "I promise."

He walks slowly up to the bar. "Does your beautiful friend have a name?"

*Beautiful* friend? "She does. It's—"

"Tayler," my best friend says, holding her hand out to him. "We've met, though."

"I know. You were here last Wednesday." His voice just dropped an octave, I swear.

"I... uh, yes, I was."

"You've also been here a number of times with a man."

I respond before she can. "Her ex. He cheated on her. Can you believe that?"

"No." Luke looks at her for a good long time. "He's a fucking idiot."

"Right?" I say, then laugh. Neither of them is listening to me. As a matter of fact, Luke's now leaning over the bar so far that if Tayler leaned in, they'd be kissing. "Welp, I guess I'll move along." I laugh again as I head off to help another customer. Peeking back at them, I see they're now talking.

Damn, matchmaking is fun.

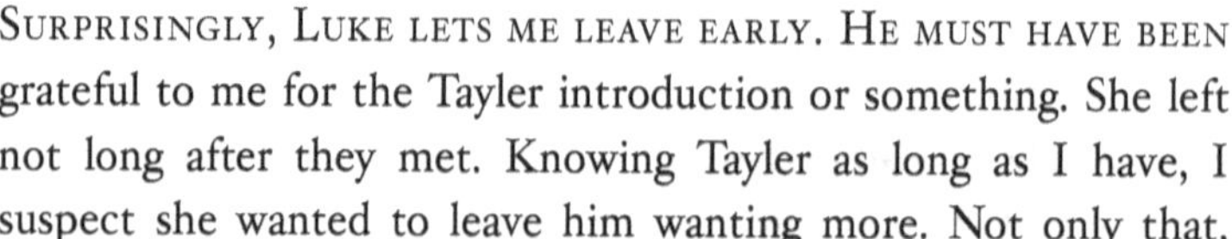

SURPRISINGLY, LUKE LETS ME LEAVE EARLY. HE MUST HAVE BEEN grateful to me for the Tayler introduction or something. She left not long after they met. Knowing Tayler as long as I have, I suspect she wanted to leave him wanting more. Not only that, she'd want him to make the next move. Clever girl. Now we'll have to wait and see.

The party is still going strong when I grab my sweatshirt and purse. I catch Cooke's attention and point at the door. As he follows me, the rugby guys slap him on the back, sad to see him go.

"You're all done, then?" he asks, taking my hand in his. It feels very natural to hold hands with Cooke Thompson. I should probably be wary of any feelings I have for this man, though.

"Luke let me leave early."

"What shall we do now? The night is young."

It's just past ten on a school night, but I'm not about to say a word about it being late. "We could...." I shrug. "What would you like to do?"

"First, I want to see where you live. I'm feeling peckish, so after that, a bite would be lovely."

"Peckish?"

"Yes, I'm hungry."

I could make him some ramen, but I'm afraid to bring it up. "Oh, okay."

Cooke leads me down the street to a sleek black sports car.

"Nice ride."

"Aye. I've had a bloody time of it trying to drive on the wrong side of the road *and* sit on the opposite side of the car."

"I could drive." *Oh, please let me drive.* I've never driven anything remotely as fancy as this thing is.

"Be my guest." He holds the driver's side door open for me. When I sit down, I practically fall backward, he's got the seat so far back. As I adjust it, Cooke walks around the car and slides into the passenger side. Once I'm set, I search for the key slot.

"Press the button," he explains.

"Ooh, this is cool," I say, admiring all the leather and faux wood details. There are so many buttons, lights, and other gadgets in this thing, I'm tempted to play for a few minutes before taking off, but he's "peckish," so we need to get a move on.

I've got the uncontrollable urge to put the pedal to the metal on the main road, but I don't need a ticket. Too bad.

Before we know it, we're at my house. It's not perfect or even pretty, but it's a solid house with lots of room for us. Pushing the shifter into Park, I smile, then turn to look at Cooke. "This is a sweet-ass ride."

It must have been a funny thing to say, because Cooke bursts with laughter. "It is indeed, love." Taking my hand in his, he lifts it to his lips and kisses the top of it. I felt it through my entire body. It practically singed my skin, it was so electrifying. I'm staring at his face—well, his mouth, as it still sits about an inch from my hand. He slowly releases it and I sigh, wishing he'd do that again, but this time on my face in general, my mouth in particular. But that's never going to happen.

Reaching for the door handle, I find it and tug until it clicks. Then I push the door open. "Come on, I'll show you my subterranean slumber chamber."

He chuckles as he steps out of his side of the car. "Spiders included."

"Well, they may have all died in the great flood of '19."

Cooke holds his arm out, and I place my hand in his again. It's becoming a habit already. One I like very much. God, it's going to suck when this is over.

# CHAPTER TWENTY-SIX

"Bloody hell," he says, pulling his shirt up to cover his nose and mouth. He points to my shirt, but there's no way I'm doing that. It'll rise and show my secrets. And by secrets, I mean my belly that I've kept strategically hidden beneath lots of fabric. "That smell?" He points into the room. "It's mold. Please tell me the landlord is going to remediate."

Remediate? "Um, I—"

"Love. You can't live down here with mold. It's dangerous."

"I moved upstairs." I grab his hand. "Come on, I'll show you my new digs." I pull him up the basement steps and through the kitchen, into the living room, to the stairs leading to the top floor. "See?" I point to my little area known as the niche.

"Love." Cooke's face is scrunched up. "You can't live like this."

"What's wrong with it? It's warm and dry." And there aren't any spiders to speak of. Well, there was one, but he was a little guy.

"Darling." He places one hand on each of my shoulders. "I can't have you living like this."

"Huh?" What does he mean by that? "This is fine. The girls aren't loud—well, very loud."

"Quinn." Cooke bends down until we're face-to-face. "I—"

Just then, my stupid phone rings. I want to ignore it so I can hear what he was going to say, but he smiles and says, "Answer it." He nods at the ringing phone. "Go on."

I quickly find the phone in my small purse. "Hello?" The second I know who it is, I add, "Oh, hi, Gage."

"Who's Gage?" he mouths, frowning.

Holding my hand over the phone, I tell Cooke, "It's the police officer who's looking into my scooter."

His frown is still there.

Turning back to my phone call, I hear Gage say, "I have some news."

"You do? What?"

"I was able to locate the person who damaged your scooter."

"Okay." I wait, but he says nothing. "Can you tell me, or is it not allowed?"

"It was Kara Becker."

I'm shocked, sort of. I suspected her, but in my mind, I didn't think she would go that far. "Do you know for sure?"

"Her vehicle had damage, and traces of paint from your multi-colored scooter were on her car and most importantly, your helmet was jammed up between the frame and the muffler."

"You're kidding."

"I wish I were. She was adamant that she had nothing to do with it until we took her car in and got it up on a lift. Your pink helmet was right there."

I so want to ask if it was okay, but I think I know the answer. "So, what happens next?"

"We've charged her with hit-and-run."

"Is that serious?"

"Very. Leaving the scene of any accident is frowned upon by law enforcement."

"I doubt it was an accident."

"She claims it was."

I know different.

"This combined with the other assault report filed, she's in serious trouble. I'm going to need you to come in tomorrow to sign some papers."

"What time?"

"It's my day off, so just text me when you plan to come, and I'll meet you here."

"Are you sure? It's your day off." I look up at Cooke, whose expression has turned from a frown to downright stormy.

"It's not a problem, Quinn. Talk to you tomorrow."

"Okay. Thanks, Gage. Bye."

I press End and look up at Cooke. I'm going to ignore the flaring nostrils for just a second. "Kara is the one who ran over my scooter. Her car had my paint on it, and my helmet was caught up underneath it." My poor helmet.

"So, you call the police officer Gage?"

That's what he took from that. "He's nice. A friend."

Cooke runs his palm over his face, then through his hair. "You have a lot of friends."

I smile because it's a nice thing to say, but by the look on his face, he didn't mean it like that. "I do."

"Men friends."

"I have both. Male and female friends."

"Are you sure they only want to be friends?"

I snort. "Well, yeah. Nobody wants to be more than that with *me*."

"What the bloody hell are you talking about?"

I roll my eyes to keep myself from tearing up. God, this is embarrassing. "Guys don't like me... like that." I shrug. "I get it. I'm not attractive to you... them."

"Quinn," he says softly, his face changing from cranky to something much gentler. He steps closer to me, bringing his finger up to touch me right below my chin... chins. "Love." With slight pressure, he pushes my face upward. "You're bloody beautiful." Then he does that thing I wished he'd done earlier. He kisses me. I close my eyes so I can really concentrate. His kiss is soft. Sweet. It's just a brush of his lips over mine. I'd love to savor it, but it's over before it starts.

I open my eyes. He's still so close, I can see the color of his irises. They're light brown, almost the color of his hair, but there are flecks of gray and green in them too. They're like nothing I've ever seen before. "You have really pretty eyes."

Cooke chuckles. "So do you. They're as blue as an azure sea."

"That blue, huh?" I giggle because I have no idea what that is. I'm definitely going to google "azure sea" the first chance I get.

"Aye. That blue."

He hasn't moved. He's still an inch from me. What should I do? Should I kiss him? Should I wrap my arms around him and drag him down to my twin mattress? I start to laugh at that notion just as he moves back and away from me. "Let's go get a bite. I'm starving."

Refusing to overthink the kiss or anything that just happened, I make my way toward the stairs. "I'd offer to cook for you, but all I have here is stale bread and ramen noodles." I turn my head, adding, "Trust me, you don't want that." Continuing down the steps, I say, "So, I'm going to let you buy me dinner."

"It would be my honor, Q."

## CHAPTER TWENTY-SEVEN

"Best pizza ever," I say with my mouth only half full. I was able to get a to-go order in to Great Plains Sauce and Dough Company before they closed. I've never had it before due to the price, but I've always heard good things. And wow, it's so good. "Do you like it?"

He nods and smiles as he dips part of his crust in a dish of honey. He's devoured over half the pizza, which is saying something since we ordered a large and it's exactly that, *large*.

"I'm glad." And relieved. I chose the place not having any idea what kind of food he might like.

We're at Cooke's hotel, sitting at the small dining table in the second living area of his two-room suite. I'm not sure it's as fancy as the places Cooke usually stays, but he hasn't complained. I mean, the room is nice. I took a little tour when we first got here. There's a king-size bed with a big wall-mounted television, closet, and sitting area in the other room. This room has a larger living area with an even larger TV, along with a kitchenette and this dining table. All in all, I think it's not bad.

We've been quiet for a few minutes. Part of that is me not wanting to ask him how long he's staying, but I need to know so I can plan fun things for him to do. "So"—I place my half-eaten piece of pizza back down on my napkin—"how long are you staying?"

He nods, chews, and then swallows his big bite. "One more night. I fly out the following morning."

"Oh." What did I think? He was going to stay a week or two? Of course not. "Well, what would you like to do tomorrow? I don't work." And I can skip my afternoon classes. Probably.

"I'd like a tour of your campus, I promised the rugby lads I'd visit their practice tomorrow evening, and I'd love to take you to dinner."

"I'd like that." The conversation lags, so I ask, "Are you having a good time so far?"

He smiles between bites. "I am. I'm just knackered."

Oh, I know what that means—he's tired. "That's right. You're on UK time. I'm so sorry. I should go and let you sleep." I quickly stand and search for somewhere to throw my trash.

"Stay."

I halt. "St-Stay?"

"Stay. It's a big bed. I won't even be tempted."

I feel the flush hit my cheeks instantaneously. "Of course not." Why would he be tempted by me? Sure, he kissed me, but I swear I've had a more passionate kiss with my brother.

Wait. Don't... I didn't mean it like that. All I meant was his was barely a kiss. It was a peck, like when you see your grandma and grandpa kiss. Like that. Geesh. I'm not a perv. And neither is my brother. You know what? Forget I said anything. All I mean was his kiss was nothing. A tiny blip on the giant radar of life.

"Quinn."

"No, I think I'll, uh, call an Uber."

"Quinn, love."

I throw my things away, trying to keep busy. I must be tired too, because this shouldn't make me emotional. It's just that sleeping in a room with the lights on almost all the time has been difficult. The girls aren't noisy, mostly, but there's a lot of activity on the upper level. I'm sort of used to the dungeon I called home for a month or so.

"Quinn?"

I turn and he's right there.

"What?" I snap.

"Don't go."

"You need to sleep. I have to get up early. My stuff is at home. I'm not at all worried that you'd be tempted by me. Not in the least. I just prefer to sleep in my own bed." Lies. All Lies.

"Fine." He releases a gust of air. I feel it on my forehead. "I'll drive you."

"No." Grabbing my purse, I head to the door. "See you tomorrow?"

"Damn it, Quinn. Stay." He's running his fingers through his hair angrily.

Why? Why would *he* be angry? *I'm* the one who should be angry. At myself. Every time a guy pays any attention to me, I get lofty, romantic ideas in my head. I'm stupid. Pathetic. I need to stop with the optimism and turn to realism. Life isn't a fairy tale. It isn't a romance novel where the big girl gets the hot man. It's just not how things work in real life.

I reach for the door handle and start to turn it when I feel myself being pulled away from the door. The next thing I know, my back is firmly against said door, and Cooke's mouth is on mine in a decidedly un-grandfatherly kiss. It was so sudden that my mouth was open when he started it. His tongue slips into my mouth, and I do what anyone would do—I touch my tongue to his. I haven't had a chance to figure out what to do with my hands, so they're just down at my sides. His hands are in my hair. I should put mine in his hair, but when I try, I can't get them there. That's when he takes my hands in his and lifts them until they're up above my head. It's shocking and sexy, so I moan and press myself against him, getting as close to him as I can.

"You have—" He stops talking to kiss his way down my neck. "—no idea how fecking beautiful you are." His mouth moves down the middle of my chest to my little bit of cleavage thanks to my V-neck tee. "The second I saw you—" His lips slide up the other side of my neck to my ear, where he suckles on my lobe. "—I knew."

What? What did he know? "Oh my God," I pant. This feels better than anything ever has in the entire world.

"You like my mouth on you, love?"

"Yes." Hell, fuck, yes. "Don't stop." Don't ever, ever stop.

But he does. The big jerk stops. When I open my eyes, he's staring into mine. "Stay."

Stay. Stay?

"I promise you we won't do anything you aren't comfortable doing. I just want you in my bed. I want to hold you. I want to kiss you and wake up next to you."

"That was much better, Cooke."

"Better?"

"Yeah, better than 'I won't even be tempted.'" I say it in a deep voice to make it sound like it's him who's talking.

"I'm tempted. Believe me." He looks down at himself, and my eyes follow until they reach his crotch region. His jeans look sort of uncomfortable right now.

I giggle, because nerves. "Oh. Dear."

Smiling, Cooke takes me by the hand and leads me to the bedroom part of the suite.

"I, erm, don't have anything to wear," I mumble.

"I've got something."

I watch as he digs through his suitcase. Pulling out something red, he steps back over to me. "I brought this for you."

Taking it from him, I unfold it to see it's got his team logo on it. He turns it around so I can see his number, 10, and his name, Thompson, printed above it.

"Wow, Cooke." My first concern is if it will fit. I don't want to look at the tag to see the size, but gauging just from holding it up, I think it will. It'll most likely be snug around my ass, but I can't do a thing about that. "Thank you."

"Go on, then." He points to the bathroom. "You use the loo; I'll undress out here."

I step into the bathroom and quickly shut the door, all the while biting my lip. Shit. *He's undressing?* What if I step out and he's naked? What will I do? I know what he said a few minutes ago, that we won't do anything I don't want to do, but.... "Just breathe, Quinn." I'm whispering to myself so he can't hear me. I'm acting like a lunatic. "He won't be naked." And what if he is?

"You all right in there, love?"

Shit. "Uh, yeah. I'm good."

I quickly undress, contemplating whether or not I should wear my bra. I opt not to wear it because a, it's too tight, and b... well, there is no b, so I unhook my bra and tuck it into my folded shirt. Next, I unbutton, unzip, and shimmy out of my jeans. Standing in only my nicest pair of Hanes Her Way underwear, I slide the shirt over my head. Pushing my arms into each hole, I pray this thing will fit, because I can't walk back out there and tell him, "Hey, sorry. I'm too fat to wear your ginormous shirt. Got anything in xx-ginormous?" Luckily, when I pull it down, it's a little loose on me, even over my ass. And it's long, hitting me at midthigh. "Phew," I say softly.

Now that the shirt drama is over, I look at myself in the mirror. I'm flushed, but that's probably just from changing clothes, though it could also be from that kiss. My hair has certainly been mussed because of that. I run my fingers through it to smooth it down. I lean toward the mirror and see my makeup is okay. Before I go, I decide to quickly use the bathroom, wash my hands, and rinse out my mouth. I'm ready. Now all I need to do is open the door.

"Quinn?" he calls from the other room. "Is this too much for you, love?"

Oh shit. How long have I been in here? Without responding, I open the door and step out. My eyes go right to the bed. He's in it, beneath the covers. I can't tell if he's wearing bottoms, but I can see his upper body is free of clothing. I can finally see his tattoos in real life. I could probably touch them if I wanted to.

"Wow," he says sort of breathlessly. "You look perfect."

I blink at him a few times but say nothing.

"You all right over there?"

"Sure."

That makes him chuckle. Stepping closer to the bed, I stop and look at his face. With courage I didn't know I had, I say, "I think you're the most gorgeous man I've ever seen, Cooke Thompson."

"I feel the same about you," Cooke says as he lifts the sheet and blanket for me to slide under.

I feel the cool sheets hit my bare legs and sigh. Once my body is beneath the covers, he releases them, resting his hand on my belly, over the blankets. I look back at him, and it hits me. *Holy shit. I'm in bed with Cooke Thompson.* I'm literally *in bed* with Cooke Thompson. It's too bad I'm stiff as a board. I've pulled the bedding up to my chin, but I haven't moved. He slides closer to me urging me back. I scoot over and end up being spooned. Holy shit, I'm spooning with Cooke Thompson. That's what I said, s-p-o-o-n-i-n-g.

With his mouth right next to my ear, he whispers, "Love?"

"Yeah."

"Nothing is going to happen tonight. I just want to hold you. Please relax. I don't like that you seem afraid of me."

I quickly turn my head. "I'm not afraid of you." Should I be? Maneuvering so I'm facing him, I place my hand on his face. "Cooke. I'm a virgin."

He blinks a few times, then smiles.

"Aren't you going to say anything?" I mean, I just confessed something to this man—a secret that only Tayler knew about.

"Good" is all he says right before he kisses me. It's not like the one before. No, this one is soft and lingering and sweet. Sure, there's tongue, but it's not frantic; it's fluid and exploratory. I do my best to mimic his movements. I must be doing something right, because he lets out a deep moan from somewhere in his chest. I feel his hand slide down my back to rest on my butt. He squeezes one of my ass cheeks, then pulls me in to him.

"Sleep, love. Let me hold you."

Easy for him to say. I'm pressed up against the hottest man on Earth. Everything about him is delicious, starting with his musky, earthy scent and his warm skin. Even his calloused hands and fingers feel good to me. That's not even hitting on his physical appearance, because I'm starting to think that what makes Cooke Thompson beautiful isn't his face. It's his heart.

## CHAPTER TWENTY-EIGHT

"When are you finished with your courses today, love?"

"Noon." I have class after that, but I've decided to skip since I only have one more day with him. On second thought... "Actually, make that eleven."

"You sure?" He comes up behind me and wraps his big arms around me. I'm about to say fuck it and skip everything, but I'm pretty sure I'll miss a pop quiz if I don't show up to art history.

"I'm sure. Where would you like to meet?"

"At that Hub place. You can give me a tour of campus, and then we'll get a bite."

I turn in his arms so I'm facing him. Why does this feel so natural, like we've been doing it forever? I don't have one ounce of self-consciousness or shyness with him. It's bizarre. "You've got this all planned out, don't you?"

"Aye." He leans down to kiss me softly. "One thing you should know about me, Quinn. I don't do anything without a plan."

"Hm, I'm not sure how I feel about that. Spontaneity is the spice of life." Or something like that.

With a smirk, he does two things. First, he says, "Oh, I'm spontaneous." Second, he bends slightly placing his hands right below my butt and lifting me up in the air. I squeal as he turns and tosses me back onto the bed. Then, before I know it, he's there above me, his big body between my legs. "How's that for spicing up life?"

"You can't be lifting me, Cooke. You'll hurt yourself. Then what will happen to your team?" I mean seriously. He could throw his back out.

"Please stop saying shite like that, love." Then he kisses me. Not like the one a minute ago. No, this one sort of picks up where we left off last night. He brushes his tongue across my lower lip, and I smile against his mouth, opening mine enough for him to sweep his in. I open farther and moan at our kiss. Running my fingers through his hair, I arch to get closer to his body. I want his hands on me, all over me, and the thought scares me a little.

Sadly, he pulls away. "I've got to get you home."

"I know," I mumble in a whiny voice.

"Eleven. And I've got a surprise for you as well."

"Oh?" I love surprises. "Okay." I smile brightly. "Don't forget, I need to go to the police station too."

"Right." He nods, kisses my nose, and then he's up on his feet.

Since we're both already dressed, me in the clothes from work last night and Cooke in a pair of dark jeans that fit him like a glove, a button-up dress shirt, and a zip-up hoodie that makes him look like sex on a stick, we're ready to go.

In the car, I pull my phone out of my bag and see I've got a bunch of missed texts and voice mails. I guess I never turned the sound back on after work last night. I quickly scan them and realize they're all from my roommates. The first is from Pats, not long after we left Cy's.

**Patsy:** Where are you? Where did you go?

At about thirty-minute intervals after that, all of my room-mates were texting.

**Lindsay:** Where are you?

**Kat:** We just got home and you're not here. Patsy's losing her shit.

**Patsy**: I'm going to strangle you. I'm this close to calling the cops.

**Robbi**: Jesus, fuck. We really don't know this guy. Where are you?

The last one came at three in the morning.

**Susanna**: We're going to bed, but we're sleeping with one eye open in case you call.

"Shit," I mutter. "My roommates are worried about me."

"You didn't let them know you were with me?"

"Oh, they knew I was with you, but they don't really know you." Neither do I, honestly.

As soon as we pull into the driveway, I sigh.

"Would you like me to come with you?" he nods at the front door.

"Nah. You go do...." I look at his nice clothes. "What are you going to do?"

"This and that."

"Oh, you're being mysterious. Well, don't get lost." He points to his fancy navigation screen that's bigger than my laptop was. "Yeah, you're good." I'm about to lean in for a kiss, but I suddenly feel awkward. Are we doing that? You know, kissing each other goodbye and stuff?

Before I can overthink it, I lean in a little bit and he meets me halfway, giving each other a chaste kiss. I like it. "See you at eleven."

"Have a good morning, love."

I smile as I slide out of his vehicle. It sits extra low to the ground, so I have to grab hold of the door to push myself. I attempt to do it as elegantly as possible and only sort of achieve that. I wave as I take the steps up to the front door. Looking down at my phone, I note I only have a few minutes before I need to be back out the door or I'll be late for ceramics. I'm going to have to wear the same clothes and grab my bag. When I open the door, the house is quiet, which is weird because we all have morning classes. When I start through the living room, I stop dead in my tracks. They're there. All of them.

"Oh... hey," I say weakly.

"Don't—" Patsy starts, but Robbi raises her palm to stop her, then stands.

"I've been given the metaphorical talking stick." Robbi gives Patsy the evil eye. "And please know this comes from a place of love." She sighs. "We were worried sick about you. Although we know of Cooke, we don't really *know* him, and for you to leave and not tell us where you were going was irresponsible and inconsiderate."

Oh shit. *Inconsiderate?* That sort of stings. "But—"

Robbi raises her palm to me just as Patsy's mouth opens and then closes. "We care about you, Quinn. Running off with a guy we barely know is incongruous with the Quinn we've gotten to know."

Wow, a lot of I-words from Robbi.

Robbi moves a little closer. "Next time you leave with someone, be sure to check in with one of us. Okay?"

I want to say a lot right now. I know Robbi has gone home with people a time or two. Patsy and Kat have long-term boyfriends. Lindsay and Jack are going hot and heavy, and Susanna, well, she has a couple guys she sees off and on.

"Okay?" Robbi repeats.

"Yeah, okay." I look at the girls. "I'm sorry. I honestly didn't mean to upset you guys. My phone volume was off because of work, and I was too caught up in Cooke to remember to turn it back on." Placing my hand over my heart, I add, "It won't happen again."

Patsy stands first, and then the rest of the girls follow her lead. I'm expecting words from Patsy, but it's Robbi who speaks. "They need a day or two to get over it. Then"—she winks—"we want to hear about you and that hot piece of English ass."

"Jesus, Robbi. Sexist much?" snaps Lindsay.

It makes me giggle.

"Oh, like you don't want to know," Robbi snaps right back. "Cooke is the hottest man I've... no, *we've*"—she points at every roomie as she finishes—"ever seen, and our girl here went home with him. I want details." She glares at Lindsay. "I know you do too."

She shrugs. "It's just not cool to call a guy a 'hot piece of ass.'"

"Get over it," Robbi grumbles. "Go—"

"Okay," I cut in quickly before Robbi says too much. "I'm sorry. Yes, I'll tell you all about it when you guys are ready."

As the girls leave the room, I reach out and touch Patsy's wrist. When she looks at me, I can tell she's truly upset with me. "Pats?"

"Yes?" she asks, sounding very formal.

"I'm sorry."

She sighs. "I know. I was worried, that's all."

"I get that. I had no idea." What? No idea they cared? No, I knew they cared; it's just a surprise to see the extent. I feel a connection to these girls, especially now that Kara is out of the picture. Which reminds me. "I talked to Gage last night."

"Gage?" She looks confused. "The cop?"

I nod. "I think you should know that Kara is the one that ran over my scooter."

"Shit," she mutters, looking back into the room. "Sus," she says absently. "I'll need to call Mom. Does Kara know we know?"

"I'm not sure. I'm going to the station today to fill out papers. They charged her with hit-and-run."

"Fuck."

I know she's worried about her mom's job. "I'll let you know what else I find out, okay?"

"Yeah. Okay." She steps away from me, then turns back. "You do whatever you need to do, Quinn. Kara deserves to be punished. What she's said and done to you is bullshit. I'll let my mom know so she can be prepared, just in case."

"Oh. Right." I sure hope her mom doesn't get fired because of me.

# CHAPTER TWENTY-NINE

I'm late for class. Again. Luckily, my ceramics professor is cool. Not so lucky that being the last to arrive to class means I'm forced to use the crappy wheel in the way-way back of the room. The one with the kick-wheel instead of an electric pedal. I much prefer the electric one, because I can't seem to throw a pot and use my foot to make the thing run all at the same time. I'm just not that coordinated.

Case in point, we were supposed to be working on a simple cup shape. One you could drink from, or if you add a handle to it, it could be a coffee mug. But mine didn't quite turn out that way. I'd say mine was more of a, well, a plate. No worries, I still have time to make another one next class period. I'll just have to leave extra early for class next time. Cooke won't be here, so I'll have all the time in the world. The thought makes my heart drop in my chest. I'm going to miss him so much, and we just met.

At a few minutes past eleven, I rush into the Hub in search of the man himself. When I spy him, he's standing at a tall table near the window talking to someone. Not just someone, a woman. And not just any woman. She's drop-dead gorgeous. I've seen her before, and I'm positive she's in a sorority, but not only that, I've seen her in Iowa State cheer squad gear. She's a cheerleader. I take one step back to watch them interact. Cooke is smiling and nodding at something she's saying. He looks interested. When he laughs, I feel my heart slip down further than before.

Of course he'd be interested in what she's saying. Why wouldn't he?

I'm about to turn and walk away when his attention moves from the beautiful blonde woman to me. I catch my breath at the smile on his face. When he raises his palm to wave me over, I push my shoulders back and take one step, then another, until I reach his table. The woman, whoever she is, turns her head to look at me. I don't know what I expect her to do, but she only blinks a few times before her attention returns to Cooke. "So, anyway...," she starts.

"Love?" Cooke moves around the table to stand next to me. The second he reaches me, he leans down and kisses me softly on my lips. "Quinn, meet... uh?"

"Krissy. With a K."

"Right." Cooke nods. "Krissy with a K, this is Quinn, my girl."

*His girl.* Wow, I love the sound of that.

"Really?" Krissy with a K sounds surprised.

Cooke wraps his arm around me until his palm is on my hip. "Really." Looking down at me, he smirks. "Shall we? We don't want to be late."

"Sure." Late for what? "Nice meeting you, Krissy with a K," I say as Cooke picks up my backpack and slings it over his shoulder.

"Christ, woman, what've you got in here, an anvil?"

It surprises me, making me laugh. I took a jewelry making class. I know what an anvil is. "No. I've got my mostly ruined textbook in there, plus some art supplies." Not to mention the rest of the things a student needs throughout the day.

I follow him out the door and around the building to the street that runs perpendicular to the Hub. It's also impossible to park there without getting a ticket. Actually, there's never parking on campus. But not for Cooke. Nope. His little black sports car is parked right there. I walk around the front to see if he has a ticket yet.

"How did you get away without a ticket?" I frown at him, though I shouldn't. It's not his fault.

"I spoke with the traffic warden, and she—"

"She?" I roll my eyes.

"Hm, yes." He looks at me, perplexed. "She told me I had one hour."

I roll my eyes again. "Only you would get away with that."

"How do you mean, love?"

"I just mean...." I look up at him, and his brows are scrunched up in the middle of his face. It's worry. "Nothing. I'm glad you got such a great spot." I step closer to the passenger side. "Back home, we call this rock star parking." I open the door and slide inside, waiting for him to do the same.

Cooke chuckles. "Now you can call it rugby star parking."

Giggling, I gently slap his thigh as he slides down in the car. "I will." I snap my seat belt on. "So, if we're not doing the campus tour, where are we going?"

"It's your surprise. Don't ask questions."

He pulls out onto the street, moving slowly past the main administrative building, Beardshear, and then the Memorial Union. As he drives, I point toward the large grassy area. "That day we were talking on the phone, I was sitting right over there."

"Aye, I recognized the clock tower."

"The Campanile. There's a story that says you're not a true Iowa Stater unless you've been kissed under the Campanile at midnight."

He turns his head slowly toward me. "Are *you* a true Iowa Stater?"

"No, sadly."

"Maybe we can remedy that tonight. Another first?"

I blush at his reference to last night. It can't be helped.

~

"Cooke? Why are we here?" He's pulled into a parking lot next to what looks like an old school located a little west of Beedle Drive.

He winks at me as he pushes his door open. "You'll see." I follow him into the building to an office with an elegant marble plagued on the door that reads Leasing Office. Inside, I listen to him ask for someone named Connie.

"You must be Cooke," says an older lady as she comes out from somewhere in the back.

He shakes her outstretched hand. "I am. Pleasure." He moves aside and places his palm on my lower back. "And this is Quinn."

"Quinn." She holds out her hand to me. "What a lovely name."

"Thanks." *What the hell is going on?*

Holding her arm out in the direction of the door, she says cheerily, "Shall we look at the condominium now?"

"The condominium?" I repeat.

Cooke sounds practically giddy when he shouts, "Surprise!"

"Surprise?"

"Just wait."

My God, seeing the man excited is something else. He's like a kid on Christmas morning, so I keep my mouth shut as I follow Connie and Cooke down a long hallway, past an indoor pool, a gym, and a large party room.

"This used to be the elementary school," Connie explains. "It's been unused for forty years, so the owners bought the building and turned it into beautiful condominiums, as you'll see, Quinn. They've added unique touches in each unit; for example, a portion of an original chalkboard hangs in each entryway.

"Cool." It really does sound cool. But I'm still wondering why we're here. I have my suspicions, but I'm afraid to ask.

We approach a brushed stainless-steel elevator and wait as Connie presses the button. Cooke hums as we wait. It doesn't take long for the ding to sound, and we all enter the small box. Cooke's size makes it feel much smaller than it really is. Hell, Cooke's size makes *me* feel much smaller than I am. It's nice for a change.

When we reach the fourth floor, the doors open, and Connie gestures for us to get out first. "To the right, please. It's number 410."

We move to 410 and wait for her to unlock it. When she pushes the door open, I gasp. From here I can see floor-to-ceiling windows that overlook Ames. It's not a New York City or even a Chicago skyline, but it's still pretty. As I step into the entry, I see the chalkboard she mentioned. It's framed in old wood to look original. On it, someone has written "Welcome" in chalk. It's clever.

Moving through the entry hallway, I gasp again when we reach a huge open space with the kitchen of my dreams, a living room with a fireplace, and a spot for a television. The room itself is small but there's plenty of space for the sofa and chairs they've used to stage the place. To the left of the kitchen is a small dining nook.

"There are two bedrooms and two full baths. I'll wait here in the kitchen while you two explore."

I slowly turn around, looking up and down. It's mostly white, but the ceiling is high, maybe twelve feet or more. Part of it is exposed pipes, but part of it is finished in charcoal and white. There's exposed brick on one wall in the living room, and as we walk around, I see the same brick in both bedrooms as well. But it's the bathrooms that take my breath away. Both are enormous with attached walk-in closets about the size of my bedroom at the Beedle house. There's a bathtub and a shower in one and a giant shower with multiple showerheads in the other. I don't know which one is the best, to be honest. All the finishes are white, and the counters are all white marble like the sign downstairs.

"What do you think, love?"

I choke out a laugh. "It's frigging gorgeous."

"You like it?"

I look up at him. "What's not to like?" I step closer so Connie doesn't hear me. "But what are we doing here?"

He places his palms on each of my shoulders. He beams as he whispers, "I'm glad you like it, because I'm buying this apartment. For you."

This time I really do choke. "Huh?" I squeak and cough and sputter all at once. It's not pretty. "No. You're not."

"Yes." He blinks. "Wait. What?" He looks sincerely confused.

"You're not buying me a condo." I feel my chin start to quiver, and then my bottom lip does the same. I can't control it, damn it.

"Love, you can't continue to live in that house. It's not safe."

My chin wobbling has intensified, and tears threaten to fall. I focus on his face and will them back. "It's not?"

"Quinn? Love? Are you upset?"

I shrug because I'm not sure why. "It's... I...." One tear slides down my cheek just as I hear the door close. Connie has stepped out. Good thing, because I'm about to start rambling unintelligibly, and it's going to be embarrassing enough with only Cooke to see.

"Come here." Cooke takes my hand and leads me to a fancy sofa that they used to stage the place. He sits, pulling me with him.

When I end up on his lap, I choke, "I'm too heavy."

"Shh. Now tell me what's wrong, Quinn."

So I do. Without taking a breath, I tell him how much I appreciate the offer and that it's about the nicest, sweetest thing anyone has ever done for me, but I like living with the girls even though my bedroom isn't private, and I'm hoping the owners will do something about the basement, especially since there's still standing water in some spots down there.

"The water is exactly why it's not safe. My guess is mold has already begun to grow. Have you called the landlord about it again? Because they should've already had that sorted out, love. It's been almost a week."

I look into Cooke's golden brown eyes. Sniffling, I ask, "You really think it's not safe?" Because I hadn't given that much thought. I know mold can be dangerous, but it depends on the mold, right?

"One of my mates lived in a house with mold, and he became very ill. It took months for him to recover." As Cooke talks, I run my fingers through his hair. He must like it, because his eyes close at my touch. "Would it make a difference if I told you this flat would be an investment?"

"Cooke," I say, placing my palm on his cheek. "You're so sweet, but I like living with the girls on Beedle." I lean in and kiss him softly. "What if I promise you that I'll call the landlord first thing tomorrow and ask about the basement? I'll message you with the results." Since he'll be gone, damn it.

"If they don't get to it this week, you need to leave that place." He kisses me back. "You all do. It's not safe for your mates either."

That's true. "Right." I slide off his legs and hope he can still walk. I'm also hoping that this idea of buying a condo for me is done. Changing the subject is the way to go. "Don't forget, we need to go to the police station soon. I'll text Gage when we get in the car."

"Why don't you do that now? I'll have a word with Connie."

I nod as I pull out my phone. I search for old calls and find his number listed on the date of the horrible, terrible, worst fucking day ever.

Well, it can't be that bad. It brought Cooke to me, so there's that.

I message Gage that we'd like to come in now, and he informs me that he's already at the station, which is good. I want to get this over with.

Out in the hall, Cooke is still chatting with Connie. I'm tempted to move closer, but I don't because that would be weird. I don't need to eavesdrop on Cooke. When they're done, he turns to me with a smile. "Ready?"

I nod. "Gage is already there. I told him we were on the way."

I hear Cooke grumbling, and I'm sure I heard the name "Gage" in the mix.

## CHAPTER THIRTY

"You're just in time," says Gage, shaking my hand. His eyes pan to the man behind me, and then he grimaces.

"Gage, this is Cooke." I turn to Cooke. "Cooke, this is Officer Gage Golden. He's the one who investigated my moped, erm, accident." Even though it wasn't an accident.

Before I can say another word, I feel Cooke's big warm hand slide across my back and wrap around to my hip. He tugs a little, enough for the momentum to make me move closer to him. It's also obvious that Gage notices. Interesting. Men are weird.

"Right. Well, Kara's father is here, along with an attorney. They're talking with the captain."

I want to roll my eyes. *Of course he brought an attorney.* "What does that mean?" My eyes pan the police station. "Is she here?"

"She's not here. At least not yet." I feel Cooke give my hip a squeeze.

"Why are they here?" asks Cooke in a husky voice.

"Most likely?" Gage runs his fingers through his light hair. It gives me the opportunity to look at him. He's cute in his street clothes of dark jeans and an Iowa State University tee. "They want the charges dropped."

"Will you? Drop the charges, I mean?" I ask.

Gage scowls. "I hope not. That woman is a menace; I made sure the captain knew about her earlier assault."

*Assault.* It's such a serious word, but I guess that's what it was. What else would you call it?

"What do we need to do to ensure this girl stays away from Quinn?"

Gage's head turns slowly to Cooke. "Cooke, is it? In what capacity are you here with Quinn?"

"In what capacity?" Cooke's face is priceless—part sneer, part confusion. "She's my...."

There's quite an uncomfortable silence that I end with "We're friends."

"Bollocks." Cooke grunts. "We're more than friends, love."

"Anyway...." I look at Gage. "You can talk to him. He knows the whole story." Cooke squeezes my hip again, and I want to giggle but keep my mouth shut. And good thing because right then, a door opens behind Gage and three men walk out. I'm guessing one of them is Kara's father. All three of us watch as two of the men shake the other's hand, presumably the captain. They look happy, which makes me curious about their conversation. Then the captain points in our direction. Since he doesn't know who I am, I'm guessing he's pointing at Gage.

"Shit," mutters Gage. Turning to me, he smiles weakly. "Give me a second." He walks directly to the captain and the two men.

"What do you think they're saying?" I ask Cooke softly.

Cooke growls, "Probably making a fucking deal. That guy in the dark suit looks loaded."

"Sometimes I think life is only good for the wealthy, but I know that's a cynical, jaded way to look at things. It just seems like rich people get their way no matter what. Money isn't every-thing." I shrug.

"It's nice, though, love. It'd allow me to buy my girl a new place to live."

I look back up at him with an arched brow. "I wouldn't care if you were a pauper, Cooke." Reaching up, I pat him in the middle of his chest. "I can tell you have a heart of gold in there. That's all the wealth I need."

When I hear raised voices, I quickly turn back to the four men across the room. The dark-suited man looks angry. "This is bullshit." Yep. He's angry. "We had an agreement," he spits.

Gage gestures in my direction, and I slide the inch or two needed to be right up against Cooke. I don't like this. Any of it.

Cooke must sense my unease, because he leans down and whispers, "No worries. I've got you, love."

"Thank you." I say it without taking my eyes off the four men who are all now looking right at me.

"Her?" the dark-suited man says, pointing one angry finger my way. "She's the one causing all this trouble for my poor daughter."

I snort, then scoff, and it's loud enough for them all to hear. For some reason, I grow some courage. "I didn't cause anything, sir. Your daughter has been especially unkind to me."

The man with Kara's father snickers. "Unkind? Who says shit like that?"

*I do.*

"She destroyed my only mode of transportation." And I have no money to fix it.

"That's what insurance is for," the other man grunts.

Gage has joined the fray. "It was parked. Your daughter admitted she ran over it."

Kara's dad remains silent as his friend says, "She didn't know what she was saying."

"She admitted to running over it several times," Gage deadpans.

"She was confused. Her car was caught up in the debris." Still the other guy talking.

"Enough!" shouts Kara's dad. "What do we need to do to make this go away?"

Go away? That's not right or fair.

The four men look at me. They're silent, like they're waiting for me to say something. So I say what I'm thinking. "What?"

Gage's captain speaks, finally. "Mr. Becker wants to make a deal. What's it going to take to keep you from pressing charges?"

I shrug. "How would I know? I'm not a cop. She broke the law. Isn't that something she should pay for?"

I feel Cooke vibrate behind me. He's laughing. I don't know why, though. This isn't funny.

"Are you going to press charges?" asks the captain.

"Look." I pull away from Cooke and step closer to the men. I'm over this. I'm tired of dealing with Kara Becker, and I'm not going to let her father get his way either. Not without a fight, anyway. Where my courage is coming from, I have no idea. Well, maybe it's coming from the six-five man who is now directly behind me again. I know because his palm is on my lower back. Just another gift from him, because Cooke Thompson gives me strength.

"She has had a burr about me from day one. I tried to be nice, but nothing worked." I look at Kara's father, then back to the captain. "Ask my roommates. On the morning of the assault, I was attempting to mend fences, but she wouldn't have it. When the police were there, Patsy and Susanna convinced me not to press charges or get a restraining order because they were afraid you'd fire their mom," I say to Mr. Becker, "By the way, that would be wrongful termination, and you'd get sued. I'd be a witness to that." So there.

I know all about wrongful termination. My brother claimed he was wrongfully terminated once, but it turned out he was having sex with the boss's daughter in the back room. During business hours. He claimed that if *he* got fired, so should she. I get his point. In the end, I think the girl *did* get fired, but then she was rehired not long after that. My brother wasn't happy, but by then he'd gotten another job *and* a girlfriend. "A better one" according to my big bro. I'm not sure if he meant the girl or the job.

"I don't know why she would feel compelled to destroy my scooter. It wasn't much, but it was all I had to get to work and to class. She's vindictive and irrational, and I had nothing to do with that. She's seriously unstable, and I'm afraid of her."

Turning to Gage, I say with sincerity, "Maybe I *should* pursue that protection order. If you all let her go without any repercussions, what's to prevent her from doing something worse? Especially if her father can waltz in here and sweet-talk you all into a deal."

I hear a low rumble coming from Cooke. At first, I think he's laughing again, but when I peek up at him, his face looks like he wants to kill something, or someone. Turning back to Gage, I look at him to see what his face tells me. Nothing. His face is showing absolutely no emotion. I bet he's good at poker.

Then he says, "I suggested that the day of the assault, Quinn. I think that's a good idea."

"It's not going to stop her from doing more damage to your other property." Cooke sounds as angry as his face looks.

"Jesus," Kara's dad mutters. "Fine. This is what I'm going to do to prevent all this protection order bullshit. I don't want that on her record, so I'm taking Kara home. She's... she needs to regroup."

*Regroup?* I call bullshit on that. She needs therapy. "When will she be back?" I ask with an arched brow.

"Never, if I have anything to say about it. She can transfer to another college next semester."

"What about Quinn's scooter?" asks Gage.

"How much was it worth?" Mr. Becker asks.

I'm about to say "nothing" when Gage responds. "Five grand."

*Five grand?* Is he joking?

"Fine. I'll write a check—"

"Cash," says Gage. "Right now."

Mr. Becker looks at the captain. "If I give her five grand, will this thing drop?"

The captain looks at me. I look at Mr. Becker. "I won't see her again?"

"I'll make sure of it."

I turn and look up at Cooke. "What do you think?"

"I think you need to get all of this in writing and have that guy"—he points at Mr. Becker—"and Kara sign it, making sure they understand what will happen if she shows up here." I smile up at him and nod, but he's not done. "I'd also make sure he includes something in there about your mates' mom."

"You her attorney?" asks Mr. Becker.

"You could say that."

I want to snicker, because I know Cooke admitted to nothing just then, but I remain straight-faced and quiet.

"Fine. We'll draw up the paperwork and sign it."

"In front of either the captain or Officer Golden," I add.

"Of course." Mr. Becker smiles, but he misses the mark; it's more sneer than smile. "We'll bring Kara in as well."

"Today," Cooke snaps.

"We'll have this done by five today."

Gage turns to me. "Meet me back here at five thirty. I'll have the papers and the cash so you won't have to see Kara."

"Okay." I nod. "Sounds good." I turn to walk away, but before I do, I hold my hand out to Gage. "Thank you, Officer Golden."

He gives me a soft smile. "My pleasure, Miss Maxwell."

Gah! He's such a good guy.

Cooke takes my hand in his and tugs me out the door. When we get to his car, he walks me around to the passenger side, nudges my back against the door, and kisses the hell out of me. It's been hours since he kissed me like that, and I'm not going to lie, I've missed it. Reaching up, I wrap my arms around his neck and pull myself up to get as close as possible. When he pulls away, his face still looks stormy.

"What's wrong?" I ask, concerned.

"I don't like the way that man looked at you."

"Man?" I look right, then left. "What man?"

"The police constable."

What's a... "Oh, Gage?"

"Aye. The fact that you're on first names with him drives me mad."

"Cooke," I say softly. "He's just a kind man who was trying to help me."

Mumbling softly, Cooke steps back and says, "Trying to get into your knickers, more like."

It makes me giggle. "I heard that."

"Good."

## CHAPTER THIRTY-ONE

After the police station, I asked Cooke to take me home so I could shower, change, and pack an overnight bag. I also wanted to let the girls know I'd be gone tonight, and I hoped to catch Patsy so I could tell her and Susanna about the police station and Mr. Becker's promise. I invited Cooke to wait for me, but he said he had a few things to take care of and he'd be back within the hour.

I wonder what things he needed to take care of. I could ask him, but that seems super intrusive.

True to his word, Cooke is now back to pick me up. A few of the girls are hanging around in the living room when he says, "You look lovely, Quinn. The blue looks perfect with your eyes."

"Thanks," I say with a smile.

"You do," Of course Patsy would say that, since she helped me pick out an outfit that was dressy enough for dinner but could still be worn to rugby practice. What could be so versatile, you ask? Black leggings and a light blue tunic with black stitching details. I've also slipped on my black flats and grabbed my black purse. It's not bad, at least compared to my normal clothes.

"I've packed clothes for tomorrow," I add shyly, since I'm

essentially telling him I'm sleeping with him again. I feel the heat of a blush spread over my face and neck.

"Good." He smiles. "Did you tell your mates about the meeting earlier?"

"About Kara and Mr. Becker? Yes."

"I hope he's true to his word," grumbles Patsy. "I've already talked to my mom."

"It would be wrong and probably illegal for him to fire her for something she had nothing to do with." I sound far more comfortable than I feel.

"What about the mold issue?" Cooke asks.

"I agree with you, Cooke," Patsy tells him. "Mold is dangerous."

I add, "Patsy's going to call the landlord later."

"Why not now?" Cooke asks. "We have a little time before we need to be back at the police station."

Patsy nods. "Sure." Searching for her phone, she finds it between two couch cushions. We sit silently as she searches for the number and then dials. "I'll put it on speaker."

I nod but remain quiet.

"Hello?" says a scratchy voice on the end of the line.

"Hi, yeah, Mr. Conrad? This is Patsy at 205 Beedle Drive?"

"Uh-huh." Mr. Conrad says, then coughs like he's losing a lung. I hope he's all right.

"Yeah, I was calling about the basement."

"What about it?" asks the older man.

"Well"—Patsy sounds so chipper, but her face tells another story—"there's still water down there. We're concerned about mold."

"Mold?" He chuckles. "That's ridiculous."

"No it's not, Mr. Conrad."

I feel Cooke fidget next to me. Looking over, I see his brows furrow and his lips flatten and thin. He's irritated.

"Sweetheart, we'll get to it soon enough."

Cooke stands and moves closer to Patsy. Whispering, he tells her, "Tell him if he doesn't take care of it this week, you'll all need to find other living arrangements due to health concerns."

Patsy is staring at Cooke. I wonder what she's thinking. I don't have to wait long before she says exactly what Cooke suggested.

"You have a lease, young lady. You can't move out."

Cooke appears ready to counter that argument, but Patsy holds her hand up to stop him. "Mr. Conrad. All I have to do is call someone at the city to ask them for a rental housing inspection to test for mold. It's free. If they find mold, we'll move out, and you'll be forced to remediate that mold and find new tenants."

"Don't you threaten me, young lady."

"It's not a threat, Mr. Conrad. My health and the health of my roommates is my first concern. If necessary, I'll retain an attorney to protect us against any legal action."

Smart. She didn't threaten to sue him. I know from that wrongful termination situation with my brother that threats only make things worse.

"I'll give you one more week to have the basement cleaned and inspected for mold," she continues. "If you haven't done that by this Saturday, we'll be making arrangements to move out quickly."

The crusty voice on the other end of the line isn't happy. "Fucking girl...."

"Is that a yes?" she asks smugly.

"Yes," he hisses. "A crew will be there in the morning."

"Great!" she says cheerily. "See you then."

Hanging up, she smiles first at Cooke, then me. "How's that?"

I'm in awe. "Perfect."

Cooke steps back over until he's next to me, wrapping his arm around my shoulders. With a tug from him, I'm pressed against his side. "Excellent. But if he doesn't follow through, please let me know. I may have a solution for your living arrangements."

Patsy looks surprised. "Oh, okay."

"Wait! Did you buy that condo?" I squeak.

Smiling down at me, he says, "Not yet."

"Cooke—"

"Well, we'd best be off. It's nearly five thirty."

"Oh, right."

Time to get back to the police station.

GAGE IS POINTING TO A LINE ON ONE OF THE POLICE FORMS. "Sign here, please, Quinn."

I'm staring down at a police report. "I didn't think I was going to press charges."

"You haven't. Not yet. This is merely for our records. I'm not convinced we won't be seeing Kara again. None of what they provided to us will hold up in court, and all it says in there is he'll *try* to keep her from returning to Ames."

I look into Gage's eyes to see if I can get a read on him. I don't like what he just said. "So, this isn't over?"

"It may not be." After those papers are signed, Gage hands me a brown, legal-size envelope. "This is the signed agreement you asked for and the cash. I checked it all for you, but I suggest you take a moment to read through everything and count the money. I'll have you sign a receipt for everything and add it to your file." He sighs and runs his fingers through his hair. "None of this is normal police procedure, Quinn, but we have mediated situations before. With that said, you still need to be sure you're protected."

I nod, then point to an empty desk. "Can I look at everything over there?"

"Sure. Let me know when you're done."

Cooke, who has been standing beside me in silence since we

stepped foot in the station, walks with me to the desk. Pulling out a chair for me, I sit down as he takes one from another nearby desk. Opening the envelope, the first thing that slides out are five packages of bills, each with a brown paper band that reads $1000.

I gasp. "Wow. That's a lot of money."

"Aye. Would you like me to count it while you read through papers?"

"Sure." I watch him unbundle one pack and count out ten hundred-dollar bills. When he chuckles, I look up at him. "What?"

"Read." He points to the forms.

"It's too much fun watching you count the money." I shrug. "But you're right." So I do my best to focus on the forms. It's only a page and a half. When I'm done, I hand it over to Cooke. "Will you read it?"

"Sure." He hands me the money. "It's all there." I gaze down at it like it's a newborn kitten or something. This is a lot of money. It'll help me a lot, but I feel like I got it the wrong way. It's like I extorted it from Mr. Becker.

"Stop," Cooke whispers.

I look up, blinking. "What?"

"I can see it written all over your beautiful face."

"What?"

"Guilt, love. Remember. Kara owed you the money. She destroyed your scooter."

"He's right, Quinn." I look up and see Gage standing in front of us. Damn, he's like a ninja. I didn't hear him approach the desk.

"My scooter wasn't worth near this. I could buy ten of my old scooters for this money."

"Think of it like this," Gage explains. "Insurance is supposed to pay enough to replace whatever was stolen or destroyed. In this case, you can't replace your exact scooter, so you need to buy a new one. You were inconvenienced because the scooter was destroyed, which some would call pain and suffering."

"That makes sense, I guess. I wouldn't say I suffered, but it was a pain." I snort because I thought it was funny. When neither of the guys laughs, I quickly shut up.

Gage continues, "If he'd gone through his insurance company, they would've penalized him by raising his rate just for making the claim. And if they knew it was intentional, they may not have covered it at all, and he may also have lost his policy. In the long run, this saves him time and probably money. Not to mention his daughter isn't going to be charged for hit-and-run."

"Sadly," mutters Cooke.

"Yes, sadly," Gage grumbles.

"So, I shouldn't feel bad about taking this money and buying a new scooter."

Gage nods. "Not at all." He smirks. "And a new pink helmet."

"Right." And those aren't cheap either. "So, my helmet was toast?"

"Oh yeah."

I look at the cash. "Scooters don't cost five thousand dollars," I say, sounding unconvinced.

"Some do. It's good you have the money to get what you want. If you have money left over, you can use it for real insurance."

I snort, then laugh. "I had real insurance. Liability is real."

"You'll want full coverage this time, Quinn."

"Yeah. I know." I'll get it.

After Cooke has gone through the documents, we pack everything back into the envelope and wave goodbye to Gage. "He's so nice," I say as we leave.

"Quinn," Cooke growls. "Please stop."

"What?" I giggle. "He is." I'm sort of hoping I get another passionate kiss against the car. Before I can get there, Gage calls my name from the front door of the police station. I look at Cooke and hold one finger up to let him know to wait. I walk quickly over to Gage, who's holding the door open with his body.

"Yeah?" I smile brightly.

He looks down at me. No smile on his handsome face, he asks softly, "Are you happy?"

Why do I get the sense that his question holds more meaning than it seems? "I am. Very."

Gage nods, then pats my shoulder. "Good. You deserve to be happy, Quinn."

"Thanks." I smile again. "So do you, Gage."

"I know. I hope to be. Someday."

Oh, geesh. Why does that sound so sad? Not knowing what to say next, I turn and wave. "Talk to you later, Gage." I can't say goodbye. It's not in my DNA.

"Sure," he says with a small smile.

When I get to his sleek sports car, Cooke's standing on the passenger side, holding the door for me. He doesn't kiss me, but his expression tells me he wants to know what that was all about.

"We're all set," I chirp.

While I was hoping to get that passionate kiss at the door, I'm glad he waits until we're in the car this time. When he pulls me in, he kisses me like I'm water and he's been in the desert for days.

"Wow," I say, sitting back in my seat. I had been leaning over the center console in my attempt to get closer.

"'Wow' is a good word for it." Cooke smiles. "Now, off to rugby," he says as he starts the car. "Do you know where they practice?"

"Uh... no." I pull out my phone. "I'll send a text to Dan and ask." In seconds, I get his response. "Southwest Athletic Complex." I know where that is. "It's about a block from Cy's. Turn right here." I point in the direction I want him to go.

In no time, we're pulling up to a large grassy area filled with the same big guys Cooke met last night. The second we stop, all eyes turn to the fancy car. Bull's the first one to head our way, followed by the rest of the guys. "Cooke!" he shouts. When he reaches us, he's panting. "Mr. Thompson. Thanks for coming."

"No problem." Cooke reaches behind his seat and pulls out what looks like tennis shoes. "I brought my trainers if you want me out on the pitch with you."

"Hell yeah." Bull is outwardly giddy. I want to laugh, but I'd better not ruin his moment with Cooke.

I find a spot to sit off to the side near a small group of bystanders. I make eye contact with an older man, who gives me a smile. I smile back. With the same smile still on my lips, I look at a young woman, about my age or maybe a little older, but her face isn't as friendly. Choosing to ignore her, I turn back to the action on the pitch.

After an hour, I have two things: a much better understanding of the game of rugby and a sore ass. Sitting on the ground for most of it hasn't been fun. Even though I haven't watched the team play before, I can tell Cooke's advice is really helping them. The coach has been right in the mix as well, listening to Cooke as he shares some of his expertise. At one point, I watch as Cooke and two other guys move to the far end of the field. From the numbers on their tees, I see the number 10. That means they play the fly-half position, the same as Cooke. He spends a good twenty minutes with just them, and I can see from my grassy spot that they're eating it up.

When it's time to go, Cooke slaps the 10s on the back and shakes hands with the rest of the guys. Well, everyone but Bull. Nope. Bull gets a hug. A big slappy man-hug. I swear the big guy has tears in his eyes.

"Thanks, lads," Cooke says as he makes his way toward me. Turning at the last minute, he waves one more time. Then, taking my hand in his, he leads me over to the car, unlocking it with the key fob on the way.

"Wait!" We turn and see Bull jogging toward us. When he gets there, he wraps me up in his arms. "You're the bomb, Quinn."

I giggle. "Thanks, Bull."

He turns to Cooke. "This is the best day of my life, Mr.

Thompson. Hands down. Thank you so much for taking the time to visit us." His eyes are glistening. I was right.

Thanks, mate." Cooke pats Bull's shoulder. "I appreciate that. Quinn has your number. I'll let you know when I'm coming back."

*He's coming back? When?*

"Cool." Bull nods, then looks at me. "Very cool."

And it is. It's all very cool.

Cooke is coming back.

# CHAPTER THIRTY-TWO

"That was delicious," Cooke says, patting his hard, flat stomach. "I could get used to American food."

"It was." Even though I hardly ate, which is saying something, because I took Cooke to the most popular restaurant in Ames, Hickory Park. There are usually lines out the door to get into the place, but we went late enough that a lot of the rush was over. Not even Hickory Park's dessert was tempting. Probably because I've got nervous jitters—or maybe I should call it anticipation for spending the night with Cooke again. There are so many thoughts rolling around in my head. The fact that he's leaving in the morning is the main thing. I'm already sad about it.

But what about when we get back? Will he want to have sex? Will *I* want to have sex? Yes, I do. I knew I'd been holding on to my virginity for a reason. A special reason. And there's nobody more special than Cooke, and I can't fathom there ever will be again. Sure, I used to think Eric Mackey back in high school was the one, and let's not forget Bryant. In retrospect, I'm so glad it was neither of those guys. Nope. Cooke is the one in so many ways.

"Love?"

"Huh?" I look over at Cooke, who's chuckling. "What?"

"I've been talking to you for several minutes. Are you daydreaming?"

"You could say that."

"Penny for your thoughts?"

Oh, wow. I can't tell him my thoughts. "I'm already sad you're leaving tomorrow." That's true.

His face suddenly sad, he says, "I am as well, love." Reaching out, he takes my hand in his. His thumb slides over my wrist, and I want to close my eyes to memorize the feeling. "You should come to London."

I open my eyes and look at him. "That's...." An amazing idea. Unbelievable. And impossible. "I can't."

"Why ever not?"

Gah, I love his accent. Just the word "not" sounds so cool. He emphasized the *t*, and it's adorable.

"For one, I've got a job now."

"That's an easy fix. Ask for leave."

I roll my eyes inside. "Two, I don't have the money."

"I'd buy your—"

"No."

"Yes. I'd buy your ticket. You have a free place to stay and free transportation. All you'd need is a little bit of cash for trinkets for your mates."

Okay, I'm going to call his bluff. "When? Because I've got school—"

"At the end of term."

"Christmas?" What about my family? Christmas with them is my favorite time of year.

"How much time after the term ends before Christmas?"

I pull out my phone and look for the college calendar. "Um, there's a week between finals week and Christmas. There's also time after Christmas." I look up at him. "Do you do anything for New Year's Eve?" I've never gone to a New Year's Eve party. I never saw the point. I wasn't going to get that kiss at midnight, so why put myself through that?

"Aye. My mates and I usually do something." He turns his head to look at me and smiles. "But that would work for me."

"I just—"

"Just think about it. We can talk about it next week. Let's just enjoy the little bit of time we have left on *this* visit."

"Okay. Sure." He's right. There's no use fretting over that now.

"Good. Now, let's head back to the hotel, shall we?"

Oh wow. This is it. It's happening. "Sure."

Cooke chuckles, and it's warm and rumbly. I like it.

"Shall we watch some telly?"

Telly? He's pointing to the flat-screen. "Oh, television. Sure." I sort of wish he'd ravage me instead of wanting to watch TV, but what am I supposed to do, jump his bones?

Cooke flops down onto the sofa in the living room and pats the seat next to him. "Come. I'll let you choose what we watch."

"A movie?" I step across the room and sit down, leaving about a foot between us. I'm just not sure what's going on. Last night he couldn't wait to kiss me. Heck, he had me against the door, for goodness' sake.

"If you'd like."

I can't figure out from that if he wants to watch a movie or not. I mean, if he doesn't, he would've said, right? Leaning forward, I pick up the remote. I find the page with the channel guide and hit the option that says Premium Movies. I blush when I see the first option: porn. I quickly move the selection arrow down to New Releases.

"No porn, love?"

I don't turn my head, but I do side-eye him. "Do you want to watch porn?"

"I'd love to watch porn."

Now I turn to face him. When he starts to laugh, I want to throttle him. "Funny. Ha ha."

"I'm not joking. I love some good naughty secretary porn."

God, my face is on fire. "You do?" I squeak, because *gah*!

"What's not to like?" He shrugs. "You have your domineering boss and the secretary that keeps fumbling at her job. She gets her little bottom swatted, and the rest... well, it's hot."

I'm speechless. Literally and utterly speechless. And do you want to know why? Because it *does* sound hot. Gah! Again. I'm a pervert, but so is he.

Doing my best to gain whatever semblance of control I have, I shrug. "That sounds good, but I think I'd prefer to watch something more mainstream."

"Ah, of course. Like delivery man porn?"

I laugh as I reach out and swat his big arm. "Stop teasing me."

"I never joke about porn, love."

It's stressful choosing a movie for someone you don't know all that well. We've never talked about movies or music or anything like that.

Ignoring his last statement, I click on a new release, *Captain Marvel*, one I hope he likes. I wanted to see it in the theaters, but it's expensive. I mean, by the time you buy popcorn, you've dropped thirty bucks. "How's this?" I nod toward the television. "I mean, it's not MILF porn, but it's okay."

When he throws his head back to laugh and hits it on the wall behind the sofa, I lose my shit. I laugh so damn hard I nearly pee myself. When I take a breath, I see he's now slumped over his legs, his body still vibrating with laughter, but he gets out, "Oh, bloody hell, woman." He sits up and covers his face with both of his hands, trying to get himself under control. "Quinn, love, you're hilarious."

That makes me smile as I wipe the wetness from my eyes. Yep, I laughed so hard, I cried.

Cooke bends forward and reaches for me at the same time. Wrapping his arms around me, he pulls me into a hug. "Come 'ere, Quinn. Sit close."

So I do. I scoot over and lean back until my head sits perfectly between his arm and chest. No place I've ever been has felt so good.

# CHAPTER THIRTY-THREE

I must've dozed off. I wake up blinking, still in Cooke's arms, but the television is off and it's dark outside.

"Why'd you let me sleep?" I whine, because damn it, we've only got this one night.

"You conked out as soon as the movie started. You looked like an angel. I didn't want to wake you. But we need to go. I want to take you somewhere."

"We'll be back, right?" I want to sleep in his bed. "You're not taking me home yet, right?"

Cooke kisses me softly. "No, of course not."

Thank God.

Cooke takes my hand and leads me out of the room, down the hallway, into the elevator, and out to the first floor, then his car.

"Where are we going?" I mean, it's late.

"You'll see. Stop asking," he says giving me a quick kiss on my cheek.

"Fine."

Once we're in the car, I pay close attention to the direction he's going. When he pulls his car onto the road that leads around the Memorial Union, I ask, "Are we going to the Campanile?"

"Of course. I can't let anyone else kiss my girl at the stroke of midnight under that thing, now can I?"

I shake my head. I can't speak. I'm getting choked up because, honest to God, I never thought I'd ever get a kiss there, at any time.

Cooke finds a spot right in front of the Campanile, because of course he does. I pull the handle and start to push the door open when he appears at my side. "Milady," he says with a bow. My goodness, the man makes me giggle.

"Thank you, kind sir." I do my best English accent, but it sounds more like... well, not like an English accent. I'm sure I'm red from embarrassment, but it's dark, so who cares? Speaking normally, I ask, "What time is it?"

"We've got five minutes until midnight."

"Just in time."

Cooke pulls me along until we're in front of the clock tower. "Now what?" he asks, looking down at me.

I point to one of the four archways at the base of the tower. "I think we go inside, underneath, to, uh, to kiss."

We both walk through the closest archway and wait, still holding hands. "Two minutes," Cooke says, moving closer. Pulling his hand from mine, he wraps both around me, tugging me closer. "Are you ready, love?"

"I am."

We stare into each other's eyes as time ticks away. Just as Cooke starts to lower his head, the clock tower starts to gong. And by gong, I mean G-O-N-G. It's loud!

"Bloody hell," Cooke says, placing his hands over his ears. "Fecking hell."

Covering my own ears, I start to laugh. I think I know why this is such a big deal. If you can endure the bell enough for a kiss, you deserve to be a true Iowa Stater. Cooke bends and kisses me so fast, I nearly miss it. The next thing I know, I'm being dragged away from the bonging, and then we're running to the car. "Get in," Cooke yells.

I quickly open my door and jump in, slamming the door as I go. "Oh my God." I'm still laughing as Cooke slams his too.

"I may never hear again. I'll need to see an audiologist when I get home."

I wish I could tell you Cooke was laughing. He wasn't. On the contrary, he looks very angry.

"Cooke, I had no idea."

He takes a minute and does some deep breathing before he answers. "I could tell. You were just as shocked as I was, Quinn."

My voice sounds small, weak, as I say, "I'm really sorry."

He finally smiles. It's a small one, but that's something. "No need to be sorry, Quinn."

He's saying all the right things, but I can't help but worry. We're quiet on the ride back to the hotel. Maybe it's because our ears are still ringing.

I hope that's the reason.

THE QUIET CONTINUES ALL THE WAY UP TO THE ROOM. ONCE inside, Cooke offers me the first shot at the bathroom. I quickly brush my teeth and hair, then I change into his jersey. I'm out in less than half the time as the night before. When I step out, Cooke's sitting on his bed, typing something on his phone. Afraid to disturb him, I clear my throat. "I'm done."

He stands up then, sliding his phone into his back pocket. "I'm going to hop into the shower, love. Out in a jiff."

I swear he hasn't looked me in the eye since the Campanile. I must have really screwed up. In my defense, though, I had no idea we were even going there. I do my absolute best to gird my emotions by sliding into bed, the same side as last night. At first, I lie facing the bathroom door, but ogling him the second he walks out of the bathroom is kind of creepy. Then I roll onto my back, but I'm not a back sleeper, so it feels uncomfortable. I finally decide on facing the opposite direction of the bathroom, which doesn't work either because it's like I'm giving him my back. When none of the others work, I push myself up to sit with my back against the headboard. I can look wherever I want this way.

"Damn," I mumble. I wish I had my phone. I could pretend I'm doing something like checking messages or reading. I scan the room for my purse, but it's not in the bedroom. "I left it on the table."

"What did you leave on the table?"

"Oh." *Shit.* "My phone."

"Shall I fetch it?"

It's then that I finally look up. And I gasp. I'm speechless because Cooke's out of the shower, water droplets still clinging to his beautiful chest and arms. But that's not the part that leaves me mute. It's the little white towel he has wrapped around his waist. The wet and almost transparent white towel.

"Quinn?"

"Huh?" I realize I'm staring then. "What?"

Cooke walks over to me slowly. "Are you ogling me?"

"Yes. I'm definitely ogling you." As a matter of fact, I used that exact word in my head a minute ago. "You're beautiful."

"Love," he whispers. Sitting next to me on the bed, he places his palm on my cheek. "Are you okay after the bells? I feel bloody awful I took you there."

"No." I'm so surprised at his words. "I'm sorry. I had no idea they did that."

"I was attempting to be romantic and I failed. Epically."

"No, Cooke. I loved it." I stare into his pretty gold-green eyes. "I really loved it."

With his hand now on the back of my neck, Cooke scoots closer—close enough to kiss me. It's soft and tentative at first, but it quickly escalates to something frantic and hot. My god, this it hot. Doing my best to get closer to him, I kick away the sheet and blanket from my legs, and I'm up on my knees and wrapped around him in moments. I push his shoulders back until he's lying down, I lean down, kissing him back just as frantically.

He's leaving. Tomorrow.

Lying at his side, I lift my leg to wrap around his hip and skim it across the towel. He's hard. I pull away from his kiss so I can breathe. When he places his hands on my ass, I feel him urging me closer until my center is directly over his hardness. I whimper because, my God, it feels good. When he shifts and does it again, I gasp. "Don't stop doing that."

He doesn't. He keeps right on pressing himself into me as his hips move back and forth, gradually increasing his pace, each time hitting my clit.

"Oh, fuck," I moan.

"Love," he pants.

"Yeah." I pant right back. "Please don't stop." And then it hits me like a tsunami. I see stars and fireworks. "Ahhh," I say as I feel myself pulse. The feeling is something I can't describe. I know it was an orgasm. I've never had one before, but I'm not an idiot. All I know is I want more of them. Many more of them.

Cooke has stopped moving against me, but he's still there. And hard. Very hard. His breathing is labored, but he's got a huge smile on his face. "Did you like that?"

"Uh, yeah. I've never had an orgasm before."

"I know. I could tell by the shocked expression on your beautiful face."

"I liked it. I want more." He shifts slightly, and I frown. "What about you?" I nod toward his... oh wow. The towel has fallen away, only covering one leg and his right hip. It's... he's right there.

"I'm fine."

"B-But—"

"No worries, love. I'm good. I'm going to sleep with a smile on my face because I just gave you your first orgasm." He smirks. "I like being number one."

I slap his muscled arm jokingly, then run my palm over the same arm. He's warm, and his skin is smooth. "Your tattoos are amazing." On his left arm he has what looks like an old clock face from his shoulder down, and there are leaves, flowers, and other symbols weaved in and out of all the organic stuff. On his other arm he has a face. It could be Buddha, but I'm not sure. Similar vines and plantlike things are all around them. I see words and numbers in the mix as well. "They all mean something, don't they?"

"Aye."

He doesn't offer up any details, though. Or maybe he just likes being touched. His eyes close, and his breathing has evened out.

"Does this feel good?" I ask.

"Aye." His voice sounds weaker, huskier.

So I keep doing it until I hear a tiny snore. He's asleep, which gives me a chance to look at him. To *really* look at Cooke Thompson in the flesh is amazing, because one thing's for sure: he's the most beautiful human I've ever seen.

As I close my own eyes to sleep, I can't help wondering what this all means. If you had told me a day ago that I'd be in bed with Cooke, and that he was sexually attracted to me, I would have laughed. Sure, I had a crush on him since the first second I laid eyes on him, but he was a fantasy, like all the guys I've liked over the years.

So why now? Why, of all people, does Cooke like me?

I'm awoken in the middle of the night, twice, with kisses. Kisses on my neck, cheek, and then, when he knows I'm awake, on my lips. The first time, he murmured in a sleepy, sexy voice, "I can't bloody believe you're here."

I kiss him back. "Me neither."

This second time, he wraps his arms around my waist and pulls me until I'm on top of him. I'm half asleep until I realize what he's doing, and then I wake right the heck up. I try to scoot off him, but he won't have it. "Love. Stop squirming."

The second I feel his erection between my legs, I stop immediately. "Cooke. I'm too heavy."

"Bollocks."

"I-I don't know what I'm doing." I attempt another getaway, but he stops me once more.

"Shh, just let me look at you." And he does. He looks at me from the top of my head down to my knees. "Seeing you in my jersey is fecking hot, love."

"Fine." I let him look at me. It's not easy, because my self-conscious inner demons want to ruin this for me.

"Stubborn," Cooke mutters, but I don't think he's too concerned, because his hands that started at my waist move down to my upper thigh, just beneath the jersey I'm wearing. I watch as they slowly slide up farther. My mouth is suddenly dry, so I swallow hard. I should stop him before he gets to my belly, because the second he feels all of that, he'll run screaming. But then I look into his eyes, and what I see there makes me tingle. He's looking at me like he's enjoying himself, like he likes how I feel.

"So soft," he whispers.

Oh I'm soft all right.

When his big warm palms slide over my hips to my waist, I hold my breath. I didn't mean to; it just happened. He moves farther up, and I sit up straighter, I guess anticipating where he's going. The second his palms are beneath each breast, his eyes meet mine. I see heat in his; I suspect he sees fear in mine.

"You okay, Quinn?" he asks softly.

I nod because I am. I want him to touch me more than anything in this world.

Like he's torturing me, his hands move at a snail's pace. When they touch the bottom of my breasts, I press my chest out just a little bit. Enough for him to notice, I guess, because he chuckles. He stops chuckling, though, the second his hands cup each breast.

"So perfect." His voice sounds husky.

I'm not perfect, but his hands on me sure feel that way.

"Cooke," I urge, arching my back farther. I want his hands to move and squeeze me, but he's only holding them. "Please?" I whine.

Luckily, he listens and begins kneading each breast. Then he runs his fingers over the hard tips, and it makes me want to move my hips. When he pinches and tugs on them, I press down on his dick. I'm like a puppet he can control with just my breasts.

When his fingers squeeze harder and tug more aggressively, I begin to grind down on him, back and forth. I'm chasing another one of those illusive orgasms. I can feel it, though it's just out of reach. I need more. Just feeling him through my panties isn't enough. Sliding away from him, I reach down so I can touch him, but it makes him stop.

"No," I say almost angrily. "Don't stop." I want to feel him.

I half expect him to roll over and go to sleep, but he doesn't. He reaches down between my legs and moves my panties aside.

"I've never seen a naked man in person. In real life."

"Another first. Now climb back on, love."

I do it. I climb back on without another thought. He's bare against me, and it feels natural to be skin to skin. We both moan so loud, I'm afraid we're going to wake the dead.

"Move, Quinn. Please move." His hands are back beneath my shirt and on my breasts in seconds. Hands that feel frantic as I slide over him, forward and back. I'm so into it that I don't see him sit up and latch on to my nipple through the shirt. I'm tempted to pull it off, but I'm not there yet. I need to focus on chasing the orgasm that's slowly building.

I make the mistake of looking down at him just then, and what I see makes my breath catch. Cooke looks intense. His eyes are focused on my face, his lips a straight line like he's concentrating hard. It makes me smile, because I can tell he's into it. When he sees my expression, his seems to soften. What doesn't soften is any other part of him. I feel his hips move beneath me as he hits the perfect spot. "Feel good, love?"

"S-So good." I'm seconds away from the second orgasm of the night, and of my life. "Almost. Don't stop."

Two or three more moves and I'm gone. I throw my head back and release a guttural sound that I should be embarrassed about, but I can't be because it feels too damn good. Moments later, Cooke presses against me and hisses. Looking down, I see his release all over his stomach. I'm tempted to touch it, maybe even taste it, but I'm not sure I should. What I do know is I should get off him now. I'm probably crushing his pelvis.

Placing my palms on either side of his broad shoulders, I lift my leg and swing it over and away from him. When I'm on my knees at his side, Cooke smirks. "That was fun."

I giggle. "It was."

Looking down at his rippled abs, he quickly sits up, then rolls off the bed. "Back in a tick, love. Need to clean up."

I just sit there like a bump on a log, watching his perfectly round backside walk away from me into the bathroom. In preparation for his return, I lie down, facing the bathroom. This time, I don't care if I'm gawking. It's one show I don't want to miss. He doesn't disappoint, because he strides back out of the bathroom completely naked.

"Cooke, your body is *ri*-diculous." Oh shit. Did I say that out loud?

"Thanks." He chuckles, patting his abs. "That's what you get with hours and hours of training."

"I can see that."

When he slides back into the bed, he scoots to the middle,

patting the spot beside him. I move closer to him, and he turns his body enough to snap off the bedside lamp and then swings that same arm back over my hip and around my stomach. I should suck in the gut made possible not by "hours and hours of training" but by years and years of neglect. I should worry about my extra-soft middle, but I'm too tired right now. Yawning, I scoot back so we're touching, and I fall asleep in minutes.

# CHAPTER THIRTY-FOUR

God, I'm depressed. Cooke has been gone for three days, and whenever I've had a minute alone, I mope. Sure, I've cried a couple of times but that only happens in the bathroom when I'm at home, since I don't currently have any bedroom walls. And it doesn't look like I'm going to have any walls anytime soon. The landlord did what he promised. A crew came in on Saturday with a huge dumpster and gutted the entire basement. And I mean *gutted*. There's no longer a bedroom down there, nor are there walls around what used to be a makeshift bathroom. Now the toilet sits out in the open next to the sink and shower stall. They took it down to the studs, throwing away the carpeting, paneling, and the little drywall that was down there. They sucked up the water with shop vacuums, plugged in one dehumidifier, and left. That was two days ago. Patsy tried to call the landlord to see when they were going to finish the job, but he's not picking up. Big surprise there.

I have a sneaking suspicion that he's not going to do another thing down there. I guess I'll have to decide what I'm going to do. I could stay upstairs and only get about two hours of real sleep a night, or I can move back down into the basement. Sure, there might be a third option, but I can't think about that. Besides, I don't know if Cooke bought the condo, and I'm not about to ask him. It's bad enough he bought me a scooter.

Yes, that's what I said. The day he left, I was lying on my bed, trying not to think about him, when Susanna yelled for me to come downstairs. "You have a delivery."

"Okay!" I shouted back. I had no idea what the heck she was talking about, and I let my imagination run wild. Maybe Cooke sent flowers. But that made no sense. He was still in the air; how could he? Instead of overthinking it, I ran down the steps and found Susanna pointing toward the front door that was standing open. Tentatively, I moved to the opening and stepped through. Outside the door was a guy holding up a white envelope and a set of keys. Behind him was the prettiest baby blue Vespa I'd ever seen.

"What?" I squeaked.

"You Quinn Maxwell?"

"Yes."

He stepped closer before handing me the envelope and keys. "These are for you."

"Who—"

"It's all in the envelope." He waved and left. I watched him slide into a truck with a small trailer on the back.

"Who's it from?" Susanna asked.

"It's Cooke, right?" Robbi added.

*Where did she come from?*

Opening the envelope, the first thing I saw was a handwritten note.

*Quinn,*

*I saw this color and it reminded me of your pretty blue eyes. I hope you like it. If you don't, the gentleman said you could exchange it for something else. Please don't try to return it.*

*I can't tell you how much I enjoyed meeting you, love. You are so special and genuine. It pains me to leave you, but I must. Duty calls. I hope you'll consider visiting me over the holidays. The invitation is open. Just say the word.*

*I'll be busy for several days after I return with practice and meetings, but I'll call you when I can. Take care, and drive safely.*

*Yours, Cooke.*

I looked through the other items in the envelope. "Idiot." I say with a laugh.

"What?" Susanna asks.

"He bought me a new scooter, and there's a gift certificate for $500 dollars. It says, 'for helmet and other accessories' in the memo." I laughed again. "He's ridiculous."

And I love him. Before you think less of me, I don't love him for buying me a scooter. I love him for coming to my rescue and for being the sweetest, kindest person I've ever met.

"Shit. He shouldn't have done this.".

"He's wonderful," says Kat from somewhere. I turn and see three out of five roommates standing on the front step, watching me.

"He is."

He really is.

# CHAPTER THIRTY-FIVE

**Cooke:** What's a Garryowen?

I blink at the text message and smile. It's been seven long days since Cooke flew out of Des Moines International Airport, and this is the first time he's contacted me. I did send him a message thanking him for my Vespa, but it went unanswered. I know he's busy, so I haven't let it bother me. Much.

**Me**: Is that someone on your team?
**Cooke**: Love...
**Me**: Okay, hang on.
**Me**: Garryowen: An up and under kick. A high short punt onto or behind the defending team.
**Cooke**: Excellent, young pupil. We have a game against Ireland next week that should be on American telly. Probably on in the morning there. You going to watch your boyfriend play?
**Me**: Of course, I always watch Ian play.
**Cooke**. Love...
**Me**: Just kidding. I wouldn't miss watching you for anything. You're the best 10 in the world.

How am I going to watch a rugby game in the morning? What if it's on a school day? I guess I'll have to figure it out.

**Cooke**: Aye. That's better. Let Bull know, will ye?
**Me:** Yes, I'll send him a message.
It takes him over an hour to respond.
**Cooke:** I miss you.
Oh hell. Here come the waterworks.
**Me:** Me too. So much.
**Cooke:** Aye, love.

The next day, I'm awoken in the *very* early morning by the familiar chime from my FaceChat app. I've resisted calling him because I know he's busy getting ready for his matches, but damn, it's been a struggle. I quickly roll off my mattress onto the floor. No worries, it's only a six-inch fall since my bed frame was *accidentally* tossed out with the rest of the basement stuff. I'm not worried. This mattress is fine for now.

The second he comes into the frame on my computer screen, I feel my heart flutter in my chest. Cooke looks good. *Very* good.

"Why are you wearing a tuxedo?" He's taken off the tie, but he's still got on the black jacket and dress shirt. It looks as though he's gotten a haircut since his Iowa visit. His hair is almost shaved on the sides, the top styled perfectly. It's shiny like it's got product in it. Plus he's got a short beard now.

"Had to go to a fancy-dress ball tonight. I'm just leaving now." I can see a large stone building behind him and a long set of stairs. *Is that a castle?*

Wow, it's late there. "Fancy dress?" I love the sound of that. "Does that mean the ladies wore pretty ballgowns?"

"Aye."

"I bet that was fun."

"Fun? I—"

Just then, a voice sounds from somewhere on his end of the

line. "Cooke?" the voice says. I'd love to tell you it was a guy's voice, but I can't. "Cooke?" the voice says again.

I stare at the screen as Cooke starts to gnaw at his lower lip.

"Cooke, darling." The voice is getting louder.

"Quinn, I—"

And there she is. A stunning woman with long brown hair is walking down the steps behind him. A woman who would look perfect next to Cooke. Her bloodred dress sparkles as she moves, and a high slit in the skirt exposes one insanely long leg. When she gets to him, she wraps her arm around his neck and kisses his cheek. "There you are. You ready?"

I'm speechless. So many things are swirling in my head. For example, why did he call me if he's out with someone else? Did he do that on purpose? To let me down easy? I swallow hard as I stare at the screen. Sadly, Cooke isn't saying anything either.

"What's got you so intrigued on the phone, love?" she asks, attempting to peer at the screen. She's leaning over so far that I can practically see down the deep V of her dress.

I'm tempted to say hello, because why not. Cooke beats me to it. "No one, Sarina. Just my mate."

Wow. "Just my mate"? A stabbing pain shoots through my chest, like someone just used a machete on me.

Just. My. Mate.

I can't bring myself to speak so I do what any self-respecting girl would do, I shut the lid of my computer, then decide shutting down the computer is the best bet, so I open it back up. He's still there. Well, his leg or something like his leg is in the picture, along with the red sparkly skirt. It's pressed up against his pants. If I had to guess, I'd say they were kissing. But his hand, at least the one holding the phone, is down at his side.

Screw it. I quickly shut down my computer and crawl into bed. I don't have to be up for another hour, so I pull the covers up over my head, and do my utter best to fall asleep—anything but think about Cooke and *her*.

A while later, maybe fifteen minutes, I hear a chiming sound. "My phone." I flop out of bed and grab my bag to search for it. When I find it, I stare at the screen. Should I answer it? Should I just shut the phone down? "Screw it." I jab at the button and watch as his face appears. He's alone.

"Love—"

"Mate. You mean mate."

"Quinn—"

Ignoring him, I say things I never thought I could or would ever say. "I can't do this."

"Do what?"

"This." I point at him, then at me. "My self-esteem is fragile, Cooke. But I'm not stupid. I know whatever this thing between us was... well, it was going to be short-lived."

"Why?"

"Why?" I sniffle. "Because you're Cooke freaking Thompson, international rugby star. You're model gorgeous, you live in another country, and I'm...."

"You're what?"

"I'm... I'm just me. A boring, awkward Iowa girl. I can't compete with gorgeous women in red sequined dresses."

"Look—"

"Whatever excuse you're about to make, save it, Cooke. I know I'm easy prey for you."

"Prey?" he says loudly. "You're not bloody prey."

"I just mean you should be with someone like her."

"She's the club sponsor's daughter."

I stare at the phone, expecting more. When he says nothing else, I shrug. "So she's perfect for you."

"I can't bloody stand her. None of us can. But I can't tell her that."

I sniffle again. "You said I was nobody. A mate." A tear slides down my cheek.

"Because it's none of her fecking business who I talk to. She's a shit-stirrer. If she thought I had an American girlfriend...."

"What? She'd what?"

"She'd push harder."

Push harder? "To what? Pursue you?"

He nods, his mouth set in a grim expression. "Blokes have been left off the roster after rejecting her."

I stare at the phone, at him. Do I believe him? Yes. Am I disappointed? Yes. I mean, Cooke Thompson's the best fly-half in the world. If they "leave him off the roster" because of the owner's daughter, I'd think his fans would want to know that. "But you're the best."

"Right now I'm the best. But not forever."

"So, you'd rather—"

"Quinn, enough. I told you who she was and why I said you were my mate. Now leave it."

Wow. Just... wow. "Well, on that note, I need to go. Bye."

I hang up and then shut down my phone. Now instead of being sad, I'm pissed. He sounded just like my brothers. They talk to me like I'm an annoying gnat, and I'm not going to allow Cooke Thompson to do the same. Sure, I love him, but that doesn't mean I'm going to let him treat me like that.

Searching my room, I find a pair of leggings and a tee and get dressed. The girls and I are still walking almost every morning. I say almost because there are days we just can't. Like when it's raining, or if we went out the night before, or if I had to work until close. When that happens, I'm too pooped to walk, and my roommates are on the same page, usually. Since the weather's nice and I didn't work last night and no one over-imbibed, the walk is on.

I'm the first one ready to go today. I usually drag my ass out of my bed last. I guess it helps that Cooke woke me up so early. Sitting in one of our kitchen chairs, I close my eyes and run back through our conversation. Well, I guess you could call it a fight.

Our first fight? Hell, it doesn't matter; a fight is a fight, no matter how many we've had. But he was wrong this time, or at least what he said was wrong.

"So," Robbi says, surprising me, "what was that all about?"

"What?"

"Your tiff with Cooke."

"You heard that?"

"Uh, yeah. You were both talking loudly."

We were? I don't want to rehash it, so I shrug. "Long story."

She pats my back. "Lucky for you, we've got thirty minutes to talk about it. Come on."

"Where is everyone?"

"Patsy has her boy over, Kat is at Ryne's, Lindsay is across the street, and Susanna is a lazy ass." She snorts. "Just kidding. She was up late studying for her chem test."

"So it's just the two of us."

"Yep. Now let's go. And tell me everything."

## CHAPTER THIRTY-SIX

Robbi's been nearly silent the entire time I tell her about the FaceChat with Cooke earlier this morning. Now she says, "I think you did the right thing. He shouldn't have cut you off like that."

"Right?" I pause, trying to figure out how to say this. "But I think I may have overreacted."

She places her hand on my shoulder as we slow our walk. "I've had two serious boyfriends. The first one, I was too young to know what I was doing. The second time, I learned from my mistakes. And the main thing I learned was to nip shit in the bud right away, as soon as it happens. So, by hanging up on him, you let him know he can't talk to you like you're a toddler."

I nod. I agree with her, but I'm not sure hanging up on him was the right thing to do. "But I should've said something to him instead of just hanging up on him and shutting off all communication."

"Give it a day or so, then send him a message explaining your actions. See how that goes."

"I suppose that would work."

"Worth a try." She pats my shoulder. "Now, let's get inside so we can beat the others to the shower."

Now that they've gutted the basement, we're down to one shower. Sure, I could use the one in the basement, but it's sort of moist and creepy down there now. Creep*ier*, I guess I should say.

When we step into the house, we hear the shower running, and Patsy is in the kitchen making her breakfast. "Who's in the shower?" asks Robbi.

"Jeff."

"Seriously, Pats. Again?" spits Robbi. "You let your boyfriend shower here when there's too many of us for one shower as it is. Lindsay will be over here any minute to use it too. Plus, you know the hot water heater sucks. He should've showered at his place. Now we're all going to be late."

"Jesus, Robbi—" Patsy starts.

"I'll shower in the basement. That'll help. I'm sorry." Ugh, why am I sorry? Robbi's right. Jeff should have schlepped home.

"No. That's not the point." Robbi sounds angrier now. "That was inconsiderate to say the least, Patsy."

"It's just one morning," Patsy snaps.

"No it's not." Robbi has her hands on her hips. "This is the third time in two weeks."

"Well—"

"I'll shower downstairs." I run up, grab my towel, and run back down the steps when I realize all my shower stuff is in the main bathroom. Not wanting to get in the middle of the spat between Robbi and Patsy, I wait for Jeff to get out of the bathroom.

I sit for a good ten more minutes before Jeff strolls out of the bathroom in only a towel. My mind immediately goes back to that night in Cooke's hotel room. Jeff's cute, but he doesn't hold a candle to Cooke Thompson in a tiny towel.

Shaking away those memories, I make quick work of grabbing my toiletries. Stepping back out, I can hear Robbi laying into

Patsy again. "This place is overcrowded as it is now that we lost a bedroom and the basement bathroom. There's just no space for our *guests,*" she says sort of snidely, "to use up our hot water and make us late in the morning."

"Robbi, I'll take care of it. Just let it go."

Robbi isn't letting it go. "How are you going to take care of it?"

I sneak past the quarreling roommates and head down into the basement. I haven't been down here since the day they gutted the place. When my feet hit cool concrete, I take a whiff. It doesn't smell bad, and it looks dry. I move to the bathroom area. I can't call it a bathroom in its current state, so area is a good word for it. Setting my clothes on the toilet seat, I reach into the shower to turn it on—and scream. The biggest fucking spider I've ever seen has made a home in the wire rack that used to hold shampoo and soap. We make eye contact, my two meeting all of his. It's black and hairy, and judging by the size of him, I'd say it could sit in the palm of my hand.

Yeah, if I was fucking crazy.

"What the hell!" Robbi says from directly behind me.

I didn't even hear her come down the steps.

"Is that a spider?"

"Aragog," I say softly.

"Jesus." Robbi shivers. "I've never seen one that big before."

Like an afterthought, I murmur, "That's what she said."

Robbi chuckles, then pulls my arm away from the shower. "You can't use this. Someone needs to spray down here or something."

I grab my clothes from the top of the toilet and follow Robbi back up the stairs. "I told you guys there was something lurking down here. Now I know what it was."

"Yeah, Stephen King's incarnation lives and breathes in Ames, Iowa."

"I just hope it doesn't have a family."

"Jesus." Robbi shivers again. "I'm calling the landlord."

*Good luck with that.* "While you've got him, ask him if he plans on doing anything with the basement, would ya?"

"Will do. Now, you take the bathroom next, but hurry your ass up."

I walk to the bathroom, but the door's shut. "Patsy?" I say loud enough for her to hear.

"Yeah?" she says from behind me.

"Oh." I turn to face her. "Who's in the bathroom?

"Jeff. He had to"—she rolls her eyes—"you know."

"You're shitting me." Now I'm on the same page as Robbi.

"What!" Robbi shouts right in my ear. "Patsy, why couldn't he have done that downstairs or even upstairs? There's a toilet up there."

She shrugs. "He'll just be a minute."

"It'll be a while," says a man's voice from behind the door. "My tummy is upset."

"Tummy?" I say almost to myself.

"Yo, Jeff!" yells Robbi. She doesn't wait for him to acknowledge her. "Next time, go home to shit, shower, and shave, yeah? Now none of us will be able to get ready in time."

"Whatever," he mumbles, then moans from inside the bathroom.

"I'll just put my hair up and go like this," I say. "I'm going to be late."

Loud enough for Patsy and Jeff to hear, Robbi replies, "Me too. I guess I can't use my own goddamn bathroom to get ready for class." Then she mumbles, "Inconsiderate fuckers."

This entire thing this morning gives me pause. Robbi mentioned that we're overcrowded, especially now that the basement isn't an option thanks to the arachnid from my nightmares down there. Heck, even if the landlord *did* finish the basement, that giant fucker could be living in a crevice somewhere. With its million spider babies. They could regain control of my bedroom in a matter of hours. God, I hate spiders.

No, I need to take all of this as a sign. I need to find a new place to live. And since Tayler is going to be homeless in a few weeks, maybe I could bunk with her. The money from Mr. Becker could help me with that.

I race back upstairs and pick up my phone to check the time, but I forgot I turned it off. Quickly restarting it, I brush my hair and put it up in a messy bun. I throw on an oversized ISU sweatshirt and slip on some fake Vans. I wish I had more time to get ready. I feel gross. At least I brushed my teeth before the walk. Oh, and I'm starving, but there's no time for breakfast. I finally have some food too. Food that isn't considered a carbohydrate. I used a tiny bit of the five thousand from Mr. Becker to buy myself some healthier groceries.

When my phone comes to life, I quickly check the time. "Shit." I'm late. Not only that, I see several messages. Cooke's name is among them. No doubt he feels badly about earlier. I don't have time to read them, so I grab my bag and am out the door to my pretty blue Vespa. The pretty blue Vespa that Cooke bought for me. I used the gift certificate to buy a new helmet. It's the same style as before, but this one is baby blue, just like the scooter. The new trunk also matches the scooter. I paid a little extra to have the guys at the shop install it.

Slipping on the helmet, I straddle the bike. I've got the keys in my hand, but before I start it up, I grab my phone and quickly type.

**Me**: I forgive you. I'm late for class, so I'll write more later. Long story, but I'm probably going to have to move soon. I'll let you know where and when.

I race to campus. When I get to the Design Center parking lot, there isn't a spot in sight. "Of course there isn't."

I drive around frantically for ten more minutes. When I don't find a thing, I park illegally behind a short brick wall that separates the sidewalk from a grassy area behind the building. I've seen other scooters there from time to time, so I cross my fingers that I don't get ticketed, or worse, towed. By the time I race into ceramics, I'm sweating, panting, and my hair looks like I've been in a wind tunnel. In a word, I look hellish. Not only that, there's only one wheel left, and it's that fucking kick-wheel.

Shoulders slumped, I lumber to the back, mumbling, "I should have never gotten out of bed today."

I wouldn't find out until later, but I was more right about that than I could have imagined.

## CHAPTER THIRTY-SEVEN

**Cooke:** You hung up on me again?

**Cooke:** Childish. That's what that was. Bloody childish.

**Cooke:** Now your bloody phone is off, isn't it?
Well, you can just sod off, Quinn.

See? I should have stayed in bed. God, I'm the world's biggest idiot.

I reread his texts to be doubly sure. Yep. I can say, without any hesitation, that Cooke was not asking for forgiveness in his messages. Nope. And if "sod off" means what I think it does, I'm pretty sure he broke up with me.

In a text.

What a cliché.

I turn off my phone again because I can't take one more text. From anyone.

I *knew* I shouldn't have gotten out of bed this morning.

# CHAPTER THIRTY-EIGHT

The world's second crappiest day has turned into the world's second crappiest night at work too. Luke's in a terrible mood, so nothing I do was right. And I mean nothing. I'm not sure what crawled up his lovely, firm ass, but whatever it was, it isn't sitting well.

Example. Just now, I was minding my own business, pouring a pitcher of beer. When I finished, I turned around and ran smack-dab into Chris, causing me to drop the pitcher and get us both completely drenched in beer. Chris is laughing it off, but Luke is livid.

"What the fuck is wrong with you, Quinn?" he shouts. "Clean that shit up."

So I start to pull up the rubber mats we have behind the bar when he yells, "No, Jesus. Get the people their beer, for fuck's sake. Then clean it up." Then he literally growls, "On second thought, Chris, get their beer. Quinn, clean that shit up before you fall and break that Kardashian ass of yours and sue me."

I'm bent over and have started to lift the rubber floor mat when the words float out into the air above me.

*No.*

*He.*

*Didn't.*

My face heats, and that fucking burn behind my eyes starts, but I'm not doing it. I'm not going to cry because of something some asshole says to me. Not anymore.

Shame. I was even starting to like Luke. I rise slowly, leaving that stupid mat right where it was. My eyes meet his.

*He knows.*

I can tell by his expression that he knows he said the wrong thing. And, for once, I'm not going to put up with it. "You know what, Luke?" I'm not waiting for him to say anything, and I think he knows it, because he keeps his stupid, insensitive mouth shut. "You can go fuck yourself."

I toss the rag into the sink, something he'll be super pissed about, and start to stomp away, but the fucking mat is wet and slick, so I slip. I don't fall, though. I'm able to keep my balance at the expense of my groin muscles, but who the hell cares. With my head held high, I stomp past the customers at the bar and stop right in front of Luke.

"Luke Green, you're no better than those assholes that you yelled at about the same damn thing, and frankly, I deserve better." I'm pointing at myself when I say that last bit. "It's not okay what you just said to me. And you know what else?"

This time he answers. Clearing his throat, he says, "What?"

"*I'm* telling Tayler."

He winces. I saw it. I knew he'd react to that, because the guy has been working overtime to get her to go out with him. According to Tay, he's called her almost every night. At first it was for a booty call, so when she told him that wasn't her style, he switched gears. Now he's wooing her—Tayler's words. He even sent her flowers one day, but she still hasn't given in yet. So yeah, I knew my words were going to hit him where they hurt. In his dick. Ha!

I grab my purse from just inside the kitchen door, and I'm out of there. But not before I shout, "Kiss my Kardashian ass, Luke Green."

I BLUBBER ALL THE WAY HOME. CRYING IS CATHARTIC, RIGHT? If that's the case, I should be cleansed as fuck. No matter. As far as days go, the horrible, terrible, worst fucking day ever is still numero uno, but this one is right up there. I mean, apparently Cooke broke up with me this morning. I found out I used to live with a spider the size of a rodent, that our house can't sustain six roommates, and since I was the last one in, I'm the logical one to go. Also, I think I quit my job. Granted, I didn't say *those* words exactly, but by telling my boss and the owner of the bar to "kiss my Kardashian ass" is pretty much quitting. I'm boyfriendless, homeless, and jobless.

"God, my life sucks."

When I slow to a stop at a light, I look down at my pretty blue scooter. Petting the handlebars, I coo, "At least I've got you, Bluebelle." Yeah, I named her Bluebelle. What can I say? It fits.

As soon as the light turns green, I slowly pull away from my spot into the intersection and continue my ride home just as a large SUV in the lane next to me begins to merge into my lane. "Hey!" I yell, then press my thumb on the horn button, but the car's windows are closed and the horn isn't loud. Hell, it's not even a horn. It's more of a beep-beep sound. Whoever is driving the SUV is still moving into my lane. My only option is to swerve over to the lane to my right—into oncoming traffic. Headlights practically blind me, but I maneuver over into the other lane. The car heading my way is far enough back that I'm able to jump the curb onto the sidewalk, where I lay down my scooter into a skid. I hear the metal scrape and even see sparks. It's too bad my skin is doing the same.

When we both come to a stop, me and Bluebelle, the pain hits me like the SUV was about to. I take deep breaths to get myself under control, because I need to assess the damage and get out from beneath Bluebelle. I'm about to push her off me when I hear sirens. I look up and see an Ames police cruiser with its lights on chasing down the SUV that just about killed me. They must have been close enough to see what happened.

"Shit," I hiss. My face, left arm, left side, and left leg burn like they've been set on fire. I'm able to move some, so it doesn't seem as though I've broken anything, but I suspect I've lost skin, at the very least. Bluebelle is still resting on my leg, and I do my best to lift her enough for me to scoot out from beneath her. As soon as I do, I hear another set of sirens.

"Don't move," shouts a gruff voice.

No. Please don't tell me I'm under arrest.

I look up and see Gage running toward me. "Jesus, Quinn." When he gets to me, he slides onto his hands and knees. "I heard a call on the scanner that a motorcycle was run off the road."

"It was me."

Gage is checking me for injuries. We both gasp when we see the wound on my forearm. My sweatshirt is shredded enough to see that I've lost skin—a *lot* of skin. Blood has seeped through the fabric. Not only is there blood, but the wound is also covered with rocks and dirt.

"What happened?" he asks, looking at my leg next.

"The big SUV merged into my lane. They must not have seen me. I honked and then avoided them by pulling left and jumping the curb."

"You could've been killed," he snaps.

Why is *he* angry? I'm the one who's hurt. "Yeah." I wince as he tears the new hole in my jeans until it's wide enough to see the leg wound. From here, it looks to be about the same as my arm.

"You shouldn't be out driving this thing at night."

"I had to work."

"Then take the bus. It's too dangerous."

When he places his hand on my face to look there, he scowls. That's when I get mad. It's also when I swat at his hand, not hard, just enough to get it away from me. "You know what?" I say, doing my best to stand up. It's not working. I'm having a hard time since my left side is fucked up.

"What, Quinn?" he asks softly.

I roll over to my right side and use the scooter to help me up. I wince when I put pressure on me left foot. Something doesn't feel right there either, but I do my best to appear fine. "I'm just not cut out for this."

"For what?"

"Anything," I say, swinging my right hand in the air. I also start blubbering. Great. "Life."

"Quinn—"

"No matter what I do, life just shits on me, Gage." Yep, feeling sorry for myself. "I ruined Bluebelle." I point to my scooter. "I know I have to go to the ER, because I'm pretty sure I broke my foot, and I don't have the money for a hospital bill. I'll have to spend the money from Mr. Becker, and that sucks because I was going to use that to move into a new place because there's no room for me at the Beedle house because I no longer need it to fly to England since Cooke dumped me. Oh, and I told Luke Green to kiss my Kardashian ass, so I don't have a job with which to pay the bills I'm going to have from the ER." Just then, an ambulance pulls up with sirens blaring. "Great. Now I'll have an ambulance bill because why. The fuck. Not?"

After all that, the only thing Gage asks is "You broke up with Cooke?"

I blink away tears as I stare into his eyes. It makes me laugh, but not in a good way. No, it's more in the hysterical 'I belong in a loony bin' kind of way.

"Miss?" I look up to see two paramedics with very concerned expressions on their faces. "You okay?" asks the one closest. I feel my shoulders slump, because I don't think I can handle being around another hot guy. Now there are three of them right here.

"No." I'm not okay. I'm injured. My left side is a mess, and I'm pretty sure my foot is broken.

"Let us take a look. Can you walk over to the truck?"

"Yes." I take a step and nearly fall on my face.

I feel an arm wrap around me, and I know it's Gage. "Let me help."

I do let him help. I hop on my good leg over the small section of grass, then do the same off the curb until I'm at the back of the ambulance, or truck as the paramedic says.

"What's wrong with your foot?" the second guy asks.

I look at the badge on his chest and see his name. "Well, Bill, I think it's broken. Or maybe just sprained."

I peek over at the other guy. "Chip?"

"Yeah?" He's busy getting gear out of a box. It looks like swabs, ointments, and a syringe. I hate shots.

"Your name is Chip, or is that a nickname?" If I distract him, maybe he'll forget about using that needle.

"Charles. Chip for short."

I feel warmth on my left and look over at Gage. "Thanks for helping me, Gage. Again. You're always coming to my rescue." I roll my eyes and it hurts. Not only that, but I see Chip and Bill look at each other. No matter. The truth is, my left side hurts—my face especially. I reach up to touch it and wince. "Did I lose part of my face?" Because if I did, that would suck. It's probably my only good feature.

"Looks like it's just scraped up. I'm going to clean that up for you. I'll know more once I do that," Chip says softly. "It's gonna sting."

"Great." This day just gets better and better.

"Can you take the helmet off?"

I didn't realize I was still wearing it. I'm half afraid to look at the damage. I do it, though. As soon as it's off, I examine the top and sides. It's scratched, but there aren't any dents.

I wince when the first swipe of the antiseptic wipe hits my knee. "I really think we need to take her in," says Bill. He tried to take off my shoe, my favorite pair of Converses, but I winced and whimpered, so he stopped. "Her foot is too swollen to pull the shoe off without pain. I'll need to cut it off."

No. Not that. I finally got these broken in. They're soft and comfy and black. My favorite color, even though it's technically not a color. "Just take all the laces out." That'll open it up.

Bill mumbles something, but he does as I suggest, opening the shoe wide enough to get it off my foot.

"See?" I say, doing my best to keep the pain from showing on my face, especially when he begins to poke and prod my foot.

"You've either got a serious sprain or it's broken. You'll need an X-ray."

"See? Told ya." This sucks. I can't afford an X-ray. But what else can I do?

Gage is still next to me. He must sense my hesitation about the hospital. "The driver of the SUV will have insurance. They were at fault here."

I nod as Bill puts a brace on my foot. It hurts. Looking over at Bluebelle, I sigh. "Do you think she's totaled?"

Gage walks over to her and lifts her off the ground. "She's banged up, but I bet she can be repaired."

"That's good," I say, but there's not a lot of excitement behind it.

Maybe he's right. I should just start taking the bus.

## CHAPTER THIRTY-NINE

"Thanks for picking me up, Tayler." It's well past two in the morning by the time I'm released from the hospital with bandages on all my wounds and a big boot on my left foot. At least it's not broken. Nope, badly sprained was the verdict. But it's going to hurt for a while, since I sprained the side of my foot. I didn't know you could do that, honestly.

"No problem, Quinn." Tayler's been quiet since she strolled into Mary Greeley's emergency ward, though I haven't had a chance to ask her why before now.

"What's up?" I turn to face her as she drives down Lincoln Way.

"First. I heard about Luke. He called me and fessed up."

"Uh-huh."

"He's sorry, by the way. Says you aren't fired."

"Did you make him not fire me?" I ask with an arched brow.

"No. He said he was an asshole and that he was proud that you stuck up for yourself."

I did stick up for myself, didn't I?

"Before I left, I told him I was going to tell on him... to you."

I giggle, then wince because the left side of my ribs hurt, and laughing makes that worse.

"Well, he beat you to it." She's not laughing. Hell, she's not even smiling.

"So, what's wrong?"

"Dylan." I roll my eyes, but she can't see me. It's dark in the car. "He wants me back."

"Of course he does." My eyes roll so hard this time I bet she can hear it. "But you're not taking him back, right?" She's quiet. Too quiet. "Tay?"

"We were together for so long."

"And?"

"He's—"

"A cheating bastard. Besides, what about Luke?"

"Luke has his head up his ass."

I can see that. "How so?"

"He can't see past just hooking up. I mean, I should probably go along with it, since I was in a serious relationship for so long. I should have some fun. But I'm not made that way. Honestly, things with me and Dylan have been over a long time. We just drifted apart when we got up here, and we were so busy, neither one of us did anything about it."

I snort. "Dylan did something about it." He cheated.

"True." Her laugh is humorless. We drive in silence for a few minutes. "No."

"No what?"

"No, I'm not taking Dylan back. I'm also not going to be some guys hookup. There are plenty of girls who want that. I'm just not one of them."

"And you told Luke all of that?"

"He knows. He just can't seem to see himself in a relation-ship." She shrugs. "I respect that."

But she's sad about it. "I'm sorry, Tay-Tay."

She glances over, giving me a reserved smile. "So, you were nearly run over, huh?"

Leave it to Tayler to cut to the chase. "Oh, well, that was the good part of my day. The rest really sucked."

That gets her laughing. Hard.

We decided it was best if I just crashed—no pun intended—at her place for tonight. I already sent a text to my roommates that I was staying with Tayler. I didn't mention my accident.

When we pull into Tayler's apartment complex, I frown. "You've got stairs."

"There's a service elevator. We'll use that."

"Thank goodness."

Tayler wraps her arm around my waist and leads me through the door to the back of the main level. She presses the button, and we wait as the elevator clanks and wheezes its way down to us.

"So, where did they take your scooter?" she asks.

"The police have it." Gage took care of it for me. He was going to drop it off at my house for me. He's so sweet.

At her door, Tayler unlocks the deadbolt and pushes the door open. I step through, and the first thing I see are boxes stacked along the main hallway. "You're ready to move. Did you find a place yet?"

"Most of that is Dylan's stuff. He keeps thinking he's just going to move back in here, but I took care of that. I've started packing my stuff too." She shrugs. "Why not? I've got to be out of here. Our lease is up on the fifteenth." I must have a strange expression, because she adds, "Yeah. Dylan wanted to be in before Thanksgiving last year, so he talked the management into a midmonth move-in date." She rolls her eyes, then mutters, "Fucking tool."

I want to ask her straight up if she wants to get a place together, but I know her. It's got to seem like it's her idea. She's bossy like that. "I think I need to move too."

"Really? Why?"

Sitting down on her sofa, I put my bad foot up on her ancient coffee table and update her on the basement and the landlord. I'd already told her about the mold issue.

"That's bullshit," she growls. "I hate landlords like that. He's just spiteful."

I can't disagree. It appears he's holding out on us because Patsy threatened him. I'm guessing, anyway.

As I sit on the couch, Tayler gathers up a sheet, blanket, and pillow for me. Her sofa is comfy. I've fallen asleep on it a time or two. Setting my phone on the coffee table, I pull off my mutilated sweatshirt and lay it across the back of the couch. Next, I retrieve the small bottle of pain meds the hospital pharmacy gave me. Then I lie down in my jeans and the tee I had on beneath the sweatshirt. I'd like to take the boot off, but I'm afraid I'll bump my foot, which would hurt, so I do my best to get comfortable. It's not easy, but I find a spot that isn't bad.

"You hungry? Thirsty?" Tayler asks from the kitchen.

"I'd take some water. I need to take one of these pain pills."

"Sure."

She brings me water and a package of crackers. "You need to eat something with those things."

"Thanks, Tay."

"No problem."

I take the pills, then pull a cracker from the sleeve and nibble while Tayler stands beside the sofa. I hear her sniffle and jerk my head up to look at her. "What's wrong?"

"You could've been killed." Her sniffles are becoming more frequent.

"I wasn't."

"Fucking scooters," she snaps.

"It wasn't Bluebelle's fault. It was the idiot driver of the SUV."

Wiping her eyes, she scowls at me. "You know what I mean."

I do.

She sniffles once more. "You're my best friend. I don't want to lose you."

"I'm right here. I'm fine."

"I know." Her voice is so soft that I barely heard those two words. "You should call your boyfriend and tell him you're okay."

What boyfriend? "He's... not. This morning...." I can't seem to finish what I'm trying to say.

"Jesus, you did have a bad day, didn't you?"

"Told you."

Running her hand over my head, she whispers, "Poor Q." Sitting on the coffee table in front of me, she smiles. "We should totally live together."

*Bam.* There it is. "You think?" I try to seem surprised at her suggestion.

"Absolutely. We'd have a blast."

I smile, then wince because my cheek hurts like a mofo." We would." I hold my good hand out to her for a shake. "Roomies."

She takes my hand and beams. "Roomies."

THE SECOND TAYLER LEAVES TO GO TO BED, I PICK UP MY phone. I'd turned it on at the hospital so I could call Tayler. When I did, it dinged a bunch of times. I was afraid to read anything then, but now that I'm alone, I want to see if any of them are from Cooke. Hitting the message app, I see a couple from Luke sent not long after I stormed out of Cy's. But there are none from Cooke. Damn.

**Luke:** I'm sorry. I was an ass. I deserved that. Don't quit. You're a good bartender.

Then another one from Luke.

**Luke:** Having a Kardashian ass isn't an insult, by the way. People pay thousands of dollars for that ass. You got it for free. (I assume.)

God, what an idiot. I quickly shoot him a text.

**Me:** My ass was home grown, *thankyouverymuch*. I won't quit, but I was run off the road tonight, and I'm pretty beat up and now wearing a boot, so we'll have to talk about it when I can come back.

Then I decide to put myself out there about my best friend.

**Me:** And by the way... WTF are you doing with Tayler? She's not a booty call kind of girl. She's the forever kind.

Okay, I said it. It's done.

**Luke**: I know.

If he knows, then what is he doing? Gah! Men are so frustrating.

I glance down at my screen and see a bunch from Kat, sent a few minutes ago.

**Kat:** Okay. Have a fun slumber party.

Then another one immediately following that one.

**Kat**: Wait. Why was your scooter just dropped off by that hot cop? Where are you?
**Kat**: I went out to move it into the garage for you. What happened to it? It's all smashed up.
**Kat**: CALL ME!!!!

**Me**: I'm fine. Had a little accident. Tayler picked me up from the ER. I'm fine.

**Kat**: The ER???!!! I'm telling Patsy.

**Me**: Please don't wake up Patsy or anyone else. I'm fine. I'll tell you all about it tomorrow. I'm beat. Just took a pain pill and need to sleep.

**Kat**: A PAIN PILL???!!!

**Me:** I'm fine.

**Kat:** You promise?

**Me**: Promise.

**Kat:** Ok. I guess.

**Me:** Night, Kat.

**Kat**: Night, Quinn.

## CHAPTER FORTY

I've got the girls in the living room for a powwow a few days after my accident. In that short time, a lot has happened. First, the driver of the SUV had insurance. Unfortunately, the guy was a huge asshole. The officer who wrote out the accident report had to remind him, several times, that he could have killed me. I don't think the guy cared one way or the other. The good news is his insurance company is paying to repair Bluebelle and taking care of my hospital bills. They also offered me a settlement, but I'm hesitant to take it. Gage told me not to be naïve, saying, "It's how these things work."

So I went ahead and took it, adding ten thousand dollars to my bank account. I'm uncomfortable taking the money, but it's needed since I won't be able to work for at least a couple more weeks. It also gives me the courage to do what I'm about to do.

"Ladies," I say from my perch in one of the side chairs. "I'm moving out."

"What!" comes from everyone.

"I've heard more than one of you talk about how cramped it is upstairs and how the bathroom situation sucks. It does. Not only that, Tayler needs a roommate. She can't afford to live alone, and her lease is up on the fifteenth." I breathe in and out. "I won't leave you in the lurch money-wise. I'll pay my rent until—"

"No. You shouldn't have to pay rent for a room you don't have anymore," Patsy says with a frown. "I understand. I should've tried harder to get the asshole landlord to do something about your bedroom." She sighs.

"It's not your fault he's a jerk, Pats."

She wipes a tear from her cheek. "I don't want you to move out."

"I know. I love you guys." I really do. "We're looking at places close by so we could still do our morning walks, and I'll definitely go out with you when you want. I...." A wave of emotion comes over me. "I really love you guys."

"We love you too." Robbi isn't crying, but she does look angry. "I'm sorry I complained about the bathroom."

"No. It's fine. It is fun being upstairs with you all, but I can't really sleep up there."

"We're sorry." Susanna's turn to sniffle.

"Stop, you guys." They're making me feel terrible. "You haven't gotten rid of me."

"Good." Kat stands first. Making her way closer, she wraps her arms around me. "I saw the spider. I don't blame you."

Patsy laughs. "We *all* saw the spider. I took a picture for the landlord. No reply."

"Did anyone kill it?"

Kat shivers next to me. "Fuck no. You know the second you try to kill it, you'll miss and it'll freak out, run up your arm, and eat your face."

I giggle and nod at everything Kat's saying because those were my thoughts exactly. "Right?"

As the girls disband, I pull Patsy aside. "You sure this is okay?"

"Yeah. I meant what I said. You're paying the same as the rest of us, but you don't even have a bedroom." She pats my arm. "We'll figure it out, Quinn. No worries."

As she starts to step away, I ask, "What about your mom? Is she okay?"

"Yeah." Patsy laughs. "She got a promotion and a raise."

"Oh?"

"I don't know what went down with you and Mr. Becker, but thanks."

"I didn't—"

"Kara's going to Iowa in the spring term."

"Oh, wow. I should feel bad for them, but then again...."

"I know." Patsy laughs. "Kara has gotten away with a lot over the years thanks to her dad. I'm just glad she won't be around here anymore."

I hope she's right.

I haven't heard from Cooke in so long. I know he's busy playing a tournament—or a fixture, as they call them—but that's not the reason he hasn't called. Part of me still wants to reach out to him, update him on the changes in my life, but he sounded so angry that night of his fancy party. He hasn't tried to talk to me, so I don't feel I should bother him. Besides, there's nothing pressing that I need to tell him anyway. Sure, I was in an accident and I had to go to the hospital, but I'm fine. See? It's not pressing. I need to find a new place to live, but again, that isn't anything he needs to worry about. I'll just text him my new address once I know what it is. After that, it'll be up to him to make the next move.

My shoulders slump. Everything I said just now... it's a lie. I'm bummed that he hasn't tried to call or text me. I'm sad because I feel like it's over between us. It seems like it was months ago that he visited when it was only weeks ago. In those weeks, everything just fell apart. *Maybe I should've had sex with him.* Then maybe he'd—

What the hell am I doing? I need to just remember the good times with Cooke and let him go. End. Of. Story.

# CHAPTER FORTY-ONE

"What about that place?" I ask Tayler as she pulls out of the apartment complex.

"It was dirty," she says glumly.

"We could clean it." Right?

"Who knows what's lurking underneath the carpet." She shivers. "God, disgusting."

I didn't think it was that bad. Yes, it needed a good scrubbing, but the bedrooms were big and the kitchen looked decent. "We have one more place left, right?" We've been looking at places off and on for almost two weeks. Every place in our budget either needed to be condemned, or it was only big enough for one person. A small one.

"Yeah. If this one doesn't work out, we're screwed. I'm going to have to live in my car or crash at your place."

I don't think that would go over very well with my roomies, but I don't say it aloud. No need to add to her bad mood.

I watch as she pulls into a parking lot next to a three-story brick building. It reminds me of the old school with the condos that Cooke and I looked at, but this one hasn't been remodeled.

Actually, that building isn't far from here. Down a block or two. Too bad that place is out of our price range.

"Here's hoping," Tayler mutters.

I push the car door open and step out on the gravel lot. I follow her to the front door, where a sign tells us the rental office is on the main level, to the left. We enter and walk down a long hallway, finding the office at the end. It's certainly not as nice as Cooke's building. This corridor needs a coat of paint and a good mopping.

At the door marked Manager, Tayler tries the knob, but it's locked. Next, she knocks. We wait for a minute or two, and then Tayler knocks again. She's about to do it a third time when we hear a gruff voice yell, "Hold your damn horses."

Tayler and I look at each other, but our expressions remain stoic.

When the door creaks open, a man about my grandpa's age stands in only a pair of old jeans and a satin robe a la Hugh Hefner. "What?" he snaps.

When Tayler doesn't respond, I say, "We're here to look at an apartment."

"I called earlier," Tayler finally says. "My name is Tayler."

"Tayler's a man's name."

"It's also mine, uh, sir."

"Fucking confusing if you ask me." He reaches back, and I hear the clanging of keys. When he steps out of the apartment, he's holding a huge ring of them. "Top floor, girls."

We follow him to a set of wooden stairs that have seen better days. There are cracked boards, and several planks are completely missing.

"Stairs are gettin' fixed next week."

Sure they are. "Is there an elevator?" I ask.

"Nope. Exercise would do you good, girl."

Fuck. Doesn't he see the boot I'm wearing? Besides, I didn't ask for commentary on my exercise habits or my body. God, I'm sick of people. "I exercise. Don't judge a book by its cover."

He snorts. "If I did, you'd be *War and Peace*."

I stop in my tracks. "That's rude," I say to the crusty old fart.

He's stopped moving too. Turning around slowly, he says, "Pardon?"

"I said that's rude. You don't know me. You don't know one thing about me, so don't presume to say something as callous as '*War and Peace*.'" I use an old guy's voice for emphasis. "Someone your age should have better manners than that."

"Well." He chuckles. "You're a spitfire, ain't ya?"

"Yes." At least I'm starting to be.

"You're a pretty thing." Then, lowering his voice, he adds, "For a big book."

Fuck this guy. I'm about to turn around and leave when he stops in front of the door at the farthest end of the hallway on the top floor. "This'n needs to be cleaned up and painted."

"Oh, great," Tayler grumbles.

"It's a nice one," the old guy replies. "Lots of people want to live here."

"Uh-huh." I don't believe him.

When he turns the key, I hear the door unlatch. He pushes it open and steps back so we can walk in first. When we get all the way in, we both gasp.

"It's beautiful," I say first. And it is. The living room is huge with extra-tall ceilings. The walls and ceiling are white, but they look like they need a fresh coat of paint. The hardwood floors are a medium color and mostly shiny except for the parts that need cleaned. They look like they're in great condition, just a little dusty. On the outside wall are large windows that run across the entire space. It's so sunny, it makes me smile.

I turn toward the area designated as the kitchen. Most of the appliances and sink are all opposite the window wall. There's a gas stove, large fridge, and even a dishwasher. All the appliances are white to match the walls, but the cupboards are dark gray, almost black. Not only that, there's a large kitchen island that faces the windows.

I look over at Tayler as she opens the cabinets one at a time. She hasn't said a peep yet.

Stepping out of the living area, I walk down a short hallway into the first of two bedrooms. This one is huge with the same large windows along one wall. The floors from the living room have continued into the bedroom. I pull open a door and see a giant walk-in closet with built-in drawers along the back wall. "Amazing," I whisper. I suddenly feel nervous. What if someone else has already filled out a rental application? What if the old guy picks them instead?

Shaking off the doubts, I walk farther down the hallway past a bathroom with a giant bathtub that also doubles as a shower. The black-and-white tile in the bathroom reminds me of the old houses I've seen on *House Hunters*. Everything is in good condition. It just needs to be cleaned.

Moving on to the next bedroom, I notice it's just slightly smaller than the other one. It's also not as sunny, because the windows are on the opposite side of the apartment and there aren't as many. I pull open the closet and see the twin of the other one. I like this room. I think I'd sleep better in a less sunny room.

Moving back out into the hallway, I bump into Tayler. "What do you think?" She looks up at me, and there are tears in her eyes. "What's wrong?"

"I love it. It's perfect." She pauses. "Right?"

"Yeah. It's perfect. The price is a steal too." I wouldn't be paying much more than I was at the house. "I wonder what the catch is."

"I've been wondering the same thing," she grouses. "I mean, was someone murdered here? Is it haunted? Does it leak?" She looks up at the ceiling and smiles. "Shit. Tin ceilings."

"I know. This place is amazing. There's got to be a catch."

As Tayler continues her tour, I move out of the living room where the old asshole is standing. "So," I say with caution. "What's the catch?" What? I might as well cut to the chase.

"Catch?" He chuckles. "You sure are a spitfire."

"Uh-huh. So? Is it haunted? Is it a murder apartment? Does the neighbor have a thing for college girls?"

"The neighbor is a professor at the college. I don't think he's got any weird fetishes." He shrugs. "Who knows these days. Am I right?" He chuckles again.

"What's your name?"

"Vic."

"And you manage the place?"

"I own it, hon."

"And the stairs?"

"Carpenter is coming on Monday."

"And what about utilities?"

"Included. So is cable. I've also got WiFi."

"Shit," I mutter. "It's too good to be true."

He chuckles again. "Sometimes something good can be true too, love."

Love. He called me love.

God, I miss Cooke.

"We'll take it," I say suddenly. "How soon can we move in?"

"Well now, you'll need to fill out an application. I've got others interested."

"See?" I say, irritated. "I knew there was a catch."

"No catch." He leans a little closer. "You're my favorite by far, girly. I'm rootin' for ya."

I don't know why, but that makes me laugh. Hard. "Vic," I say after I've calmed down. "We need a place to live. Tayler's boyfriend cheated on her, so she's got to move out. I was living in a basement with a spider the size of my fist." I hold my fist up for reference. "This is the best place we've seen. We need an answer now."

"My goodness, you do remind me of my beloved Mary."

"Your wife?"

"Pitbull. She's the love of my life."

I start to giggle again just as Tayler steps back into the room. "We'll take it."

Oh God. My giggle turns into full-on laughter with tears. I swear I'm about to pee myself. Once I get myself under control, I look him in the eye. "Vic. Please?"

"Tell you what," he says, scratching his scruffy face. "If everything checks out on your applications, it's yours. It'll take me a day or so. Then I've got to paint and clean."

"We'll do that," I say suddenly. I know Tayler only has a couple of days left on her lease.

Tayler nods. "Yeah. We'll paint and clean."

"Interesting." Vic scratches his chin again. "I'll let you know tomorrow. Is that good enough?"

"Yes!" we say at the same time.

We follow Vic down to his home and office. Waiting in his gorgeous kitchen with granite countertops and stainless steel appliances, I stare at Tayler, whispering. "Can you believe this place?"

She shakes her head.

I'm about to say more when I see a dog the size of a small horse run right for me. I quickly push my legs out into a wide stance, anticipating the force of the dog. When she gets to me, though, she stops suddenly, sits down, and wiggles her tail, all the while looking up at me.

"You must be Mary," I say, petting her head. Scratching behind her ears, I add, "You're a good girl, aren't you, love? Such a good girl." Her head moves with my hand, seeking more rubs and scratches. I move down to one knee, the good one. "Oh, you're such a pretty girl, Mary." When she leans up and licks my face, I laugh and hug her. "I see what Vic sees in you, girl. I think I love you too."

"You're in." Vic's voice sounds sort of scratchy. "She's n-never done that before." He clears his throat. "She's a rescue. Abused somethin' terrible. She's scared of everyone." He sniffles. "But not you, spitfire. She loves you. And in my book, dogs read people way better than humans. You're in. I'll have the paint and supplies up there for you tomorrow. First and last month's rent before I give you a key. You can move in tomorrow."

I'm staring at Vic while still petting Mary. Looking down at her again, I say, "Did you hear that, girl? We're going to be neighbors." Mary barks, and I laugh. Standing up, I reach out to shake Vic's hand. "Thanks, Vic."

"My pleasure, spitfire."

I follow Tayler out of the apartment and down the hallway. When we get to the car, Tayler turns to me. Smirking, she says, "Who are you?"

"What do you mean? I'm me."

"You're much more than that."

I'm not sure what she means, but that's okay. "We have a home," I squeak. "Not just any home either. It's the coolest place I've ever seen. I can't wait to decorate."

"Which reminds me. We're going to need help moving. I doubt you and I will be able to move furniture up those stairs, especially with your boot."

"My boot can come off any time. I'm just nervous about it." I roll my eyes because I know I'm being a wimp. "I could call the rugby guys." They owe me, sort of.

"Perfect. I'll also ask Luke if he knows anyone."

"Luke?" I arch my brow. "I thought...." Well, since I haven't been back to work yet, I guess I'm out of the Luke loop.

"We're friends. Nothing more. He's still petrified of commitment. We talk. That's all."

～

As soon as we're buckled into Tayler's car, I pull my phone out of my pocket. *I'm just going to do it.* I send Cooke a text. The first communication from either of us in ten days.

**Me**: Good news. Tayler and I found a new apartment. It's amazing and cheap!

I add a photo of the main living room and send it to him. Even though he hasn't bothered to message me, I feel like I need to try one more time. If he doesn't respond, then I can accept that it's over.

Over before it really began.

## CHAPTER FORTY-TWO

"Thanks, Dan. Can you put the chair right over there?" I point to a spot in the far corner of the living room. We want things out of the way so we can move around. Furniture will be the last thing we'll arrange once everything else is put away.

"This place rocks, Quinn," Dan says, wiping off some sweat from his brow.

"It does," Bull agrees as he passes by holding three boxes, all Tayler's. She's the one with all the stuff. Mine fit in one trip in Tayler's car. When he comes back empty-handed, he's quiet for a second, like he's apprehensive about something. "Sorry to hear about Cooke."

*Sorry? To hear about Cooke?* Did he hear we broke up? No. That's impossible. "What do you mean?"

"His injury."

"His injury?" I squeak. "What injury?"

Bull and Dan look at each other, then back at me. "Yeah. Playing Ireland. It was gnarly."

Oh my God. "W-What? Ireland?"

Bull looks a little perturbed. "I figured you watched it online or something."

Shit. No, I didn't. I look first at Bull, then at Dan, "How bad was he hurt?"

Dan pulls his phone out of his back pocket. I watch him impatiently. I want to yank the phone out of his hand to see what he's doing. "Here's an article."

Holy shit. I take the phone from him and squeeze my eyes shut. I had no idea. I've been so caught up in my own life, feeling sorry for myself, whining and bitching about him not contacting me, that he hurt himself and I had no idea.

"I'm the worst girlfriend."

I scoff. I'm not his girlfriend. A girlfriend would care about her stupid boyfriend more than she does about her fucking scooter. It had to have happened around the time of my accident.

Stepping into the bathroom for some alone time, I sit on the toilet seat and start to read.

---

*England National Rugby's fly-half, Cooke Thompson, suffered a season-ending injury last evening in a match against Ireland. The team representative stated that Thompson would undergo surgery at Royal Orthopaedic Hospital in Brockley Hill later this week.*

---

I stare at the words. Cooke is hurt. I try to swallow, but my throat feels like it's closing. My heart is beating in my chest so hard, I think it might burst. "Cooke," I say to myself. "I've let you down." My stomach drops, and nausea swirls inside. I need to gather myself. I'm going to finish moving; then I can figure this out.

I look at the clock on Dan's phone, then hand it to him. "Thanks." When I do the calculations, I realize it's late evening where Cooke is. I need to talk to him. At the very least, I need to send him a message.

Moving away from the two men, I search for my phone. Running into the bathroom, I shut the door and lock it. Staring down, I wonder if I should FaceChat or text.

Text.

**Me**: I just heard about your injury. Are you okay?

I want to ask him why he didn't tell me, but that seems insensitive. It's not like it's his job to tell me. I was supposed to be watching him play. Heck, I told him I was going to watch his match and that I was going to text Bull. I never did. Why didn't I do that?

I stare down at the phone, willing him to respond. God, I feel sick.

When I hear voices in the living room, I shove the phone into my back pocket and return to the job at hand. If he replies, I'll feel the phone buzz in my pocket. In the meantime, I need to get this done.

I pass Dan in the kitchen, holding a large box. I should be doing more than freaking about Cooke since these guys were the only two we could find to help us on a weekday. I start to reach for a box when Dan asks, "Did you watch the press conference?"

"There was a press conference?"

"Yeah. After the surgery."

"No. But I will after we're done here." I can't watch it right now. It's too much.

Bull steps up to us. "You going to go see him?"

I'm about to say no, but that's not the word that comes out of my mouth. I look at Tayler, who's been listening to our conversation. "Should I?"

She's got concern written all over her face. "So he wasn't ghosting you." It wasn't a question.

"No. I guess not." I thought he was blowing me off, but it was really the other way around. "What if he needed me? Or needs me now?" I should have been there for him like he was there for me.

*God. I'm so fucking selfish!*

"What about school?" asks Tayler.

"I'll text my professors. I'm always there... pretty much. I can make things up when I get back." And if I flunk a class or two, so be it.

I can read Tayler's face so well. She still looks worried. "You'll need a passport."

"Right. I have one from my senior trip to Mexico. It's at home. Aren't they good for ten years?"

"Yep," says Bull.

We wait for him to say more, but he doesn't. A man of very few words. Speaking of.... Pulling out my phone, I peek at the screen. Still nothing from Cooke.

"I can run you home to get your passport tomorrow."

"Thanks, Tay." I swallow thickly. "I'll need to sit down and talk to my parents about all of this anyway." I can't just fly off to another country without their knowledge. "I'd best book my flight." And tell Luke I'm not coming back for another week. He'll be pissed, but this is important."

"Do it. Call the airline. Tell them it's an emergency. See if they can give you a better deal. Buying a ticket this close to you leaving could be expensive."

"Let me check one of the discount travel sites first." Tapping away, I enter the pertinent information. I find a flight that leaves the day after tomorrow at 11:45 a.m. and gets to Heathrow at 9:05 a.m. "It's $2,349."

"Not terrible." Tayler shrugs.

It is sort of terrible, but I've got the money. "I'm doing it. I'll fly back the Friday before Thanksgiving, which will give me three days to make up any work I missed before break."

I know I should talk to Cooke first, but I can't wait to see if he responds to me. I need to do this now; there's something gnawing at me, like I need to get to him. I select my flights, and before I know it, I'm booked round trip for a week in London.

I hope he lets me stay with him. Hell, I hope he's there. What if he flew off to some tropical island to recover? I've never been one to take chances—putting myself out there, risking it all. But I'm doing it now. For Cooke.

# CHAPTER FORTY-THREE

"Ladies and gentlemen, as we start our descent, please make sure your seat backs and tray tables are in their upright position. Make sure your seat belt is securely fastened and all carry-on luggage is stowed underneath the seat in front of you or in the overhead bins. Thank you."

*This is it.*

"Flight attendants, prepare for landing, please."

I'm clutching the arm of my seat and staring out of the window. I can see land moving closer and closer, and all the while my heart is beating faster and faster. I hate takeoff, but landing makes me want to puke. When I feel the bump from the wheels hitting the runway, I release a gust of air from my lungs. I was holding my breath all the way down.

"Ladies and gentlemen, welcome to Heathrow International Airport. Local time is 8:58 a.m., and local weather is partly cloudy with a temperature of fifty-nine degrees Fahrenheit, fifteen degrees Celsius."

It's chilly. I'm glad I'm wearing layers. Slipping on my cardigan sweater, I lean forward in my seat, waiting for my turn to deplane. I'm so ready to get up and walk around. My ass is numb, and I'm starving. Plane food isn't the best. One good thing is the inflight entertainment. I had my own small television embedded in the seat in front of me and was able to watch several new releases and some episodes of some old favorite shows.

In all, the flight was good. I have only one complaint, and it relates to the person sitting in front of me, a person pushed their seat back to recline, which took away a good six inches of space from me. Space I couldn't really afford to lose. It's rude. I wish they didn't even have that feature. So, if you're listening out there, please think of those behind you the next time you decide to recline. Please be kind, don't recline. Catchy, right?

When it's my turn to exit, I grab my small carry-on and make my way to baggage claim. I brought a smallish suitcase, but I must have packed a lot of heavy things, because it weighed almost fifty pounds. If I buy any souvenirs, it'll be over the limit on the way back. I'll have to figure that out later. Right now, I just want to get my bag and hop into a taxi. I've got Cooke's address memorized, sort of like Dory had the dentist's office memorized in *Finding Nemo*. "35 Haliburton Road, Twickenham, TW1 1NZ. 35 Haliburton Road, Twickenham, TW1 1NZ." See? Memorized.

Outside, I find a long row of taxis, but they aren't like the yellow ones you see in the US. No, these are mostly black, and they look old, like from the 1940s, even though they're new. I guess you could call them retro.

When I get into the line of people waiting for a taxi, I bite my lip and run my tongue over my teeth. I feel gross. I should have stopped in the restroom to brush my teeth and clean up a little bit. I feel airplane cooties all over me. But there's no time.

Sliding into the taxi when it's my turn, I bite my lip again, worrying about how far away Cooke lives and how much this is going to cost. "35 Haliburton Road, Twickenham," I say to the driver. I attempt to sound assured, like I know where I'm going. I'm not sure I'm convincing, but only time will tell.

As the car moves along, I stare out the window. The area

around the airport is all hustle and bustle, but it doesn't take long until we're driving through a more residential area. It's almost provincial, with quaint brick homes and a few with thatched roofs. I love it.

In less than thirty minutes, the taxi has stopped in front of a two-story brick home. "There you are, miss."

I blink at the driver, then back at the house. This isn't what I expected. I assumed he'd live in some sleek, modern building with a doorman or something. He's famous here, yet he lives in a somewhat modest home. Granted, it's a *large* modest home.

"That'll be twenty-six quid, miss."

I turn to the driver. "Oh, right." I pull out my wallet and count out thirty British pounds. Luckily, Tayler reminded me to get some currency from the bank before I left Iowa. Handing the money over the seat, I open the door and slide out as the driver jumps out to retrieve my suitcase from the trunk. "Thank you," I say with a smile.

"Good day, miss," he says with a little bow.

I smile, then turn to face the house. I'm not sure what to do now. I was so frantic to get packed, email my professors, get currency, find my passport, and explain to my parents about my impromptu trip without telling them too much that I didn't consider what'd I do once I got here. I mean, what if he hates me? What if he takes one look at me and slams the door in my face? Or hell, what if he's not here? He could be anywhere, and since he never replied to my text, who knows what his reaction's going to be?

"Only one way to find out."

Pushing my shoulders back, I grab my wheeled suitcase, hitch my other bag over my shoulder, and march toward the door. "Here I go," I murmur.

Passing through an adorable metal gate, I step onto a brick walkway right up to the door. I scoff. "You'd think he'd have security."

Then it hits me. What if this isn't even his house? What if he just gave me some bogus address because he really did think I was a stalker?

I roll my eyes. Of course he didn't give me a bogus address. I sent him the Iowa State rugby tee and he got it. "Duh."

Talking to myself is not wise at this juncture. I look sort of crazy as it is, with my hair like a rat's nest on top of my head and wrinkled clothes as a bonus. "Why didn't I tell him I was coming?" I groan.

*Because you were afraid he was going to tell you not to come.* Yeah, that's why.

"Just do it," I say determinedly.

So I do. I step up to the door, raise my hand, and grasp the brass knocker tapping it against the door three times—tap, tap, tap. I let my arm rest at my side and wait. Leaning in, I attempt to listen for footsteps, anything. I hear nothing, so I repeat the knock—tap, tap, tap. When I hear nothing again, I'm tempted to bend down and push the mail slot open to yell through it. Something like "Hello? Does Cooke Thompson live here?" But then I decide against it.

There are two glass panes on either side of the knocker, but they aren't clear. They're more like stained glass with lilies or irises or something.

I chew on my lip, trying to decide what I should do next. I could walk down the road to see if I could catch another taxi, but where would I go? I could try texting Cooke or maybe try to FaceChat him. But first, I'll try knocking one more time.

I raise my hand and blink because I see a doorbell on the right side of the door, hiding in some ivy. Instead of knocking, I press on the button and hear a pretty chiming sound coming from inside the house. I do what I did before, leaning in until my ear is next to the door and listening for movement. I smile because this time, I hear something, and that something is getting louder the closer it gets to the door. I still don't know if Cooke lives here, but it's something.

As the door begins to open, I open my mouth, prepared to explain who I'm looking for, when I see him. Cooke Thompson. The first thing I see is the crutch at his side and the long cast that runs from his foot up to his knee. That's not the part that makes me pause, though. It's the other thing on top of the cast. It reminds me of a metal armature used in sculptures. An armature is an internal support, only this one is on the outside. I want to bend down and look more closely at it, because from here, it looks as though there are thin metal rods going into his leg. Into. His. Leg.

I quickly let my eyes move up his body. He's wearing shorts and a loose tee that appears to have some stains on the front. When I finally see his face, I'm speechless. He's got an almost full, scruffy beard, but that's not terrible. It's the rest of him that looks, well, like utter shit. Worse than me after flying for sixteen hours.

"Cooke?" I ask softly.

"Quinn?" His voice sounds hoarse. "You're here?"

"I am. I'm sorry I didn't know about your injury, I—"

I don't get to finish my sentence because he's got me wrapped up in his arms. I hear the clatter of something metal hitting the ground and realize it's his crutch. He's holding me so tightly I can barely breathe. That's okay. I don't need air right now. Not only that, I'm positive he's crying.

"Love," he croaks out.

Bringing my arms up and around his neck, I pull him closer. "I'm so sorry, Cooke. I would've been here sooner."

"No. It's okay. I should've told you. I-I just wasn't ready."

"My poor baby," I whisper softly, then kiss his cheek that's covered with fuzzy hair. I'm not sure it's the right thing to say, but it's what my mom always said when we were hurt. It always comforted me. And from the sob that just came out of him, I'd say he needs to hear it too.

We stand in his doorway, holding each other for several minutes. When he pulls back, he's still got his hands on my arms. He's smiling. No, he's beaming. "I can't bloody believe you're here, love."

"Me neither."

We stare at one another a little longer when it finally hits him. "My manners. Come in, come in."

I turn to grab my suitcase, but he hops, one footed, over to it to pull it inside.

"No, you're injured."

"I've got it. But if you'd grab my stick, love."

"I assume you mean your crutch. I'm going to have to get used to the language gap."

"Aye."

I scurry into the foyer of his house and wait for him to roll the large suitcase inside. Once he's got it over the threshold, I take it from there. "Where should I park this?" I point to the luggage.

"My bedroom." He gestures to the left. "Last door on the left."

Turning around, I grab my suitcase and let my jaw drop. "Is that a pool?" It is. It's a freaking indoor pool.

"Aye."

"Not going to lie, Cooke. From the outside, this place looks like an ordinary house." But inside, it's all modern and streamlined, just like I pictured his home to look like.

"A hidden gem. It's why I chose this one."

"Wow." I turn and look right at the kitchen. It's white with marble countertops and extra-fancy appliances. It's open to a very large living room with an entire wall of windows. That's how I saw the pool.

"Follow me. I'll show you to the bedroom."

So I do, trailing behind him as he moves quickly on his crutch.

"There are two full baths down here." He points to one in the hallway. "That's a guest bath."

When he pushes a door open at the end of the hallway, I gasp. "You have got to be kidding me."

"Swanky, yeah?"

"It is." There's a gigantic bed at the far end of the room. It's got a canopy on top with soft white fabrics draping from the top down. It looks like it would be heaven to sleep beneath all that fluff. He's got tables on either side of the bed, and two large dressers flank the bed on either side of the room.

"Here is the master bath."

My eye follows the direction he's pointing. Stepping into the bathroom, I want to choke. It's massive, with a tub big enough for two people and a shower big enough for four. "This is amazing, Cooke."

His reply is soft, almost shy. "I'm glad you like it."

He clears his throat and continues the tour. "There's a master closet through that door there." He points to the far end of the bathroom. "Be warned. I've got a bit of laundry backed up. I usually just toss it there."

Since I'm a snoop, I step closer to the door and open it. "Shut. Up!" I shout. "This is bigger than my bedroom." And he's right. Clothes are strewn about on the floor and hanging from hooks.

"So, you like it?"

I scoff. "What's not to like, Cooke? This place is amazing."

"There's a study next door to this bedroom, plus three more bedrooms up top and another bath as well."

"It's a big house."

"Aye." He takes my hand now that I'm free of luggage. "Let me show you the back garden. It's where I spend most of my time on nice days like this one."

Cloudy and cool is a nice day? I guess it is. Especially now that I'm here with him. I can't remember a better day than today.

Well, maybe the one when he showed up at the Hub. That day was better than nice.

I follow him through the living room and out the sliding glass door onto a brick patio that overlooks a decent-size yard and… what's that? A freaking river? "You've got a river." And there's a small yellow paddle boat pulled up into the yard. "Do you take your boat out?"

"The dinghy, aye. Or I did before." He points to his leg.

I look down at the cast and the metal contraption that's swirling around his leg, then back up at him. "What happened to it?"

"Broken fibula and tibia."

"Are those pins…?"

"It's called an external fixator. The rods are inside, holding my bones in place so they'll heal."

I wince but try not to let him see because he looks rather pale now. "It must hurt. Let's sit you down." I point to one of the cushioned lounge chairs he's got on his patio.

"I think I will rest. I'm a bit winded from the shock of seeing you." He lowers himself into his chair and raises the leg with the brace. I search for something to put underneath it. Finding a small pillow on the ground, I set it beneath his knee, right above the metal contraption. "Thank you, Quinn," he says laying his head back and sighing. "This last couple of weeks has been brutal."

"I bet." I push his hair away from his face and run my palm over his cheek. "I like the beard."

"You do?" he asks, one eye open and peering up at me.

"I do. It's sexy."

"Sexy, eh?"

"Yep," I say, popping the *p*.

"You'd better kiss me, then. If I'm so sexy."

"Not before I brush my teeth." And shower. "Mind if I go clean up? Then I'll make you something to eat."

"Aye. I'll stay put." He sounds drowsy. I bet my arrival and house tour is the most he's done since his injury.

"Be right back." I race back into the house, down the hallway, and back into his bedroom. Pulling my suitcase over to an out-of-the-way spot, I unzip it and grab my toiletry bag and a change of clothes. Searching the bathroom cupboards, I locate a towel and a cloth. Then I have the daunting task of figuring out how to use his fancy-ass shower.

When I think I've got one showerhead working with warm water, I strip down and step in. I moan at the feel of the water sluicing down my body, removing the airplane grime. I stand still, just relishing the water splattering over my tired muscles, relaxing me. I scrub my body and face, then wash and condition my hair until I'm clean. Using a plush towel, I dry myself, brush my teeth twice, and dress in comfy leggings and an oversized sweatshirt. I feel renewed. Folding up my dirty things, I lay them in my suitcase and hang the towel over a hook on the bathroom door.

When I head back outside, Cooke is snoring. "Poor baby," I whisper as I touch his hair again. I make my way back into the house and start to scrounge through his cupboards and fridge. There's not much to work with. He's got eggs and bread, at least, so I scramble eggs and make toast. I'll need to go to the store for him, get him all stocked up.

Carrying out his plate with a fork and a cloth napkin I found in one of the drawers, I nudge Cooke's shoulder.

"What?" he snaps.

Oh, wow. Cranky. "I made you food, Cooke."

I watch him settle back into his chair and fall back to sleep. No doubt he's tired from the pain. It's hard to sleep when you hurt.

I set his plate on the large outdoor dining table, then retrieve mine from the kitchen. Sitting on the lounge chair next to him, I eat my breakfast while he snores. I feel like I should wake him up so he can eat, but since I don't know for sure, I stare at him some more. "Screw it." I lean over and shake his shoulder.

"What the feck?" he says, opening his eyes. When they first see me, they pinch together in a scowl. Then, like a light bulb switching on, he smiles. "Love."

"You're grouchy when someone tries to wake you up."

"I know. My apologies. I'm an ass when I don't get enough sleep."

"You weren't when you were in Ames."

"Blame it on my pain capsules. My sleep is out of sorts."

"I can see that." I look at his leg, then back at his face. "I made you eggs and toast, but it's probably cold now. Let me warm it up."

"No, it's fine. I need to eat something."

Picking up the plate, I set it on his stomach. "I'll reheat it."

"No." He takes a bite and smirks. "Delish."

"Liar." I giggle. "I need to get some groceries for you. Your cupboards are bare."

"I get them delivered. I haven't placed an order in a while. I can do that later."

"Oh. Okay." That sounds like a nice service. "I should do that. It'd keep me from impulsively buying goodies like ice cream and cookies now that I have a little extra money." I laugh again. "I could lose a ton of—"

"No, Quinn." He's stopped chewing. "You're perfect just as you are."

<hr>

# CHAPTER FORTY-FOUR

I've been at Cooke's for two days. So far, it's a romance-free zone. In that time, I learned how to order groceries, cleaned both his downstairs bathrooms, changed his sheets, cooked five meals, and did his laundry. All while Cooke slept or lounged outside on his patio. I take that back—he left for two hours yesterday after a black car picked him up. He waved at the door, saying, "Off to physio, love."

I waved and smiled. Then, as soon as the door shut, my smile fell. I'm starting to feel a little sorry for myself. All I've done is housework. Heck, I haven't even slept in the bed with him because I'm so worried I'll bump into his metal exoskeleton and hurt him. The thing is... where is his family? I know he has a mom and a sister. Where are they? I sure haven't heard from them. I've no clue if he's got a father in his life. He doesn't mention him. And what about his teammates? They haven't stopped by. Hell, no one has even called him. I can't figure it out.

Then there's the fact that Cooke barely notices me. He literally sleeps all day long. I'm sure it has everything to do with those pain meds. I know they can make a person drowsy.

I'm not sure what I expected. I knew I'd be here to help him, but please. I also thought there'd be some cuddles, kisses, and cozy time in front of the telly. Heck, he refuses to watch TV. He says it gives him a headache. Gah! Nope. There's nothing romantic about flying in to be with Cooke during this trying time.

Okay, maybe I'm being unfair. It hasn't been completely unromantic. We've shared a few kisses here and there, but it's weird. I don't feel like a girlfriend right now. I'm more like a nursemaid. Yes, I wanted to make sure he was okay, and if that meant I'd be cooking and cleaning, then so be it. But now that I'm on the third day of my six-day stay, I'm getting a little irritable. I mean, I'm in London, for crying out loud. A place I've never been before and may never see again. I spent thousands on this trip, and all I've seen is the inside of Cooke's house.

Mind you, it's a very nice house.

I need to stop complaining. I can make this work. It's not like there's nothing else to do here. I could take a swim. Except I didn't bring my suit because I didn't think he'd have one in his house. I could throw on my shorts and a tee and swim, but I'm half afraid to ask him if it's okay. His mood, well, it isn't great. That first morning when he was a bit snappy was just a prelude to every morning here at Chez Cooke. I could attribute that to the pain pills as well, though. I remember when my middle brother broke his leg in high school. They put him on some pretty potent pain meds, and he got all squirrely and cranky. He was high and happy one minute, surly and bitchy the next. I assume that's what's happening with Cooke. At least I hope that's all it is.

Sighing, I dish out a bowl of chili I made from scratch. Dad's recipe. I carry the bowl, spoon, and some crackers out to the patio. He's asleep again.

"Cooke?" I say close to his ear.

I must startle him, because before I know it, his arms are flailing around, hitting the bowl of hot chili. My first instinct is to keep it from burning him, so I fumble with it until it's upturned and on top of my shirt. "Oh, fuck." I almost scream but do my best to hold it inside.

"Bloody hell, Quinn. Why'd you wake me?"

*Because it's lunchtime.* But I don't say it. I can't due to the fact that my lip is quivering. I concentrate on making it stop. I quickly turn away from him and release the bowl. It falls to the ground, breaking apart into a million pieces and splattering chili everywhere.

"Jesus, you just dropped the bowl! What's wrong with you?"

*He's only being an asshole because he's hurting. It's not him.*

I'm chanting that to myself, but it's not working. I slowly turn around to face him, the tears already falling. Without a word, I lift my chili-soaked shirt so he can see my red skin. "I-It was burning me."

"Love?" Cooke's voice sounds panicked. "You're burned."

In an attempt to keep myself from completely losing it, I drop the shirt. "I'm fine. I'll... I'll take care of it." I saw a first aid kit when I was cleaning the other day, so I turn and race into the house and down the hall to the master bathroom. When I spot the kit, I search it for any kind of burn relief. Luckily, there's a small packet of aloe. Lifting my shirt, I end up with chili on my face and hair, but it can't be helped. Tearing open the package, I squirt the cool gel onto my chest and stomach and rub it gingerly. It hurts, but I don't think I'll die, and the aloe helps.

"Quinn?" Cooke says as he appears at the bathroom door. He blinks, then looks at the first aid kit. "How did you know where the aid box was, love?"

"I saw it when I cleaned the bathroom."

"You cleaned the bathroom?" he asks, scanning the room.

"Both bathrooms on this level. I also changed the sheets, did your laundry, and started on the kitchen."

"Darling." He chuckles. "That was unnecessary. I have a cleaner. She comes in every Wednesday."

That's tomorrow. "Oh." God, I feel stupid.

He's laughing harder now, and it makes me want to punch him in the nuts. "That's all I've done since I got here, Cooke. You didn't notice?"

How could he? He's either been out on the patio or in bed. His bed with fresh, clean sheets. Sheets that I hung out on the line, right next to his lounge chair, so they smell extra nice.

He suddenly stops laughing. "I'm sorry, no."

Yeah, how could he know?

I'm not sure what to say right now. I'd like to tell him off, but he's hurt, and it's not like he asked me to come. Or to clean. I did that all on my own. So I need to let it go.

Taking air into my lungs slowly, I release it just as gradually. I need to calm myself before I say something I'll regret and don't mean. I think I just need to get out of the house for a bit. "I'm going to go out for a while. I'd like to see some of London before I go home. Do you think you'll be okay here by yourself?"

He blinks as he stares at me. "Christ," he mutters. "I'm a fucking git."

"No you're not. You're hurt. You need to rest and recuperate."

"I've been a terrible host, Quinn."

"You didn't invite me. I just showed up. Don't feel badly because you aren't able to show me the sights. I'm more than capable of figuring things out on my own. I flew here by myself. I can see London by myself." I grab my chili-soaked shirt. If I throw it in the laundry now, I might be able to save it. "Will you be okay for a while on your own?"

"Sure. Of course." He's still just looking at me like he can't figure out what he should do.

# CHAPTER FORTY-FIVE

London is as amazing as I imagined it would be. And it wasn't hard to get to the heart of it from Twickenham. The bus practically goes from Cooke's street all the way to the center of the city. I, however, hop off the bus at Hyde Park. There are some cute shops all around the park, as well as pretty gardens, and since it was my first outing, I decide to take in the sights. I buy some fish and chips from a street vendor and sit on a park bench, watching and listening to people. There are lots of English accents, but there are others too. Sitting in the park is like experiencing a mini slice of the world.

After my lunch, I continue walking through the neighborhoods around the park. I stop and pick up some small souvenirs for myself and my friends and am happily surprised to find one boutique that carries the most enviable collection of nail varnish —or nail polish as I know it—I've ever seen. Since I neglected to pack any, I decide to buy red, white, blue, and silver along with remover, clippers, a nail file, and clear coat. I've already decided what I'll do with the polish, and it has everything to do with England and Cooke Thompson.

I notice several tour companies that use double-decker buses.

I'm tempted to take one of those tours, but I feel like I need to get back to Cooke. Now that I know how to get here, I can do that tomorrow. Searching for a bus stop, I find one only a block away and wait for my bus to take me back to Cooke.

When I step into the house, it's dark and quiet. Did he leave? I hope he didn't get upset and leave, or worse, fall and injure himself.

"Cooke?" I set my purse on top of the kitchen island and decide to check the bedroom first. "Not here," I whisper to myself. He must be on the patio.

As quietly as I can, I push open the screen door and step onto the patio. "Cooke?" I say just loud enough.

"Here, love."

Moving around the corner, I stop in my tracks at the sight before me. Cooke is sitting at his patio table, but it doesn't look like it did before. Now it's covered in a white cloth with candles glowing in the center. It's set with pretty dishes and silverware.

"What's this?" I ask, stepping closer.

"It's my way of saying thank you and I'm sorry all at once."

Our eyes meet. "You don't need to do either thing."

"Quinn." When I reach him, he wraps his arms around my waist and says, "I've been angry and an arsehole to my friends and family since my injury. Hell, I ran off my mum and sister after two days. They said they couldn't stand the sight of me after I treated them poorly." Cooke chuckles. I don't. "I'm a broody, selfish bastard since I was released from the hospital— long before you surprised me, love. My mates are staying far away from me as well. And I don't blame any of them. But then you knocked on my door, and for some reason, I felt better. At ease. So much so, I slept for the first time in a week."

"Cooke." I run my fingers through his hair. "I'm glad."

"So, that's about all I've done since you stepped foot in my door, and I'm sorry. It's your first time abroad, and all you've done is work those pretty fingers to the bone." Taking one of my hands, he brings it to his mouth and kisses it.

"I haven't. I came to do what I could to help."

"I don't want my girlfriend to fly across the ocean to clean my toilet, love. I want you to sit with me. Cuddle. Take a hired car and sightsee. We'll do that tomorrow. I've already arranged it. My sister is coming along to do things I can't with this blasted brace."

"Cooke, no. I'm fine going alone. I figured out—"

"No." His tone sounds cranky again. I pull away slightly.

"Yes," I say in a similar tone. "The bus takes me right into the center—"

"Please?" Crap. He's got puppy dog eyes. "Allow me and Saffron to escort you."

"Your sister's name is Saffron?"

"Aye. We call her Saffie, though."

"Okay. If you really want to do that. I don't want you to do anything to jeopardize your leg, though. Promise?"

"Promise. Now." He claps his hands together and turns to face the table. "Are you hungry?"

"Yes. I'm extremely peckish."

He smiles at my use of his terminology. "Well, then," he says, lifting a domed silver lid that sits in the center of the table, "dinner is served." His smile lights up his face. "Shepherd's pie. One of my favorite traditional English meals."

I lean forward and peek at a square casserole dish. The top of the contents looks white and fluffy. "What is it?"

"The top is mashed potatoes."

"Yum," I hum with approval.

"Beneath that is layered, shredded meat with onion and other veg." He looks up at me expectantly. "Good?"

"It sounds wonderful, Cooke. Did you make it?"

"I called the pub up the road. They delivered."

Sitting next to him, I point to the silver lid. "Is that silver from the pub?"

"It was my gran's. I wanted to make it look romantic."

I scoot closer to him. Leaning in, I kiss him on the cheek. "Thank you so much, Cooke. It's very romantic." I swear he blushes, but I can't be sure since the sun is setting.

Cooke places a piece of the shepherd's pie on my plate, and I wait for him to serve himself. When I know he's ready, I lift my fork and take my first bite. Closing my eyes, I moan. "Mm, good."

Cooke's staring at me. When he sees I'm looking back at him, he smiles brightly. "I love the sexy noises, love. You mean it? You like it?"

"I love it. Thank you for giving me a taste of one of your favorite things." There's still so much I don't know about Cooke Thompson.

"Before you leave, we're going to know a lot more about each other, Quinn. I promise you that."

## CHAPTER FORTY-SIX

Sitting in my seat on the plane, I'm doing my best to calm down. I've started to pick away at my nail polish, a nervous habit. The Union Jack design of the British flag I painted on my thumbnail is nearly gone on my right hand. I've been beyond emotional since I woke up this morning. I was dreading the ride to the airport with Cooke because, honestly, I don't want to leave. I want to stay. But I can't. I've got responsibilities at home that include school, my new apartment with Tayler, and my job. And it's not like Cooke asked me to stay. He didn't. Why would he? We're not anywhere near ready for something as serious as me moving to London. It still hurts, though. It feels like my heart is cracking and crumbling, the pieces falling and landing in my stomach. It's why the thought of eating makes me physically ill. Hell, I may never eat again.

I sniffle thinking about this last week. Sure, at first it wasn't great, but after Cooke woke up—literally and figuratively—he became the perfect host. He did as promised, inviting his sister, Saffie, along on our tour of London. I was nervous to meet her, but it only took a minute to see that she was funny, sweet, and kind. Plus, she didn't take any shit from her brother. Saffie spent much of our tour telling me what a twat he was after the surgery. "He ran us all off, the git."

She had me laughing the entire time with stories about Cooke as a boy. Then, while Cooke waited in the car, Saffie and I saw some of London's famous landmarks. I declined the offer to go to Madame Tussauds wax museum, because wax people aren't really my thing. We did visit Sherlock Holmes's house, which was cool. I took lots of pictures for my dad. He's always loved Sherlock Holmes mysteries, so he'll get a kick out of seeing the pictures. There wasn't time to visit the National Gallery because, according to Saffie, you need a week for that. So when I come back again someday, I'll plan to do just that.

Cooke didn't sit in the car the entire time, though. He had the driver put his wheelchair in the back so he could join us for some of the excursions. One of the things all three of us did was ride on the London Eye. That's the giant Ferris wheel in the center of the city. I'm not great with heights or Ferris wheels, but this was a slow ride in a very large, enclosed capsule, so it wasn't too bad. London was breathtaking from the top. I hope to do that again someday, but at night. I bet London at night would be a sight to behold.

Cooke wanted to take us to a fancy restaurant for lunch, but I wasn't dressed for that, so he took us to The Queen's Head pub located in Piccadilly Circus. Let me tell you, it was amazing. I wasn't sure which British fare to try, so Cooke ordered a selection so I could have a taste. It was all so good, I'm not sure I could pick a favorite. Well, okay, I think I could. It was the asparagus, broccoli, broad bean, and goat's cheese pie. It may not sound good, but believe me, it was delish. Sticky date pudding with toffee sauce was damn good too.

After our outing, Saffie went home. I was bummed when she left, as it reminded me that my time in London was running out. Not to mention I was home, alone, with Cooke. And even though he was exhausted, he stayed up long enough for us to cuddle on his bed and watch the telly. I can't even remember what we watched because we spent most of the time kissing. Sweet, soft kisses.

*Sigh.*

The day after that, we had a lazy day at home together. He had a physio appointment that he rescheduled to the day after I left. I don't think the team doctor was happy with him, but Cooke didn't seem to care.

"I'm fine here if you need to go," I'd said after I overheard his raised voice on the phone.

"There's nothing they can do with me at this stage. I don't know why they make me go. All they do is massage my upper leg. I lift it up and down until they tell me I can leave." He sighed. "That can wait."

That day, we lazed about on his patio. I took a swim wearing one of his mom's old swimsuits. Thankfully, it was a modest one-piece in all black. It was too tight, but I wasn't about to say a word about that. While I swam, Cooke sat in a chair next to the pool and watched. He talked too, telling me more about his mom and even his dad.

"He buggered off when I was eight and Saff was six. The bastard," he'd said.

"Where is he now?" I asked, floating on my back.

Cooke's eyes were trained on my chest as he responded. "He lives in Scotland with his other family."

I stopped floating and moved to the edge of the pool nearest Cooke. "I'm sorry, Cooke."

"If you're truly sorry, you should slip out of that skimpy little suit and swim."

I blushed. Oh my goodness. Even in cool water, I knew my face and chest must have been magenta.

I swallowed hard, then laughed. "Cooke...."

"Please?" he asked with those eyes again.

"Really? You really want me to swim"—I lowered my voice to finish—"nude?"

"I do. I really, really bloody do."

We stared at one another for a good minute. It was a tense minute. His eyes were hooded and broody all at once.

"Fine," I whispered. Slipping off the shoulder straps, I let them fall to my upper arm. I then wiggled and pushed down at the same time until it was sliding down my legs and off. Reaching down, I picked up his mom's suit and tossed it out of the pool at his feet. "Happy?" I said snarkily.

"Very." Scooting his chair closer to the edge, he leaned forward. "Now back float, please, love."

I snort, then laugh. "You're a pervert."

"Aye."

I must be a pervert too, because I did it, and guess what? I liked it. Cooke then slipped off his pants. I held my breath as he used his palm to slowly stroke himself up and down. I had to stop swimming just to watch him.

"You should step out of the pool and help me with this." He looks down at his hard dick.

Without hesitation, I stepped slowly to the ladder that led out of the water and walked, completely naked, to his side. Grabbing the towel I brought from the bathroom, I set it on the ground and knelt next to him. His eyes never left mine. It was intense and erotic. Then, when I pushed up onto my knees, leaned over, and kissed him *there*, Cooke nearly slid off his chair.

"Is that okay?" I asked, unsure.

"Bloody hell," he hissed. "Yes."

"More?" My words were gone. One was all I could muster.

"Please." Obviously Cooke was in the same predicament.

Nervous, I leaned over him again and kissed the tip once more. Then I swiped the head with my tongue. Cooke moaned and leaned back in his chair. I pushed his hand away so I could use my own. Stroking him up and down, I couldn't believe how warm and smooth he was. There were veins here and there that all led to the head. I licked him starting at the base and working my way up. I knew I was getting somewhere, because Cooke said all sorts of dirty things to me. Dirty things I'll never forget.

"Fucking hell, love. Yes. Lick my cock."

When I placed my mouth over the head and sucked, he nearly came unglued. "Suck me. Suck all of me. Fecking swallow my cock, Quinn."

He had me so frenzied, I did what he said, choking several times. I didn't care because the man was saying my name right along with all that filth. I loved it. Having my mouth on Cooke's cock was a pleasure for both of us.

I did it several more times while I was there, each time Cooke telling me I was a "fecking natural." It makes me blush and giggle at the same time whenever I think about it. And feel a little proud, to be honest. Mind you, I'm not sure I'd like to do that with just anyone. I think it's best if you love the person, but that's just me. No judgment here. To each his own and all that.

Besides the blow jobs, we also watched my first porno together while lying on his bed, and let me just say office porn is not terrible. Well, okay, it is terrible, but in a good way.

It's official. I'm a sex fiend.

Last night, my final night in London, Cooke made me dinner —omelets and toast. It was perfect. I was glad we chose to stay in, as I didn't want to share him with anyone. Well, that was until half of his rugby team showed up at the door at ten at night, all of them completely plastered. I guess they were celebrating a win against their biggest rival, Wales. I'm not sure why Cooke didn't want to watch it on the TV, but he didn't. Hell, I didn't even know there was a match.

Anyway, that doesn't matter. What does matter is I got to meet his teammates. Ian remembered me from our first Face-Chat. He told me once again that I had great baps. I now know baps are breasts, but I wanted to die of embarrassment last night, because when he said it, I just said, "Thanks," since I had no idea what he meant. It had all of them laughing hysterically. The arseholes. At least he said they were nice.

As for some of the other guys, they kept their opinions about my baps and everything else about me to themselves. I did catch one guy giving me the stink eye and a couple of the others checking me out. I didn't like it, and from the look on Cooke's face, he didn't much like it either. I think that's why he told them all to "Go on, lads. Leave me with my woman."

"Aye," said Ian. Clapping his hands together to get the drunken group's attention, he led them out the door to the two SUVs waiting at the curb.

"At least they aren't driving," I said as I shut the door to the last of them.

Before I knew what was happening, Cooke had my back up against the door, my arms over my head, and his tongue down my throat. Of course I kissed him right back. Why wouldn't I?

"Those bloody twats," he said as he kissed me right below my ear. "Looking at you like you aren't mine." His hands were magic. When he pulled at my nipples, I felt it in my core. Then when his hand slid down into my leggings, seeking my clit, I moaned and nipped at his neck.

"Cooke," I whined.

"I've got you, love." And he did. He used his fingers to bring me to orgasm. After I came down from that high, I reached down to touch him, but he stopped me. "No. I just wanted to make you feel good."

Still trying to get my hands on him, I whispered, "I do. Let's feel good together."

Taking my hand in his, Cooke led me to his bedroom. "Lie with me. Let me hold you while we sleep. Tomorrow is coming too soon."

Well damn. I knew sex was out of the question, since he couldn't do anything that would jeopardize his leg, but I thought at least we could do something more. I understood, though. I was just happy to be with him for one more night.

So, when I woke up the next morning, Cooke was already up, making breakfast. Alone in his bed, I started to sob, but I gathered myself as I showered and packed up my things. I rolled my suitcase out to the living room and was overcome with sadness until I saw Cooke had his dining table set for breakfast. He even had fresh flowers in the middle of the table.

"Breakfast, miss?" He bowed next to my chair, then pulled it out so I could sit.

"Th-Thank you, Cooke." I sniffled as I sipped my juice. I pretended to nibble on the eggs and toast, because my stomach was in knots.

Cooke moved closer to me, taking one of my hands in his. "Now," he said all businesslike, "make sure you text me as soon as you land in the States, and again when you land in Iowa, and again when you get back to Ames."

"I will."

"I'll FaceChat with you in a couple of days as well."

"All right."

"And, Quinn?"

My head was down, staring at our hands. When he said my name, I looked up at him. He was leaning in, close enough to kiss. "Yeah?"

"I love you."

Oh shit. That did it. I immediately starting bawling, and it wasn't pretty at all. Ugly criers, you can relax. I win.

I jumped up from my chair and wrapped my arms around his neck, pulling him as close as he could get to me with his contraption. "I l-love you too, Cooke. So much."

He wrapped his arms around me and held me just like that for a long, long time. At least until the waterworks were done. Then the kissing started. So many lovely kisses. The man has the most amazing lips. They're soft yet firm, and they know what they're doing.

When it was time to leave for the airport, the black car appeared once again. Cooke rode along with me in the back seat, where we held hands and looked at one another almost the whole way. At the airport terminal, the driver parked the car, and I felt like I was going to be sick. Literally sick. I swallowed down the bile and wrapped my arms around him. "I'm g-going to miss you so much."

Placing his hands on my cheeks, he said, "I miss you already, love." Then he leaned in for another kiss. The final kiss.

I checked my bag and made my way through security. It took twice as long as it did in Des Moines. Not surprising, since Heathrow is massive. When I got to the gate, I heard my name over the loudspeaker. They were calling me up to the counter. Taking my carry-on with me, I waited in line. When it was my turn, I said, "I'm Quinn Maxwell."

"Hello, Miss Maxwell. May I see your ticket and passport, please?" the woman asked.

When I placed both on the counter, she looked at them and said, "Thank you."

I was starting to worry that I'd done something wrong. I watched her type on her computer for a minute, and then she printed something out. "There you go, miss." She slid a new ticket toward me. "You've been upgraded," she chirped happily.

"Upgraded?"

"First class."

"First class?"

"Yes, miss."

"Why?"

"Your name was flagged. It said you'd been upgraded."

She doesn't need to explain. I know what happened. One Mr. Cooke Thompson pulled some strings.

**Me:** Did you upgrade me?

**Cooke**: Aye. Only the best for my girl.

**Me**: **eye roll** Stop buying me things. With that said, thank you.

**Cooke**: You're welcome.

**Me**: I love you. I miss you.

**Cooke:** I love you too. I miss you more.

I slept most of the way home in the most comfortable seat in the world. The food was good too. But I'd have given it all up to have Cooke by my side. No contest.

# CHAPTER FORTY-SEVEN

"So, how was it?" Tayler asks on the car ride back to Ames. She was nice enough to pick me up at the airport.

"Amazing." I sigh. "Perfect. He told me he loved me."

"Shut the front door!" she shouts so loud it makes my ears ring. "Did you say it back?"

"I did. I do love him."

With her eyes back on the road, she smirks and says, "What's not to love?"

I snort. "He's not perfect."

Tayler slowly moves her head until she's staring me in the eye. "Oh. My. God."

"What? And can you keep your eyes on the road, please?"

"This one is real."

"What's real?"

"Cooke. He's the real deal."

"Yeah. He's real." *What the heck is she going on about?* I watch out the window as Tayler slows the car enough to take an exit off the interstate that isn't ours. "What're you doing?"

She pulls the car onto the shoulder of the road. Turning to me, she says, "I needed to pull over for this." Then she reaches out and hugs me.

I should warn her about airplane cooties, but instead I ask, "Did you miss me that much?"

Pulling away from the hug, she smiles. "You haven't put Cooke on a pedestal. You said it yourself, he's not perfect."

"He's *not* perfect, but he's perfect for me."

"But every other guy you've ever lusted after was *perfect*." She says it in kind of a snooty way. I don't appreciate that. "Nothing was ever wrong with them. Take Bryant." She snorts. "You thought he shit sunshine."

"Gross." I laugh. "I did not."

"Yes you did. But this guy... the hottest man to ever walk the planet, not to mention he's a professional athlete, loaded, I assume, and British. *That* guy isn't perfect?"

"No. He's sort of a slob, and he's super cranky in the morning, and—"

"See?" she practically squeaks. "This is fucking awesome." Putting the car back into Drive, she looks back to make sure no one is behind us and pulls out onto the road.

"You're crazy."

"*You're* crazy." She laughs. "By the way, Vic has been asking about you every day. It's getting on my nerves, so you'd better stop in and tell him you're back."

"Aw, that's nice."

"He loves you for some reason. Hell, he can't even remember my name."

"He calls me spitfire."

"He called you Quinn to me."

For some reason, that makes my heart feel all warm and fuzzy. "Maybe I'll take Mary for a walk or something."

"You should. Find out the story about her, would you? All Vic said was she was abused. I want to know if the fuckers who abused her were punished."

"I'll try."

"Good."

I fall asleep for the rest of the ride home. Tayler wakes me up as soon as we're in the parking lot, so I decide I'd better send Cooke a text letting him know I'm home.

**Cooke**: I'm glad you're home safe & sound, love. Miss you. <3.
**Me**: Me too. I'm beat. I'll message you after I've slept some. Love you.

God, it feels so weird to say that to him.

**Cooke:** Love you more.

And even weirder to see him saying it back to me. How did that happen? The question I have now is, how are we going to stay together? I've always heard long-distance relationships never work out, and this distance is... well, it's extreme, to say the least. I can't just jet off to see him whenever I want to, and neither can he.

No. I refuse to think negatively. In my heart, I know... if anyone can do this, we can.

~

"You just took off on a moment's notice to be with your injured man?" Lindsay sighs and rests her head on her palm. "That's so romantic."

It's Monday morning, and I'm sitting in the kitchen of the Beedle house, waiting for Susanna to get her ass out of bed so we can go for our walk. I really don't have time to walk, though, because I've got so much homework to make up that I feel like my head might explode. No worries. I can do it. Just throw it on top of the two exams, three quizzes, and the ceramics pieces I need to make before I head home for break.

Don't get me wrong, I'm not whining. I knew I'd have a lot to do once I got back. No regrets. Absolutely none. I'd fly off to help Cooke again in a heartbeat.

"Did you hear me?" asks Susanna, who finally appeared.

"No, sorry. I was thinking about all the shit I have to do this week." Oh, and Luke wants me to work Wednesday night as well as next Friday, Saturday, and Sunday since Chris is going home to Indiana for the weekend. Again, I'm not complaining. It's the least I can do. I'll ask Tayler if she wants to head back to Ames early. It's no problem if she doesn't; my hometown is only about an hour and a half from here, so one of my brothers can drive me.

"I asked you when Cooke's coming back to visit."

"Oh, I don't know. He'll have the brace on his leg for a long time. Months." Something that surprised me, honestly, that he's got to deal with that external brace for that long.

"Well, he should totally come here to rehab. I bet he doesn't even go to practices."

"No." I scoff. "What would he do there?"

"Exactly." Susanna smiles and nods. "You should ask him."

"Oh...." I can't ask him to come here. What would I say? *"Oh, hey, you should totes move here for a few months while you rehab. And by the way, there's no elevator in my building, so you'll have to schlep up three flights of stairs to my place."* I look at Susanna. "I don't know how that would work."

"It doesn't hurt to ask," Robbi interjects. "Maybe he could rehab with the ISU athletic department. The rugby guys could put a good word in for him. They'd probably love having a professional athlete hanging around."

"You think?"

Robbi shrugs. "Like so many things, I'm just throwing shit out there. Shootin' from the hip, as they say." She gives me the pistol fingers, winks, then says, "Pew, pew, pew. Now, let's go get this fucking walk done."

Giggles break out from the entire group.

Our walk was a blast. I've missed the girls, even though I just moved out. They filled me in on the landlord drama. He's not going to do a thing about the basement. No surprise there.

"And Aragog?" I ask with a shiver.

Robbi answers my question. "He's still down there somewhere. That web in the shower is massive."

Patsy sighs. "Robbi's right. I saw it too. I can't help wondering what he's trying to catch in that thing."

"A small human." Robbi smirks. "Watch out, Susanna. Aragog is hungry."

"Shut up." She laughs. "I'm not stepping foot in that basement."

Changing the subject, I tell the girls that Tayler and I are planning a little housewarming slash dinner party. "A week from Thursday. I'm not sure of the time, but I'll let you know. It's BYOB, but Tayler and I will cook something good."

"Ooh, a dinner party? Fancy." Clapping, Lindsay asks, "Can we bring a date?"

"Of course. Invite Jack and the other guys. I'm going to invite Bull and Dan."

"Mm, Bull," says Robbi with a husky voice. "That's a whole lotta man."

Laughing, I pat her on the back. "Go for it."

"I think I will."

Hopping onto a banged-up Bluebelle that I need to get fixed, I wave to the girls as I head for my new apartment so I can get ready for class. "See you guys later. Happy Thanksgiving!"

# CHAPTER FORTY-EIGHT

"To the swanky new digs," Robbi toasts, holding up her can of cheap domestic beer.

The rest of the group hold their drinks up, muttering their agreement.

"Thanks," Tayler says with a smile. "Dinner is almost ready. I hope you all like spaghetti."

That was my idea. It was either that or chili, and I figured it would be less expensive in the long run to make pasta since our invitation list kept growing. Besides, pasta is filling too.

"I'm starved," growls Dan. "It smells fucking amazing."

"Garlic bread?" Bull grunts.

"I made the garlic bread," says Robbi, who magically appeared next to Bull. She's even smiling up at him. Robbi isn't super demonstrative, but she seems to be workin' it with Bull.

"Yeah?" he says, looking down at her.

"Yeah." She winks at him. "You gonna sit by me, Bull?"

I'm doing my best not to watch their interaction, but I can't help it. Especially now that Bull's face is the same color as our red sauce. "You want me to?" he asks Robbi softly.

"I'd love it." Sliding her arm through his, she pulls him over to the sofa and points down for him to sit. When he does, she slides right between his legs and onto his lap.

"So that's how it's done," I whisper, hoping nobody heard me.

"With someone like Bull? Yeah. You've got to be completely obvious." Tayler snickers. "Hell, with all guys. Spelling it out is a must."

Spell it out. Maybe that's what I need to do with Cooke. I still haven't suggested he should come here. I don't think there's any way it's possible. He can't leave England and his team. Right?

I nod toward our living room. "Are you spelling it out for Luke?"

She sighs and looks a little defeated. "Trying to, but... I don't know."

When my phone chimes in my pocket, I snatch it up and quickly press the FaceChat app. Cooke knew about our little party. He said he might call so he can say hi to Bull and everyone else. I smile at his handsome face as soon as he comes into view. "Hi."

"Allo, love. Is your dinner party in full swing?"

"It is." I flip the phone around so he can see everyone. "Say hi to Cooke, everybody."

"Hi, Cooke," the group shouts.

When I turn the phone back to me, I say what I probably shouldn't say. "I wish you were here."

"Me too, love."

I'm about to ask him about his leg when Robbi comes up on my right. Leaning over the screen, she says, "Cooke. You should come here to rehab."

Cooke is quiet. "Well—"

I feel my phone being pulled from my fingers by some long thick ones. "Cooke. It's Bull."

"Hey, mate."

"We've got a state-of-the-art facility here, man. I bet if I talked to Coach, he could pull some strings."

"I'm not—"

"Let me check on it, man. You could work with us even from the sidelines. That would be fucking epic, dude."

I'm speechless. Not because Bull has taken the phone but by the sheer number of words that just came out of his mouth. He's a downright chatty Cathy with Cooke.

"I'm not sure I can, Bull. My contract may prohibit me, but I'll check. I'd love to be there with Quinn and you lads."

Oh my God. I'm practically shaking from excitement. I want to jump up and down and tell him to come. To please come. But I can't. Where would he stay? He wouldn't be able to do the steps here, and a hotel is out of the question. That's too expensive.

Bull hands me the phone. "Talk him into it, Quinn."

Is Cooke nervous? "Sorry about that. You've got a lot of people who care about you here. Me included."

"I'm not opposed to the notion. I'll have to give the front office a call."

"Are you really interested?" I can't believe this.

"I am. But don't get your hopes up just yet."

"I won't."

When there's a knock on the door, Tayler rushes over and opens it. "What's all this racket?" asks Vic. His brows are furrowed, and his voice sounds scratchy. The old fart.

"Hang on, Cooke." Setting the phone down on the counter, I put my hands on my hips. "It's seven o'clock, Vic. We don't even have any music on. We're not making a damn racket. Don't be a party pooper."

He chuckles. "Spitfire, where have you been all my life?"

"Around. Now, do you want to join us for dinner, or are you going to be a cranky old fool?"

"I smelled it all the way down at my place. Course I'll eat." Then he adds softly, "If you'll have me."

"You're always welcome, Vic. You and Mary."

"She don't like crowds."

No, I bet she doesn't. I found out that she was in an underground dog fighting ring. The poor thing was left for dead. Thankfully, a whistleblower led the police to Mary and several other dogs. Some weren't as lucky as she was. How can people be so cruel?

"Love?"

*Oh shit.* Picking up the phone, I smile. "Sorry." I giggle. "Here, meet Vic." I step over to the old coot as he talks to Robbi. "Vic, say hello to my boyfriend."

"Boyfriend, eh? Where's he been? I ain't seen him around. If I was yours, I'd never let you outta my sight."

"Vic." I laugh. "That's creepy as hell. You'd lock me up or something?"

Everyone laughs.

Vic puffs out his chest. "I'm not a creep. I'm just saying—"

Interrupting Vic's mini rant, I say, "Cooke, meet Vic. He owns our building." I turn the phone and hand it to Vic.

"You tryin' to steal my girl, Vic?" asks Cooke. I'd love to tell you his tone was jovial, but it wasn't.

"Nah. You look like you could kick my ass."

Now Cooke laughs. "I live in England, Vic. Otherwise, I'd be there watching out for my girl 24-7."

"Creeeeepppyyyy," I singsong.

Everyone laughs again, even Vic. Even Cooke.

Taking back the phone, I turn it to face me. "I'd better go. Dinner's ready. Call you later?"

"I'll be here." He chuckles. "Have a good supper, love."

Turning away from everyone, I whisper to him, "I wish you were here."

He whispers back, "Me too, love. Miss you."

"Miss you too."

After we hang up, Tayler and I start dishing out the grub. When Robbi makes her way to the front of the line, I give her my stink eye.

"What?" she asks, feigning innocence.

"Bull did not come up with that idea for Cooke doing his rehab here on his own."

"Well, I may have suggested it. But he loved the idea." She shrugs. "Now, let's see what happens."

"Don't break his heart," I say softly as she takes her plate. "Bull, I mean."

Robbi blinks at me. "I've had my eye on him since the party at the rugby house. I'm serious about seeing what happens if he is."

"Oh, he is." I nod toward the couch where Bull is sitting. He's not eating, even though he was the first in line. Instead, he's watching us. More specifically, he's waiting for Robbi. "Go on. He's waiting for you."

"He's seriously hot," she mumbles. "And sweet."

Dishing some food up for myself, I eat at the kitchen island with Patsy and Tayler since there's no room anywhere else. As I look out at the group in my living room, a sense of satisfaction comes over me. I've got friends. Good ones. And they're all right here with me. All but Cooke.

Hell, even Luke showed up. He's got to head back to work right after he eats, but I feel like that was a big step for him. I know he's not here because of me; he hasn't left Tayler's side since he walked in the door. I'm proud of my best friend, holding her ground even though I know she wants to jump his bones. I'll just have some faith that things will work out for her. For now, I'm going to appreciate what I have. Because I'm happy.

"Fine food, ladies," says Vic.

"Deli-fus," says Dan with his mouth full.

"There's cake too," I tell them.

The room is quiet for a moment until Bull shouts, "Fuck yeah!"

"Eat up," I say, sipping my water. "There's plenty for seconds."

Now it's Dan's turn. "Fuck yeah!"

## CHAPTER FORTY-NINE

"Can you believe it?"

I look up from my textbook at Dan as I study for my final exam in art history. It's going to be a bitch. My grade is a solid B, so I hope I don't screw that up. The chances of me giving it a bump up are slim to none since Dr. Connolly's classes are notoriously tough. No, I'll happily take a B, but I'll have to slay this exam in order to keep it.

"Believe what?"

"About Cooke."

I set my pen down. God, is he hurt? If so, how did Dan hear about it before me? I've talked to my boyfriend almost every night, and if we don't FaceChat, we text. So, if there's anything to hear about Cooke, I'd know.

"Believe what?" I ask again.

"Coach told us he's coming here. He's going to work with the team."

Okay, this is all news to me. What the hell? "When did you hear about it?"

Dan holds up his phone. "Bull sent a text about five minutes ago."

*So Bull knew Cooke was coming to Ames before I did?* "Word spreads fast, huh?" I'm not about to admit to Dan that I'm in the dark about this since I knew nothing about his injury in the first place. "Cool, right?" I chuckle.

"It's awesome. Well, gotta go. I'm late for a test." I watch Dan turn on his heel and jog out the library doors.

A week ago, at our dinner party, Bull suggested Cooke rehab here. In that time, Cooke hadn't brought it up again. I thought it was because he a) didn't want to or b) found out he couldn't. Cooke did ask for Bull's phone number, which I thought was a little odd but not really. The two of them had become friends, of sorts. But this is all a shock. And the fact that Dan and Bull knew before me?

"I'm going to kill him."

I grab my phone, making sure it's on silent so the dinging of text messages doesn't disturb anyone.

**Me:** You're coming to Ames to help the rugby team?

I don't have to wait long.

**Cooke:** Bloody gossips. I told them to keep it to themselves. I wanted to surprise you.

Oh, that's kind of sweet.

**Me:** So, you're seriously coming to Ames? For real?
**Cooke:** It's real, but not forever, sadly. But our physio, an American, worked it out with your uni. They've never rehabbed someone with my injury, so they think it will be an educational opportunity for your physio students.
**Me:** That makes sense.
**Cooke:** And I'll help the rugby lads from time to time.

**Me:** They'll love that. Well, if Dan's reaction is any indication, they're thrilled.

**Cooke:** Aye. I'm thrilled too. But not for that reason. I'll get to be with you for a few months.

A few months. But then what?

**Me:** I live on the top floor. There's no elevator.

**Cooke:** I'll stay at my place. There's an elevator, remember?

**Me:** At your place? I thought you said you didn't buy that condo.

**Cooke:** When you asked, I hadn't yet. But I wanted it in case you needed it. Now I'm glad I did. Then you can move in too.

**Me:** Cooke, I live with Tayler. I signed a lease. I can't just move out.

**Cooke:** Then you can stay with me as much as possible.

**Me:** I guess I could.

**Cooke:** Bloody brilliant.

**Me:** When will you be here?

**Cooke:** I've got some things to do here. The plan is before New Year's. Saffron's going to house-sit after she gets back from the States.

**Me:** ?

**Cooke:** She's going to fly over with me to help me with the travel part of it. She'll stay a fortnight to help me get settled. Then she'll stay here and take care of my flat.

**Me:** It'll be fun to see Saffie again. I can't believe you're coming here and you didn't tell me. You'll be here for New Year's Eve?

I'm vibrating I'm so excited.

**Cooke:** Aye. We'll bring in the new year together.

**Me:** I can't wait.

**Cooke:** I'll let you know my flight information. We'll rent a car, so no need for you to do a thing.

**Me:** Okay. I love you.

**Cooke:** I love you more.

~

I can't study. How can I when I Cooke is coming back? But I must. Saying softly, "You can do it, Quinn. Focus," I open my book again and stare down at the page. Gothic architecture. Since the exam is comprehensive, I need to review everything from the beginning. I remember telling Cooke about this chapter, and he mentioned the Notre Dame Cathedral in Paris. *Paris.* Maybe we could go sometime. It's just right over the English Channel. Well, under it. The Chunnel takes you to France. I'd also love to go to Italy to see the Sistine Chapel.

"Focus," I growl to myself. Pulling out my notes from early in the semester, I turn to the page I need and smile. I doodled "Quinn Thompson" in the margin. "What a silly girl."

I stare at the swirling letters for a second or two when it hits me.

For the first time in my life, those doodles aren't crazy.

## CHAPTER FIFTY

**C**ooke: Be there in ten minutes.

I stare down at his message as butterflies fill my belly. Cooke is ten minutes away from his new home. I'm waiting just inside the door because it's as cold as a witch's tit outside. At least the storm that was forecast has held off long enough for his plane to land. I know he knows what snow is, but I don't think he's ever experienced an Iowa winter before. I urged him to tell Saffie to drive slowly and carefully on the way home and to be cautious on bridge overpasses because they freeze first. He assured me that she was a skilled driver and not to worry.

I've still worried.

I concentrate on my breathing because I've been a nervous wreck all day. Checking my phone again, I see movement from the corner of my eye. My head jerks up just as a large black SUV pulls into the driveway. I know it's him because the thing looks like it's probably worth seventy-five grand. Just kidding. It does look expensive, though.

I push open the door and step onto the sidewalk that has been cleared of snow and salted to melt the ice. I'd like to run to him, but I know I'll wipe out if I do. Just then, Saffie jumps out of the car first, squealing, "Quinn!"

"Saffie." I move to her and wrap her up in my arms. "I'm so glad you're here."

"It's bloody frigid here, Quinn. You should've warned me. I didn't pack for this."

I roll my eyes. "I told your brother."

"Figures," she mumbles.

Then I see him through the windshield. His face is so handsome. He's still got his beard, which will be good for the winter months, but the smile peeking out from his furry face is what takes my breath away. "I love him so much." It's just a whisper. I'm saying it to myself, honestly. But Saffie hears me.

"He loves you too."

Turning to her, I smile. "I know." Then I scurry over to the passenger side of the car and open his door. I don't give him a chance to speak, just wrap my arms around him and kiss him like he's my only sustenance in weeks.

He kisses me back until I hear Saffie mumbling something like "Bloody get a room."

Laughing, I pull away and look into his golden irises. "I'm not sure I'll be able to let you go this time, Cooke."

"I know, love."

Helping him out of the car, I grab his "sticks" as he calls them and keep my hands on him as well on the walk to the building. It's a slow process, but we get there eventually. While Cooks sits on a bench, I run down to the office to get Connie, the woman who sold Cooke the place. She grabs the keys and follows me back.

"Mr. Thompson." She beams. "It's so good to see you again."

"Same," he says with a nod.

"I think I've got everything squared away for you. I hope it's to your liking."

What is she talking about?

"I'm sure it's fine." Cooke pushes up to standing, and we all head to the elevator. Connie pushes the button for the fourth floor. When the doors open, I start to head right, like before.

"It's this way, Miss Maxwell." Connie points in the other direction.

"Oh. All right." *I thought he bought the one Connie showed us.*

I follow behind the group, keeping one hand on Cooke. When we reach number 425, Connie opens the door and we all step inside.

Saffie walks in first, and I hear her gasp. "Bloody brilliant," she says with a squeal.

Cooke stops and motions for me to go next. I peek around the doorway and gasp just like Saffron. "Wow."

The three of us make our way to the living area while Connie stays by the door. It's twice the size of the other place we saw. There's a fireplace, the decor is similar, and the ceiling, kitchen cabinets, and countertops are done in white like the first place, but this one has a larger kitchen to go with the larger living room. Not only that, there's furniture. Nice furniture. There's a big comfy-looking sectional in the living room, a coffee table, and a huge television mounted above the gas fireplace.

I peek into one bathroom and see it's outfitted with white towels and gray rugs. In the spare bedroom, there's a queen-size bed with pretty linens in grays and whites. Two dressers and two nightstands that all match the headboard complete the room. There are white blinds on the windows, but they're up right now, so lots of light is streaming through.

"Love," Cooke calls for me from the other room. He's standing in front of the other bedroom door, waving me over.

I follow him through the doorway and gasp once again. "This is amazing."

"Do you like it?"

"I love it." There's a king-size bed in this room and the same dressers, nightstands, and headboard. But this one is painted a pale blue color. The linens aren't plain either. Instead of the gray and white from the other room, the bedding is swirling lines and shapes all in various shades of blue.

"To match your eyes, love."

That's it. I've been holding in my stupid emotions for hours. No, days. Then, when he stepped out of the car, I had to concentrate to keep the tears tucked away. But I can't do it anymore. Once one tear leaked out, the rest just came like a torrent. "That's... that's the sweetest."

"Love," he murmurs. Leaning down, he kisses my lips softly.

"It's beautiful, Cooke."

"Did you see our bathroom?"

*Our* bathroom? Oh my God. This man is going be the death of me.

"Not yet." I sniffle, then step into the bathroom. I'm speechless. It's set up a lot like his home in England with a separate bathtub and a shower the size of my room at home. There are two sinks, and on the wall, blue towels hang from a towel warmer.

Back in the kitchen, Saffie is making a sandwich.

"How did you get this place ready from England?" I ask.

"I did it, Miss Maxwell," says a proud Connie.

"It's perfect. Cozy yet classy."

Connie chuckles. "I'm the interior designer as well as the agent for this project, so I'm pleased you see what I intended for these units."

"You did a brilliant job, Connie. Thank you." Cooke is smiling, but he looks tired.

"Babe, why don't you go lie down? I can bring your things up for you."

"You have two parking spaces beneath the building. I've left the codes for you on the counter." Connie points to a spot next to the fridge. "If you park inside, you can bring everything up in the elevator. There are dollies in the garage as well for larger loads. Let me know if you need anything."

With that, Connie leaves, and we're all quiet for a moment.

"This place is perfect, Cooke," Saffie says with a mouth full of bread and cheese.

Turning to Cooke, I ask, "Are you hungry?"

"Let's bring the things up, and then I'll eat."

"You're not doing a thing. You're going to go lie down. Saffie and I'll bring things up. After that, I'll make you something to eat."

"Bossy," he mumbles.

"Get used to it. You need to rest."

"Aye."

I lead him to his—no, *our* bedroom and help him undress down to his boxers and tee. "Sleep," I say, kissing his lips as he lies down on the bed. "I'll check on you in a few minutes."

"Aye, love." And then he's out, snoring softly.

"Poor baby," I say softly as I move hair out of his eyes. I touch his face gently and gaze down at him. "So glad you're here."

"You know," Saffie says form the door, "he wants to stay here."

I smile. I know he wants to be here. "I know. Until—"

"No. He wants to stay here. With you. Forever."

I step out of the room and shut the door behind me. Saffie's got my interest piqued. "He does?"

"He does. I've never seen him like this before. Neither has Mum. You should know he's had loads of girlfriends."

"He has?" Who am I kidding? Look at him. Of course he has.

"He never talked about any of those birds. He tolerated them. But he won't shut up about you. How you met. That it was fate or some shite." She chuckles. "I love him, but he's full of it."

My face must show what I'm thinking, because Saffie says, "Wait. I didn't mean it like that. He couldn't have met a better girl, Quinn. I adore you. And when Mum comes to visit next month, she'll feel the same way."

His mom's coming?

"All I mean is he's never been like this before, so I know he means what he says. He doesn't want to leave you again."

"I don't want that either. But what about the team?"

"Did you see the injury? The video?"

"No." And I don't want to. "I can't."

"He's done. He can't come back from that. He'll be in that brace for seven or eight months. Then the real rehab will start."

"Eight months? I knew it was months, just not quite so many."

"He doesn't like to talk about it."

"I get that," I say as I look out the window to check the view.

"No worries. He was always right savvy with his money. You won't be broke."

"Huh?" My head jerks up. "You think I care if he's got money?" Hell, I still have the Visa gift card he gave me months ago. "Cooke and I, well, it's never about money."

"Bloody hell. I keep putting my foot in it. All I meant was he won't have to worry about money if he can't play anymore. He can do something else since he was so smart with it."

"Oh. I see." I nod. "That's good. I'm sure the ISU rugby guys would love to have him work with them."

"Aye," she says, smiling nervously. "Quinn." She steps closer, placing her palm on my shoulder. "He loves you. I can see why. You're a nice girl. One who loves my brother for himself, not for his millions."

"Millions?" I squeak. "What the fuck?" He's got millions? My body flushes with heat. I had no idea.

Saffron throws her head back and laughs. "Yeah, you're perfect."

# CHAPTER FIFTY-ONE

"Ten, nine, eight, seven, six, five, four, three, two, *one!*" everyone shouts at the stroke of midnight.

I lean down and kiss Cooke. It's our first New Year's Eve together, and it's been perfect. "Happy New Year," I whisper in his ear.

"Same to you, love." He kisses me again, and then we both turn to look at our friends.

We're having a New Year's Eve party at Cooke's new place and invited the entire gang, including Vic and Connie. Everyone seems to be having a good time. Not everyone could make it, though. Luke is working. Luckily, he hired another bartender to take over some shifts since I'm "flaky and unreliable." His words. No worries, I'm not fired. I plan to work a lot next semester, even though Cooke wants me to quit. I can't do that. Not yet.

The sound of holiday music is floating through the air thanks to the wireless stereo system I bought for Cooke as a housewarming gift. Sure, I used the Visa card he gave me. At least the money went to something for him. I'm okay with that.

I smile down at Cooke, then back to the party. The Beedle

babes are here with their boyfriends. Bull and Robbi seem to be going strong. I think he's completely smitten with her, and Robbi seems to be all smiles lately. Patsy and Kat, along with Susanna and Lindsay, are all here with their men as well.

I look around the room in search of Saffie. When I see her, I snicker. "Yo, babe," I whisper down to Cooke. "Your sister and Dan."

"I see them," he grumbles. "I have a feeling she's never going to leave now."

"They just met." I roll my eyes. Then I remember. "I guess I fell for you right away."

"You guess?" He scowls. "*I* knew."

Kissing him softly, I decide it's a good time for me to find something to do. Back in the kitchen, I replenish the platters of appetizers for the group while he remains camped out on the sofa with his leg propped up on an ottoman, while also being protected by two chairs on either side. Drunk people around external braces is scary stuff.

When I feel a hand on my ass, I jump. "Cooke," I hiss, then laugh. "You shouldn't be up walking around with all this"—I wave at the crowd—"going on."

He takes my hand in his and tugs on it. "Come into the bedroom with me for a second."

"Are you okay?"

He nods, but I follow him anyway. Once inside, Cooke shuts and then locks the door. "Is anyone in here?" he says loudly. When no one answers, he pushes me up against the door, raises my arms above my head, and kisses me. "I fucking adore you."

I'm gasping for breath. We haven't done anything since he got here. Saffron is always underfoot, as they say. "Me too."

"I need you," he says, licking my neck right below my ear. When he takes my earlobe in his mouth and sucks, I nearly jump out of my skin. "God, I want to fuck you."

"Me too." I do. I want to do it. "But your brace."

"I read an article."

I start to giggle, though it could be because his hands tickle as they make their way up into my shirt. "About having sex with a brace?"

"Yep. There's even a couple YouTube videos. Who knew?" he says, taking my mouth again in a deep, searing kiss as he tugs the edges of my bra down with each hand until my baps are free.

"I've missed these," he says, sliding his fingers over my already hard tips.

"I've missed your hands."

He tweaks each nipple and I squeak.

He lifts my shirt, then slides his head between my stomach and the fabric until his lips land on my right nipple, sucking it into his mouth.

"Oh God." I moan. "Don't st-stop. Please?" He has me practically begging him and he's barely started.

I attempt to reach down between us so I can feel him, but he moves my hand away from his dick. "If you touch me, there's no stopping me. I want you, but not with a house full of people."

"So, after they leave?"

His mouth is still very busy with my chest. "The second they leave." He licks. I moan. "I'm locking us away in here, stripping you naked. We've waited long enough, love."

"What about Saffie?"

"Saffie can sod off. She has headphones."

I giggle at his angry tone. I know he doesn't mean it. He adores his little sister. "You'd better stop, Cooke. I can't take much more."

With one more swipe, he pulls his head out of my shirt. "As soon as they leave, meet me in here."

"But the mess."

"Will wait."

"Yes." I kiss him softly. "It will."
Now, how do I get rid of my friends?
Just kidding.
A little.

___________

# CHAPTER FIFTY-TWO

___________

C*ooke*

I'VE BEEN WAITING FOR MONTHS FOR MY TURN TO SPEAK. YOU have no idea what it's been like for me. Well, now is my chance to say it's been hell. I wasn't joking when I told Quinn it was love at first sight for me. I guess it wasn't for her. I know my girl, though. She's too afraid to admit it, fearing the truth will somehow impact my feelings. On the contrary, it would make me feel more secure.

Sure, I'm confident about many things, even women, but not when it comes to the beguiling Quinn Maxwell. The night of our first chat, I couldn't sleep afterward. I was tempted to call again just so I could see those piercing blue eyes and the sleepy hair and hear her voice, like an angel's, soft and sweet.

When I finally did work up the nerve to call her, she shocked the bloody hell out of me with her sense of humor. She's hilarious. In my experience, women aren't that funny. Now, before you tell me I'm being sexist, let me explain, or maybe clarify. The women who hang out with professional rugby arseholes aren't funny.

There. Better? I'm sure I'm overgeneralizing. Saffie's funny, after all, but she's my sister.

Anyway, back to that night I first saw her. Ian knew I was in trouble that day. For one, he couldn't believe I'd called her back. And at the gym, no less. That was intentional. I wanted her to see the team space, the logo. I wanted her to know I was *somebody*—a professional athlete. It worked too, except the girl knew nothing about rugby. My efforts to show her I was wealthy, famous, and sought after fell on deaf ears. And that, my friends, was beyond appealing.

The night she called, distraught, because of her scooter, her basement, and that woman, I was so angry, I wanted to break something. I'd still like to ring Kara's neck. But Quinn was so far away, it seemed impossible to help. But I went against team rules and flew to the States to do what I could to help her. I had hell to pay when I returned. Benched at first, but they needed me badly, so it was short-lived. My mates were mad as hell too, but when I explained to Ian and the lads what had happened, that I went to help my girl, tensions eased a bit.

From the moment I landed back in the UK, I wanted nothing more than to turn around and fly back, to stay with Quinn. It's why I bought the flat here. I wanted a place to stay when I visited. A place Quinn could live in if she needed one—which she did. That fecking landlord. Add him to the list of people I'd like to see in a scrum. But leave it to my girl to figure herself out without my help.

That's another thing I love about Quinn. She's independent and capable of handling all sorts of issues without any help from the likes of me, but she's also the most caring person I've ever met. She'd help a stranger if they needed it. There isn't a mean bone in her gorgeous body.

Ah, her body. Damn. Quinn's body is made for sin. She's lush and soft and curvy in all the right places. I've kissed and touched almost all of her. Feeling her wrapped around me... well, nothing feels better. There's still more we need to do. Tonight. Tonight is the night I make her mine. I only hope Quinn's friends—our friends—leave soon. Thinking about sinking into her is making me irrational.

"Yo, Cooke," says a drunk Bull.

"Mmhmm," I say, trying to keep my dick in check.

Slapping me on the back, he belches. Lovely. "We're taking off, man."

I look behind him and see one of Quinn's former flatmates and Dan. I scan the room and find Saffie sitting alone in a chair, looking a bit forlorn. I'm tempted to ask Dan to take her with him, but that'd be wrong. Right? I shake my head. Of course it's wrong.

"You're not driving." It's not a question.

"Nah, man. Freshman on the team is the designated driver tonight. He's on his way."

"Good night, then."

I wave them off and count the number remaining. One-two-three-four-five-six-seven-eight-nine. With Saffie, there are ten, because I know Vic left right after midnight, as did Connie. All that's left are her current flatmate, Tayler, and the former ones with their men.

Standing from my chair, I make my way into the kitchen. Quinn's asking her friends if they want to take some of the leftovers. "There's more in the fridge, so you guys can take this." She points to the plate of vegetables and one with meats and cheeses.

"Sure, we'll take it," says Patsy.

I see what Quinn's doing. She's putting the idea in their heads that it's time to go. Bloody brilliant if you ask me.

I reach into a drawer and pull out some plastic bags. "Here, let's fill these up."

*God, I want to fill Quinn up.*

My dick is unrelenting. I move behind her and get as close as I can to hide my hard-on while also letting her know I'm in dire straits.

She pushes that round bottom of hers up against me and it's on. I pinch her arse, and she laughs. "Naughty lass," I whisper in her ear.

Another eternity passes, but we finally get everyone but Saffie out of the house. I send Quinn off to bed, but before I go, I warn Saffie to wear some headphones.

"What?" Then her face scrunches up in disgust. "No. Now I can't unsee it. Don't ever say shit like that to me again, ever, you fecking git."

I chuckle all the way into our bedroom, then stop immediately because Quinn was on the bed, wearing my jersey. I swallow hard because I've got mixed feelings about that now. I may never play the sport again. Odds aren't in my favor. But she looks sexy as fuck, so I'm going to do my best to think only of the beautiful body that's touching my clothes.

Pushing the door closed behind me, I press the lock and limp toward her. Setting my stick next to the bed, I sit beside her. "Love."

"Happy New Year, Cooke."

Leaning closer, I take her top lip between mine and suckle it. Her lips are plump and soft, always glossy, always delicious. She brings her hand up to my cheek and touches me gently. I peek down at her fingernails and smile. "Like what you did this time." She's painted them in pale shades of glittery blue. Like snow and sparkle.

"Pretty simple, but I thought it was appropriate for the holiday."

I lift her hand to my lips and kiss the tips of her fingers. God, I can't wait until she's wearing my ring. Soon. I hope it's soon.

"So, tell me about this YouTube thing you watched?"

"Well." I pull her off the bed and place her between my legs, my brace off to the side. "First, this has to come off." I point to the jersey.

She places her hands on the bottom edge and slowly lifts it past her gorgeous breasts, over her face, and off, tossing it on the floor behind her. I stare at her. She was completely nude beneath the shirt. Her chest moves up and down, and it's flushed pink. Starting at her neck, I slide my palm down over each breast to the tip, watching it harden with just a touch. They're too tantalizing to pass over without the attention they deserve. Leaning forward, I lick all around one areola, nibbling some after that. Suckling on the nipple comes next. The sounds Quinn emits when I devote time to her breasts make my body hum.

I focus my attention on the other side while still touching her with both hands, pulling her closer so I can touch as much of her as I can. "Your skin is so soft, love."

"I m-moisturize." She can barely say the words as I nip beneath her left tit.

"It pays off."

She giggles and I smile, kissing her from her chest down to her stomach. My hand seeks the warmth in her center. "You're wet." I moan at the feel of her. Using my middle finger, I swirl and press her clit. She widens her legs without my asking, which allows me to slowly enter her with one finger. I know tonight is the night, but I don't want to hurt her. Right now, I want my beautiful girl to come on my hand.

"Feel good?" I ask, focusing my attention on her needy clit.

Her hands are on my shoulders, but her head is thrown back. "Yeah. Feels good."

Her hips begin to work in tandem with my fingers. She's getting close. Taking her breast in my mouth, I work her into a frenzy until she breaks. Her body vibrates against me as my fingers are soaked with wetness.

This is it. I can't wait any longer. With her help, I stand and pull off my tee. I've taken to wearing those athletic pants that snap on either side of my legs, which means I can take them off without fussing with the brace. It also means that in seconds, I'm completely nude and harder than I've ever been. I sit on the bed and scoot farther into the center while still having my feet on the ground.

"What next?" she murmurs.

Lying down, I reach for her hand. "Climb up onto the bed, love. Straddle me."

"Cooke." She sounds nervous. "I—"

"Shh, come on. This will work fine. I've done my research."

She snorts and giggles. "YouTube is research?"

"Bloody right. I learned how to fix my kitchen faucet thanks to YouTube."

She giggles again as she places her knee on the bed on my left side. When she's all the way on the bed, she kneels next to me. The view from here of my naked girlfriend is making me harder.

"Love. I'm desperate here."

Taking a deep breath that I find completely charming, she brings one leg over to my other side until she's hovering over me. I'm stroking my cock at the sight before me. "Fuck, you're gorgeous like this."

"Cooke... I don't know what to do."

I run my finger through her folds, locating her clit again. I'll bring her to orgasm one more time so she's ready.

"Kiss me," I say as I feel her move with me.

Quinn leans down and takes my mouth in a hungry kiss. It tells me her nerves have lessened and she's getting more comfortable.

As soon as I feel her release, I use one hand on her hip to nudge her back and the other to place the head of my cock at her entrance. "Sit, slowly. You're in control, Quinn."

"Okay. It's just—"

"I'll help. Talk to me."

As she slowly moves downward, I breach her until the head of my cock is inside her warmth. "God." I can't believe how good it feels already. And then it hits me. "Shit. Condom."

She stops. "I'm on the pill."

She's on the pill? I'd wonder why she's on it, but I know my sister started taking it because of cramps and such related to her cycle. I suspect it's the same for Quinn. "You okay with no condom, then, love?"

She nods. "Are you?"

"Fuck yes," I hiss as she starts to press down farther and farther. I want to fucking move but I can't. Not yet.

When I'm just over halfway, she stops and pants. "I think you should help me. Can you press up as I press down? I just want... I'm overthinking, worrying about the pain."

"Aye." I place my hands on her hips. "Tell me when you're ready."

"On three," she says, blowing air out through her puckered lips. "One." She breathes in deeply, then out. "Two." She repeats her breathing exercise. "Three."

I wait until I feel her moving, and then I thrust up until I'm completely seated inside of her. I hear her whimper, so I look up as I rub her back and hips. "Okay?"

She's doing her breathing exercises, but they're quicker now.

"Love, I'm sorry."

"No. It's fine." She smiles down at me, but it doesn't reach her eyes. "It's not as bad as I thought it'd be. Just... don't move yet. Give me a sec."

"Tell me when you're ready to move. I'll wait." Forever.

After a minute or two, Quinn nods down at me. "Ready."

Placing my hands on her hips, I urge her to move up, using her knees to lift. When she's up several inches, she presses down again, and I see fucking stars. "Yes, Quinn. Again."

My girl is a quick study, because in no time she's moving up and down faster. She's so tight and warm and wet, I don't think I'll make it long, so I reach down and rub her little nub again.

When she suddenly stops moving, I feel her squeeze me so hard, I think I could pass out from the feeling.

"Quinn," I shout as I come with her. Pressing in as far as I can, I release deep inside of her, wondering what it'd be like to be a father.

# CHAPTER FIFTY-THREE

"Wow, Cooke." I smile down at him from my perch above him.

"Brilliant," he says, still touching me, his palms exploring my skin.

It makes my breasts peek again. I'm not ready to do that again just yet, so I push myself up and feel us disconnect. I'm okay with that, because I'm a little sore down there. Lifting my leg back over him, I scoot off the bed and make my way into the bathroom. I know there's probably blood. I'd heard it was possible. When I get inside, I shut the door and find a cloth. I'm moist and sticky, so I clean myself up.

I feel warm hands slide around my waist until he's holding me. "You okay, beautiful?"

I look up and see us both in the mirror. "Yeah. You?"

"I've never been happier in my life."

"Really?" I smile brightly at his reflection.

"Really."

Turning in his arms, I wrap my arms around his neck, push myself up on my tiptoes, and kiss him. Not a sexy kiss, just a soft one. "I love you, Cooke."

"I love you more, Quinn."

"Impossible."

Cooke slaps my ass and kisses me quick. "Let's get to bed. I'm wiped out."

"Me too." I'd like to say I'm ready to do it again, but I'm not. My lady-land feels out of sorts. But I liked it. I liked it a lot. And that's probably because it was with Cooke. I can't imagine doing it with anyone else. I let my imagination go for a second, thinking of Bryant and me. It could never be him. Or anyone else for that matter. Nope, Cooke is the only one.

Sliding beneath the sheets, still nude, I scoot closer to him, placing my palm on his chest. I feel his warm hand cover mine and squeeze; then, with a sigh, he says, "I've never been happier in my life, love."

"Same here." And I mean it. Before I met Cooke, my life was uneventful. It was me constantly trying to figure out life. Falling for the wrong guys, clinging to a fantasy rather than reality. I laugh to myself, because if I could tell the Quinn from six months ago that real life was so much better than fantasy, she probably wouldn't believe me. But it's true.

I feel Cooke's arm wrap around me to pull me closer, so I go. Why wouldn't I? Hell, I'll go anywhere this man wants to take me.

"Love?" Cooke's voice sounds unsure, tentative.

"Yeah?"

"Do you want children?"

I press my arm down against the bed and push myself up to sitting. "Now?"

"No. Not yet. Someday?"

"Yes. I'd like one or two. Do you?"

"I do. With you."

"Oh." My voice cracks. "Cooke." I sniffle. "I want them with you too. I can picture some mini Cookes out there on the pitch." I settle back down and curl up against him as he wraps his arm around me, pulling me even closer.

He sighs contentedly. "I hope they look like you. Stunning. With dark hair and azure blue eyes."

Damn. I meant to look that up. "There isn't anything better than hearing that the person you love wants you to have their children."

"Same, love. I feel the same."

# EPILOGUE

## Six Months Later

"This is it," I say, attempting to be as perky as possible.

"It is."

I can tell Cooke's nervous, because his good leg is bouncing up and down on the exam table. In case you were wondering, we're back in England for the summer so Cooke can have his brace removed. It's been a long time coming, let me tell you.

"Good afternoon, Mr. Thompson," says the orthopedic surgeon as she enters the room. "Are you ready for this?"

"I am," Cooke says with confidence.

I'm not. This entire thing is scary, because they need to put him under anesthesia to remove the brace. He'll be in pain afterward, and there will be some swelling after the pins are removed. I know he'll do fine, but it's still nerve-racking.

Then there's afterward. *What will happen next? Will he be able to play?* Those are the questions we keep hearing on the telly since we've been back in England. The rugby pundits are all speculating on his return. I wish I could tell you that everything's been settled, but it hasn't. Once this brace is off, he'll start intensive physical therapy. He'll have to learn to walk, literally, before he can run. We know he won't be back for this season, and it remains to be seen about the next one, but I think Cooke's fine either way. Honestly, I'm terrified of him playing again and reinjuring his leg, but I'll need to trust the physicians and Cooke to do the right thing.

I have one more year of college remaining, and I plan to finish my degree. It may be difficult with everything Cooke will be going through, though, so we'll have to wait and see. In the meantime, Cooke still has his place in Ames, and I'm still living with Tayler —sort of. I'm not there very much, but I pay my half of the rent and stay with her when I can, so it's all good, especially since Tayler's got her own drama happening. Boy troubles. I try to help when I can, but being away from her and my other friends, and even Vic and Mary, is hard. FaceChat is handy, so I can see and talk to them, anytime I want. Even Vic is set up for it now. I think he did it more for Mary than himself because she seems to enjoy looking at my face on his laptop as I talk to her. She's such a good girl.

My hope is that we can fly back to Ames for his therapy. They've been great, and his trainers here in England are pleased. If that's approved, I'll be able to get another semester under my belt, at the very least. No matter what they decide, I'm not leaving Cooke so I'll have to figure things out. I'm good at that. No worries.

"We're ready if you are." The doctor chuckles.

Leaning over him, I kiss his lips. "I love you. I'll be waiting right outside this door." I kiss him again. "Your mom and Saff are here. Saff wants the chance to give you a pre-surgery pep talk."

He chuckles, then nods and gives me a smile I recognize. It's a fake one. He's nervous. Maybe Saffie can help with that since I'm doing my best to hold it together. When I step out of the room, I smile at her and Caroline, Cooke's mom. "They're getting ready to take him back."

"Right." Caroline stands, straightening her dress. The woman is always dressed to the nines. I guess she must dress the part since she owns her own business—a cute dress shop not far from Twickenham. I like her, and she seems to like me. Cooke and Saffie both say she does, and I don't think they'd lie. I haven't spent enough time with her to be sure, however. When she visited Cooke in the states, I did my best to let them have time together. Besides, I was busy with school and work. The time I did spend with the two of them proved how much they care about each other. That their little family was a tight-knit group.

The same is true about Cooke and my family. He's gone home with me several times, and it's gone well. My dad's the one who's having trouble warming up to the big Brit. I think he's worried I'll fly off to live in England, never to return. Well, the first part might be true, but I'll always come back. I'd miss my family too much, even if my brothers are a pain in the arse.

I look down at my leggings and long tee and sigh, thinking about Caroline's outfit. Comfort. That's all I was thinking about, because I knew I'd be here the entire time with Cooke. Running my palms over my shirt, I attempt to rid it of some wrinkles, I smile at the sparkle on my finger. Holding my hand up in front of me, I stare at the pretty sapphire and diamond engagement ring Cooke gave me just yesterday morning. He said he chose the sapphire to match my eyes. It's beautiful, just like his proposal.

It wasn't anything crazy. It was at the breakfast table, the one where he'd held my hands in his and told me he loved me for the first time. Like before, he prepared scrambled eggs and toast. There was juice and coffee and my handsome boyfriend on one knee. His good one. Holding a small box, he opened it and smiled while I gasped and covered my mouth in shock. Honestly, I wasn't expecting it.

Holding the box, he simply said, "Love. You're my everything. Marry me and make me the happiest man in England. The world."

"Yes." Tears were streaming down my face, because of course they were. "Yes. I'll marry you." Before I even took the ring from the box, I stood and wrapped my arms around his neck. "How did I get so lucky?"

"I'm the lucky one, love. And all thanks to a wrong number."

"Right?" I laughed, helping him up from the floor and into his chair. "We should probably invite Maxwell Quinn to the wedding. Did you ever find him?"

"Ian found him. Said he was a right git."

I coughed, then laughed. "Well, it's lucky you got me that night instead, huh?"

"So bloody lucky." Cooke pulled me closer until I was standing between his legs. I gazed into his beautiful golden brown eyes. Bending down, I touched my lips to his for a sweet, soft kiss I'll remember for the rest of my life.

"You did it, babe." I say as I lean down to kiss him.

"It's off?" he asks groggy from the anesthesia.

"Yep. You weren't even in there two hours. They said you were perfect." Except now the hard part begins. Rehab.

"I'm glad that thing is off. I was starting to forget what life was like before I had it," he chuckles.

"Your mom wants to come in. Then Saff. I'll come back in after that. They'll be moving you into a room soon."

"You're staying with me, right?" His voice sounds a little sad. Scared even.

"I'm not going anywhere, love." Yeah, I've started using the endearment as well. I like it.

Squeezing my hand, he smiles, and with a sleepy voice, mumbles, "Good. Don't ever leave me."

I squeeze his hand. "Never, love." Not ever. I watch Cooke sleep for probably longer than I should. Caroline wants to see him, but I'm going to take just a little longer so I can be sure he's comfortable. Running my fingers over his forehead, I push some of his hair away from his handsome face. His beard is gone, sadly but I suspect he'll grow it back from time to time.

Moving in closer, I say in his ear. "I love you, Cooke. I don't know what I did in my last life to deserve you." I'm getting a little misty-eyed now. This day has been a long time coming and Cooke has been nothing but a champ throughout. "I'm so glad you called that wrong number, because if you hadn't, I'm positive I would never have found love like this."

Cooke's eyes flutter open and a smile slowly appears. "I'm the lucky one, Quinn Thompson."

I don't know why but hearing him say my first name with this last makes me gasp. "That sounds amazing."

"It does."

Feeling the need to confess, I say, "I doodled that in one of my notebooks not long after that wrong number. Did I ever tell you that?"

I see his eyes water as he shakes his head. Searching the room for a tissue, I look back down at him, a tear is sliding down his cheek. "Do you remember our second conversation? The one at the gym?" he asks.

"Of course. How can I forget half-naked rugby players?"

He ignores my joke. "Well, right after we ended the call, I turned to the lads and yelled at the top of my lungs. 'Gents, that was my future wife. I'm going to marry that lass.'"

I feel misty-eyed again, damn it. "You did?" I squeak.

"I did."

"And you are." I pause. "You're going to marry that lass."

"I know. The question is, when?"

"Soon. I can't wait to be yours, Cooke Thompson."

"And I can't wait to be yours, love."

# BOOKS BY KAYT MILLER

## <u>The Palmer Sisters</u>

Lainie

Agatha

Sadie

Cortland

Keely

Violet

Molly

## <u>Standalones</u>

The Art of the Game

The Virginia Chronicles

One of a Kind

The Portrait Painter

Game Changer

Bedhead

## <u>The Flynns</u>

Out of the Blue

Mick'sology

<u>Vested Interest</u>

The Importance of Being Ernie with Bonus Book The Importance of
Being Kennedy's

Quirky Girl

## <u>For a complete list of Kayt's books, visit:</u>

# ACKNOWLEDGMENTS

Thank you to Virginia and Barbara at Hot Tree Editing , particularly Kristen and Kim, for editing this book from start to finish.

And an extra special thank you to Becky at Hot Tree Promotions for your advice, expertise, and her positivity.

And for my beta readers, Kay, Katy and Elizabeth. Thank you so much for your time and feedback!

# ABOUT THE AUTHOR

How did it all start? Well, I love reading and one day I was searching for a book. A book about a certain type of woman and a specific kind of man and I couldn't find it so, I wrote it. I called it Game Changer and it couldn't have been a more appropriate title. It changed my life in many ways. While my real job is teaching young people, my fun job is conjuring up characters and situations to write about.

My goal, as a writer, is to write stories that relate to all of us, to make readers laugh and maybe cry sometimes. I hope my readers can escape into a fantasy, one that's actually possible. Sure, some of the stories could be dubbed "Insta-love" stories but that's okay. I fell in love with my husband pretty damn fast and with my daughter the second I saw her. So, it's a thing, I swear.

Please Follow Me on these social media sites. Following on BookBub to learn about special book deals.

I love hearing from you!

facebook.com/authorkaytmiller

twitter.com/kaytmiller1

instagram.com/kaytmiller1

bookbub.com/profile/kayt-miller

# THANK YOU!

Thank you so much for reading Quinn and Cooke's story! When I start a story, it begins with an outline, notes, and lots of crazy thoughts running through my head. When I actually start writing, the characters take over, leading me through the story like they're holding my hand—guiding me. The process is exciting and cathartic. With that said, I hope you enjoy the story.

If you did, please go to my website, www.kaytmiller.com, and join my newsletter so you can be the first to know what's coming up next. And...

*Please, leave a review!*

SNEAK PEEK: FARMBOY

Coming soon...

## Chapter 1

"Mm-mm-mm. They sure don't grow boys like that out east."

My friend and co-working, Rose, and I are both staring at the same man. "Yeah, well, *he's* not the typical Iowa farm boy."

"I think you mean *man*. Farm *man*. Because there's no boy left in that." She points at his backside since he's walking down the long corridor away from us.

I snicker at her words because it's what I do when I get nervous. I giggle, snicker, snort, or straight up laugh out loud. It's my coping mechanism in situations that are too awkward for me to handle. "Even when he was a teen boy, he looked like that." Tall, blond, muscled, beautiful. Also known as Nashville Watson, but everyone just calls him Nash.

"God, Izzy, how did you not throw yourself at that man back then?" She arches her brow. "Or now. *You're* single."

"Easy. He was a friend of my brothers and two years older than me." Not to mention I was not the kind of girl he went with. Cheerleaders and prom queens. Those were his type.

Rose scoffs, "Two years is nothing now. I heard he's single."

"He is." And the last I heard he wasn't looking for anything serious. "I think he's playing the field."

"I'd play in his field…"

"Shh." I giggle. See? Nerves. "Someone will hear you." And that's definitely not what we're supposed to be doing on Open House night at our school. "We're professionals." I give her my haughtiest look, nose in the air and everything.

"Nobody can hear us way back here." Our classrooms are the last two doors in the main hallway. Rose is our Special Education teacher, and this is my first year as the Title 1 Reading teacher at Honeywell Elementary School. Heck, it's my first year of teaching, period. I just graduated last spring. I wasn't sure about coming home. I'd hoped to find something in city or at least a town closer to civilization but nothing panned out and believe me, I tried. Luckily, I grew up in this town and the superintendent is a friend of my folks otherwise, I'd probably be unemployed. Which equals working as a waitress like I did in college. No thanks.

I'm torn. Part of me is glad to be back, a small part. The other part wished I'd found a job somewhere else, somewhere nobody already knew me. So, I could be anyone I wanted to be. Instead, I'm back here and I'm still Izzy Harmon—boring, old Izzy.

At least I have a job in my field. That's more than I can say about some of my friends from college. It's great because I love kids and I'm looking forward to working with all these little humans. I know some of them are children of people I grew up with so that will be good, I guess. *Think positively, Izzy.*

It *will* be good.

I feel my body lurch forward and realize Rose must have pushed me into his path. When he looks down at me, I blush and fumble with words, "Oh." Giggle. "Hi, Nash."

"Hey." He says walking past me like he doesn't know me. The thing is, he *does* know me. He saw me practically every day after school for years because Nash and my brother, Isaac were best friends and as far as I know, they still were best friends. Nash was Isaac's best man a couple years ago. I know because I was there. I haven't changed *that* much. Yes. I have gained a few pounds in college but other than that, I'm the same Izzy Harmon he used to ignore back in high school.

You know what, poop on him. I don't need to be recognized by the town's most eligible bachelor and a man who smells better than I remember, like man and earth. Nope. I don't, even though I honestly considered him a friend, sort of. He's just as snobby and perfect as he was back then. Too good for the likes of me. I snort because, "I can't help saying, if he'd gotten down off his high horse, his pedestal once in a while, maybe he would have ended up with a good woman instead of in the mess he's in right now."

"Who are you talking to?" Rose whispers.

"Nobody."

I cross my arms in front of my chest and scowl at the little angel who walked up and stood in front of me. As soon as I see him, I bend so I'm at his level. He's got to be in first grade. "Hi there. I'm Miss Harmon."

"I know." He's not smiling. "I'm Marcus. I guess you're my new reading teacher."

"I am." I hold out my hand to shake his but that's a non-starter. "I'm anxious to get to know you."

Marcus doesn't hold back. "I liked Mrs. Hiller."

Yep, kids are refreshing.

"I know. Me too." I mean that. Mrs. Hiller was an elementary teacher when I was in elementary school. But she died last year. She won't be coming back, Marcus.

I don't say it because that would be rude. Unfeeling.

"Dude, Mrs. Hiller croaked."

I look up to see a boy several years older than Marcus.

"Excuse me..."

I'm about to give the older boy a good talking to when a man appears. "M.J., knock that shit off." When he looks at me, he smiles. "Oh, well, hello." He holds his hand out to me. I place mine in his and stare as he slowly bend and kisses my hand. "I'm Max Lang."

"Miss Harmon."

"Miss? Is that your first name?"

I blink a few times trying to figure out if this guy is serious or if he's trying to be funny. Assuming he's serious, I reply, "Izzy."

He chuckles. "Izzy." He leans in closely glancing down my shirt. "It's a pleasure."

I quickly pull back and cross my arms over my chest. I knew I shouldn't have worn a V-neck top. But, it's Open House. And it's not like it's low-cut or anything. V-necks are just more flattering on me. It's like all the magazines say, highlight your best features. Draw people's attention to that area. And no, I don't mean my boobs. I'm talking about my face and hair. I don't mean to brag. I'm no Ashley Stewart, that's for sure, but I'm not a troll either. Plus, my hair is good. It's dark brown, thick, shiny, wavy, and long. I like my hair.

"These two hellions are mine." Max points to Marcus and the older boy. "My ex-wife is out of the picture." He blinks at me expectantly. What? Am I supposed to say something?

And that's when I hear someone yell. I look up at to see Nash looking at me. "Come on. Let's go."

I'm about to point to myself and say, "Me?" When I realize he's gesturing to Max because, of course he is. Max then turns to Marcus and the other boy. "Come on guys. We're leaving."

My attention is drawn back to Marcus when he shrugs, turns, then walks down the hallway following his older brother. "I'm sure I'll see you again, Izzy." Max then waves as he follows his kids. When he meets up with Nash, they all take off down the hallway toward the main door. "Jerk." I mutter.

"Max?" snickers Rose.

I look over to her and smile, then laugh. "No." I'm so glad I get to work with her. We've gotten to know each other this summer since the day after I was hired, I started setting up my classroom and she was teaching summer school for extra money. We had lunch together every day I filled her in on my old life back here in Honeywell and since she's been teaching here for several years, she filled me in on school gossip, who to avoid, and who I can trust. I had no idea an elementary school could be such a hotbed of drama. It's like a soap opera around here.